INSIDIOUS

A Nate Richards Mystery
Book Three

RAY ELLIS

Insidious

By Ray Ellis

First Edition eBook: 2012
First Edition Paperback: 2013
ISBN (Kindle): 978-1-938596-09-4
ISBN (Paperback): 978-1-938596-10-0

Cover image and design by Michael Sloane. Copyright © 2012

Published in the United States of America
NCC Publishing
Meridian, Idaho, 83642, USA
www.nccpublishing.com

6022E2020130310

DEDICATION

This book is dedicated to every police officer who has ever had to undergo the turmoil and pressures of an I.A. (Internal Affairs Investigation), and had to endure the question of, *"Did You do it?"*

"A good name is rather to be chosen than great riches, and loving favour rather than silver and gold."

Prov. 22: 1 KJV

INSIDIOUS

CHAPTER ONE

(Present Day)

"PUT YOUR BADGE, I.D., AND GUN ON THE DESK."

Detective Nate Richards looked at the man sitting across from him, and then back at the plainclothes officer standing by the door. Certain he had not heard him correctly, he replayed the last sentence in his mind and cleared his throat. "You're taking my gun?"

Assistant Chief Zachary (Zack) J. Lawrence of the Treasure Valley Metro Police Department stared back at Nate, his eyes boring into him. "Nate, I need your gun…and your I.D…and your badge. I need them now."

The Assistant Chief, the A.C., had taken a breath between each phrase, making each a statement, hard—final. Nate felt each word as if it had been a blow.

"From this moment you are on administrative suspension pending the outcome of the internal affairs investigation, the I.A." A.C. Lawrence's gray eyes fixed on Nate, unflinching. The muscles in his jaw flexed and relaxed, in concert with the pulse of blood, through corded veins in his neck.

The assistant chief stood, his face hard, accented by military cut hair, graying at the temple. His broad shoulders strained

3

beneath the fine tailored dress shirt as he moved. Clipped in place by a diamond-accented tie pin, the designer silk tie swung free beneath its point of restriction bouncing off his perfectly flat stomach. With careful precision and control, he placed his large hands on the desktop. Like a defensive end preparing to attack a quarterback, he rocked forward, pressing the color away from his knuckles.

The office was a pictorial representation of the man himself. It was compact and had no windows or natural light. Clean, white walls held mementos of youthful acquisitions and memorials of manhood. Patton, MacArthur, Doolittle, and John Wayne, posted in solid wood frames, looked down from their respective perches over the A.C.'s shoulders; and all of them seemed to be staring at Nate. "Until further notice," Assistant Chief Lawrence began, "you are restricted to the same movement in this building as any other civilian."

Nate frowned and shook his head, trying to clear away the fog of emotions settling into his mind. *Any other civilian?*

"You will have no contact or communication with any employee of this department without my direct approval," Lawrence concluded.

He took my badge—my gun. Why?

The assistant chief, known to the troops as the A.C., turned to the only other person in the room, *the witness.* "Sergeant Marcus Swift, escort Mr. Rich-"

Nate jumped to his feet. "You don't really think I did this; do you, sir?!"

The assistant chief turned a wary eye on Nate. Taking a deep breath, he seemed to deflate, and then lowered himself into the large black leather armchair. For a moment the two men stared at each other. No one spoke or moved. Then the assistant chief exhaled long and slow, leaning back in his seat. He rested his hands palms up on the desk and shook his head in short quick movements. "I don't know, Nate."

Nate sagged. "It would have hurt less if you'd slapped me, sir."

Sergeant Swift stepped forward and touched Nate's elbow. "Com'on Nate, let's get you out of here. We can stop by your desk and grab whatever you think you'll need on the way out."

Nate started toward the door, but stopped and turned back to the assistant chief. "Sir—Zack, you've known me for over ten years. Have I ever given you a reason to believe this of me...that I am even capable of..." his voice broke and he looked away, "of raping someone?"

CHAPTER TWO

(Seven Weeks Earlier)

"COME ON, WE'RE ABOUT TO SING happy birthday," Sherri Richards said, pulling Nate by the hand, her blond hair tied in a ponytail at the nape of her neck.

Nate rolled his eyes in exaggerated horror before allowing himself to be towed behind his mother. "You know, Dad doesn't like being the center of attention, Mom." She ignored him while continuing toward the cake and gift-covered table. Stopping short of the food covered sheet of glossed mahogany, Nate looked back to assure his date Jackie had followed him.

Jackie hung back from the crowd, ever gracious in jeans and a pullover. Nate knew she had only agreed to come with him in honor of his father's 65th birthday. He knew she had not been happy about Amber Coles, Nate's previous girlfriend, being present as well. So far Amber had remained in the kitchen or upstairs, but Nate knew that would not be the case for the entire evening.

As if on cue, the door separating the kitchen from the dining room swung open, and Amber backed through the doorway carrying yet another cake. The arc of her neck and gentle sway of her movements caught and held Nate's gaze as she turned to face the small crowd. Smiling, she began to sing happy birthday as she sought an open space on the already crowded table.

Nate felt Jackie stiffened slightly, and then relax. He squeezed her hand reassuring her.

Singing along with the crowd, Nate looked at Jackie and smiled. He reached out to touch her cheek just as his cell phone rang. "Richards," he said into the mouthpiece shaking his head, a frown creeping across his face. He stepped away from the singing, covering his left ear with that hand.

"Yeah, Nate, sorry to bother you on a Friday night." Sergeant Clemens, the patrol evening shift-supervisor, interrupted himself with a short string of expletives. "Oh, man, I forgot it was your dad's birthday."

Nate looked back at the small group of family and friends gathered around his parents and pressed the pads of his thumb and index into tired eyes. He smiled when he saw his dad pretending not to enjoy himself. "It's all right, Stan. What ya got?" Nate rubbed his forehead as he said it. He had been looking forward to an evening off, enjoying the family and just simply relaxing.

"A robbery and rape. Happened at the Motor-Head Coffee Shop on Second Street, downtown Nampa at about 1750 hours." Stan paused. "Looks like you're back in sex crimes." He chuckled.

When Nate didn't answer, Stan continued. "Adult white female, raped and robbed at gunpoint. Minor injuries—that can be seen. But she's pretty shaken up. What do you want us to do with her?"

Nate groaned, and looked over his shoulder, then walked further away from the gathering. "Okay, no cuts, broken bones, or complaints of injury?"

"Correct."

"Okay. Get her en route to FACES for the sexual assault examination; I'll be 76 there as well."

Clemens cleared his throat. "Wait, let me get this clear, you 76 here or you going to FACES first?"

Nate leaned a hand against the wall and called the names of the on-call roster through his mind. Mac, his normal partner, had just finished two weeks of back-to-back calls and was worn out. Nate groaned again. "I'll make a call and get someone out to the crime scene. I'll meet the victim at the FACES' building."

"Hey, what's this FACES thing anyway?" Clemens asked.

Nate sighed, "FACES, Family and Children Emergency Services, it's a kind of one stop spot for victims of physical and sexual assault." How many times had he explained this to different officers. So many of them had no direct contact with victims past the initial contact at the scene.

"Like a triage station."

Nate sat on the arm of his father's La-Z-Boy. "Yes, it specializes in providing wraparound services at the most crucial time for the victim—usually women and children."

"That's pretty cool," Clemens said, then covered the mouthpiece of the phone. Nate could hear mumbling but could not make out the words.

Clemens came back online. "What's your ETA, Nate?"

"About forty-five minutes. Why?"

Clemens pulled the phone away from his ear again, this time Nate could hear voices. "I can call the on duty prosecutor, sir," a voice said. "That's what Richards seems to be saying." Nate heard Clemens explain.

"Right, Nate?" Clemens asked into the phone.

"Ideally we would have everyone there, but let's just get the exam done first and go from there."

Nate turned and found Jackie looking up at him from across the room, her eyes tight with emotion. Fear. He snapped the phone closed and walked back to where he'd left her standing near the edge of the small gathering. With a wry smile, he dropped the phone back into his breast pocket, brushed the faces around the room with his eyes, and finally turned back to her. "I've gotta go. You want to hang out here, or should I drop you off at your place?" Nate asked, knowing what her answer would be.

In the moment it took Jackie to answer, Nate looked past her and saw Amber looking at him. Their eyes held as she tucked a loose strand of auburn hair behind her ear, then turned away.

"I don't know, Nate," Jackie said, sidling up to him. Everything about her screamed don't leave me. She whispered, "It's kind of weird." Her eyes shifted from Nate to his mother.

"It's bad enough knowing how your mom feels about me, but having her here too. It's too much." As she spoke, she began shaking her head in short jerking movements, small tormented actions, subconsciously displaying her alarm and fear in her face.

Nate didn't need Jackie to explain who was meant by "*her.*" He knew Jackie was referring to Amber. Leaning forward, he kissed Jackie's upturned face. "Wait here, I'll say our good-byes."

Jackie nodded and folded her arms across her chest, relieved. When Nate returned, accompanied by Reverend and Mrs. Richards, Jackie stood up straight and fidgeted with her hands. "Oh, dear, don't feel like you have to leave just because Nate's going. We're used to that around here," Sherri said, reaching out and grasping the younger woman's hands.

"I would count it an honor if you stayed," Reverend Richards said, his dark skin in contrast to the creamy pale complexion of his wife's.

"Well…I—" Jackie began.

"I already promised I'd drop her off," Nate said, stepping between his parents and Jackie. He felt her relax beside him. "Besides, she doesn't even know anybody here, and I couldn't do that to the poor girl." Nate hugged Jackie around the shoulder and pulled her against him in an expression of exaggerated protectiveness.

"Oh, you," Sherri said as she smacked her son's arm.

"Well, thank you for coming and making an old man's birthday special," Reverend Richards said. He shook his son's hand. "Be careful, son. See you Sunday morning."

"I sure hope so," Nate said and helped Jackie into her coat. He looked through the frosted glass and noted the slush piled in the corners of the window. "It may be spring, but I will be so glad when the sun comes out for good."

Visibly at ease, Jackie's smile reached her eyes for the first time since before the party. "Well, just wait a moment or two and the weather will change," she said, stepping through the open doorway and stopping on the small porch.

Nate cupped her chin with his fingers and kissed her lips softly before turning her towards his Jeep. "Spring in Idaho." Tucking her against him, he made his way from the porch across the frost-slicken sidewalk.

After closing her door and walking around to the driver's side of the vehicle, Nate paused looking back through the window into his parent's home. He saw Amber and, for a brief moment, stood, captured by the sight of her easy laughter and the brightness of her smile. Shaking himself, he got into his car and started the engine.

Jackie looked over at Nate. "It must be hard having to leave your family like this." She touched his face with soft fingers.

"Naw, I'm used to it," he said, not sure he hadn't just lied.

CHAPTER THREE

(Seven Weeks Earlier)

NATE PARKED HIS GREEN JEEP Grand Cherokee in the south parking lot of the FACES building downtown Boise. Getting out of the vehicle and starting around the corner, Nate saw a uniformed patrol officer waving him over. The man rubbed his arms and encouraged Nate to hurry. The wind gusted around them, pushing a billowing ground cloud of snow ahead across the already ice-slick parking lot. Nate blew into his hands. "I sure hope you've got coffee ready."

"Inside." Patrol Officer Murray grabbed Nate's proffered hand and shook it, then turned and headed up the front steps where the heavy glass and metal door stood propped open. "You been briefed yet?" He asked over his shoulder.

Nate stepped through the heavy door allowing it to fall shut behind him, the magnetic lock engaging with a soft click. Walking through the small foyer, he punched in his security code to open the inner door. With a resonant snap, the lock popped and he pulled the door open.

A lone figure sat hunched over a cell phone and wrapped in a blanket—a female. The small waiting room was decorated to look more like a living room than the medical facility it was.

Giant pastoral murals covered the walls blending seamlessly into a cordoned off section by a white picket fence as play area for smaller children. Nate watched the middle-aged female sitting in one of the ornate chairs, a cell phone pressed to her ear.

The woman had a blanket wrapped around her shoulders and rocked back and forth, back and forth, as she sat crouched on the edge of the large chair. Her mid-length ash blond hair swung rhythmically with each movement. Nate made his approach. She looked up, and he could see she had been crying. He smiled at her and indicated that she should go ahead and finish her call. Walking over to a far corner, Nate turned and faced Officer Murray. "Okay, brief me."

Murray poured two cups of coffee and passed one to Nate. "What do you know so far?" Murray took a sip of coffee and smiled. "It's good," he said and shivered slightly as if savoring the first swallow.

Nate lifted his own cup and took a swallow. "Needs some creamer, but I'll live. So, what I know so far is that our victim was closing up shop when our perp came in and robbed the store then raped her. That's about it?" He took another drink of coffee and pulled out his pad from his chest pocket preparing to take notes.

Murray had his own pad out, reviewing what he had written. He raised his eyebrows and tilted his head toward the woman in the chair. "She hasn't stopped talking on that phone since we got here." He looked back toward the seated figure with his notepad.

"Is that the victim?"

"Yeah." Murray looked back at his pad and began reading, "Wanda Edna Mae Fuller, age 45 years. She was closing shop when the last customer came in. Says she called out from the kitchen that it would be a few minutes. Says when she looked up, this guy, the perp, was dressed all in black, and had a gun pointed at her face."

Adjusting the Styrofoam cup in his hand, Nate scratched notes of his own. "What's been her disposition? You think it happened?"

Murray flipped his pad closed. "Something happened. It's weird though. She doesn't act like any rape victim I've ever seen."

From across the room, laughter floated toward them. Nate couldn't see the woman's face from his position, but it appeared she had hunkered down in the blanket, cocooning it around her. Her slouched body posture stood in stark contrast to the peal of laughter that had just erupted from her.

"I see," Nate said. "What's the complaint?"

"Well, he didn't beat her up, if that's what you mean. After he robbed the place, as she puts it, for no apparent reason, he decided to assault her." Murray looked up to make sure he wasn't being watched and then smiled. "She's not bad looking; I think the perp would have made that choice first, if you get my meaning." He playfully elbowed Nate in the ribs as he laughed at his own joke.

Shaking his head, Nate smiled in return, not sure what to do with his conflicting emotions. He understood the officer's use of humor; a technique often used to deal with the harsh emotional ugliness associated with the job. But at the same time, he had difficulty in finding any humor at the victim's expense. Deciding to change the topic instead, he said, "Clemens mentioned something about force."

"The perp used an apron from the store and tied the victim up before he robbed her."

Nate was studying his notepad but snapped his head up. "Robbery...first?"

Murray snickered again. "Told you it was weird." He rubbed the corner of his chin with his notepad. "According to the victim, the guy came in and robbed her and acted like he was going to leave, but then decided to have a little extra curricular fun before exiting. Almost like it had been an afterthought." He sat his cup on the counter and folded his arms across his chest."

Nate put his pen and pad back into his chest pocket. "But-"

"Excuse me officer, but I'm done now," the woman called out, still sitting and rocking on the edge of the chair.

Nate looked at Murray and nodded. The uniformed officer took the lead. "Hi Wanda, this is Detective Richards. He's the one I told you would be coming; he'll be handling your case for you."

Nate stepped forward and slightly to the side of the woman, as not to make her feel trapped. He did not offer her his hand, instead waiting for her to establish whatever boundary she found comfortable. "Mrs. Fuller, I'm sorry that this has happened to you, but I promise you I will do everything in my power to help you."

She stood and offered a hand to Nate, and he grasped it without hesitation, shaking it briefly before releasing the grasp. She was tall, meeting Nate at eye level. An attractive woman in a plain ordinary way; her pale hair had pulled loose from the ponytail she'd worn it in. "Thank you, but please, it would make me feel so much better if you called me Edna Mae." She paused and searched Nate's face. "Do you really think you will be able to catch this guy? I mean, I didn't even get a good look at him— at his face or anything."

Murray, who had moved behind the woman, looked at Nate as if to say, *I told you she was weird.*

Nate ignored him. "Well, we'll do our best, Mrs. Fuller," he said ignoring Murray.

She lowered herself back into the chair. "Please call me Edna Mae. Besides, I'm divorced." Her cell phone rang again. "Oh, excuse me, I need to take this," she said after looking at the caller I.D.

Nate stepped away and spoke with Murray. "You call the Victim-Witness-Coordinator yet?"

"Oh yeah, Dani's on her way. She should be here soon."

Wanda raised her voice and both Nate and Murray looked back at her. "I know, Dad," she was saying. "Can you just go pick her up for me? I'm kind of busy right now." She stood and the blanket slipped from her shoulders, revealing a white cotton jacket over a black blouse and a black and green skirt that hung just below her knees." She pressed the phone against her head with her right hand and pinched the bridge of her nose with the other. "No, Leroy's still out of town. Thanks, Dad." She hung up the phone and turned her attention back to the two officers. "Sorry, my dad's being a butt." She giggled.

Nate and Murray exchanged glances. "Okay, Wanda, I mean Edna Mae," Nate said. I'm going to explain what's going to happen here tonight, all right?"

She nodded.

Nate had just begun his explanation when Dani Rivers, the department's on-duty VWC, walked in, her long brown hair bouncing loose around her face. She wore a wooly-cotton lined jean jacket and simple white button up shirt over an ankle length jean skirt. "Hi guys," she said and looked around the waiting room accessing the scene.

She nodded at Nate. "Hi there," she said, this time directing her words to Edna Mae. "I'm Dani Rivers, Dani pronounced like Danny. My dad's idea of a joke. I'm gonna be your Victim Witness Coordinator. I'm gonna stay right here beside you until this is all over. And if this thing goes all the way to court, I'll be there with you too."

Nate smiled at Dani, knowing she would do a great job getting Edna Mae onboard with the investigation while also getting her the help and resources she would need. He turned back to Murray who had taken a phone call and was busy scribbling in his pad again. Nate watched, curious.

Waving Nate over to him, Murray closed his phone. He whispered, "We might have our suspect in custody."

Nate sighed. It was never that easy; things just didn't work out for him that way. "What is it?"

"We found a guy all blacked out from head to toe, hiding in the old building supply lot just east and north of the Motor Head Coffee Shop. He didn't have a gun on him, but he does have a record for sexual assault and aggravated battery on a peace officer. This is our guy! How cool is that?"

Nate leaned against the wall. "Who has him now? Tell them to get him back to nineteen, and I'll meet them at the station to do the interview as soon as I get this exam going."

"How cool is that," Murray repeated. "How cool is that! Wrapped-up in two hours."

"We'll see," Nate said with caution. His cell phone rang, and he frowned before pulling it out of his pocket. "Richards," he said into the mouthpiece.

"Yeah, Nate, this is Al." It was Lieutenant Albert Michaels, the CID shift commanding officer. "I sent Jacobs out to the crime scene, and I had Durgins rollout as well. I know you asked for Durgins, but I thought this particular crime scene might be a bit much for him. Besides, Jacobs can teach him to do a crime scene the right way. Durgins gets the experience he needs, and we get a detective with some actual field training. It's a double win."

Nate looked back at Murray, who was writing again, and then over at Dani. She had laid a hand on Edna Mae's shoulder and was speaking in soft but earnest tones. At the end of the hall, a door opened and the SAFE (Sexual Assault Forensic Examination) nurse came in, stamping her feet and shaking water droplets from her jacket sleeves. Nate smiled at the woman and made his way to where she was standing.

"Hi, Nate Richards." Nate said and extended his hand toward the nurse.

Turning toward the coat rack, she didn't see Nate's extended hand. "Hey, sorry I'm late. I got stuck at a ballet recital."

Nate raised his palm and looked at it before returning it to his side. "I'm sorry. I hate to take you away from your kids."

The woman chuckled and with a casual gesture placed a hand on Nate's arm. "No, thank you. They aren't my kids—my husband's sister's daughter. Don't get me wrong, but you can only take so much of five and six year olds doing the dance to 'We Represent the Lollipop Guild'. So, the debt is mine." She laughed again and this time Nate joined her.

Finished with removing her outer coat, she extended a hand to Nate. "Gloria Steinem."

Grasping her hand, Nate shook it once then stared at the nurse. "Gloria Stei-"

"I know, I know, but trust me, I like being treated like a woman. You can open my door and pamper me anytime you like." She hung her coat on the peg by the door, ran her fingers through her spiky blond hair, and turned and looked up at Nate. She smiled and then looked past him down the hall. "Where's our girl?"

Nate swept his arm in a flourish, indicating the waiting area at the far end of the hall. He could see Dani standing next to the seated woman just beyond the glass door. Gloria smiled, raised her chin with an air of snooty superiority, and moved toward the lobby, and Nate followed.

CHAPTER FOUR

(Seven Weeks Earlier)

NATE SAT AND LISTENED as Edna Mae related, again, the details of, first, the robbery and then the sexual assault. "At first," she said haltingly, "I thought it would be just a simple robbery. I give him the money, he leaves, and that would be it. But then he turned and he looked at me. He just stared at me, and his eyes were hungry, they were—they were evil. All I could see were his eyes through the slots of the mask he was wearing…and I knew. I knew he was going to rape me." She ran a hand across her face, and Nate could see the slight tremble as it worked its way across her shoulders and then down her arms.

The four of them sat in the small interview room just outside where the examination would take place. The makeshift living room did little to ward off the sterile emptiness waiting in the actual exam room next door. Nate sat across from Edna Mae with Gloria to his left. Dani sat closest to the victim, ready to offer any needed assistance. With the soft lights and warm colors, the interview room could have been a family room or sitting room in any number of homes here in the valley. The large painting, hanging on the wall behind the sofa, showed a mother playing with her children in the surf; while in the background, a dog appeared to be playing fetch with an older child.

Nate resisted the urge to reach out and lay a hand on Edna Mae's shoulder; the desire to help the woman grew stronger inside him. Everything in Nate screamed at him to offer her comfort, but he knew he dared not. As she continued to describe the horrors of the attack, Nate fought to compartmentalize his anger, choosing rather to focus his energies on getting the details that would allow him to catch this animal.

Standing, Nate rested his back against the door. Reclining, he stood raking his memories, trying to call to mind something that Edna Mae had said. With effort, he rocked forward slowly, interrupting her. "Edna Mae, was there anything about this man that stood out to you?"

When he saw her puzzled expression, he pushed on. "I mean, I know you said he wore a mask and that he was covered for the most part, but if you had to say, what would be the one thing about him that stood out?"

Now she sat forward. She looked from Nate to Gloria to Dani, and then finally back to Nate. "His eyes. One was blue and the other was green. And they didn't track together. Do you know what I mean?"

Nate wrote this down on his pad. "Are you saying his eyes moved separately?" he asked as he sat near her.

"Yeah!" She said and slid forward to the edge of the sofa cushion. She placed her hand on Nate's knee. "I mean, there were times—I mean moments when I wasn't sure if he was really looking at me or not." Nate scooted back, in what he hoped was a casual gesture, causing Edna Mae's hand to slip from his knee. He and Dani exchanged a surreptitious glance.

Wanda didn't seem to notice Nate's retreat, and he continued his line of questioning unabated. "What made things stop, Edna Mae? What did he say or do that made you know he was finished, that he was going to leave you?"

She dropped her eyes and turned her face away. She mumbled her answer.

"What was that?" Nate asked.

"He thanked me."

"He what?!" Gloria blurted. Nate shot her a silencing glance.

Edna Mae looked first at Nate and then at Gloria. Nate encouraged her. "Go ahead, Edna Mae, what happened next?"

Edna Mae cleared her throat. "He thanked me for being, as he put it, an 'excellent lover'. Like I was his lover. He raped me! I wasn't his lover! I didn't want this to happen…didn't want him to do this to me!" She sat up straight, her arms folded across her chest. Her feet were flat against the floor, her legs and knees pressed hard against each other. She stared at Nate. Hot tears streaked her cheeks.

"I know you didn't," Nate said. "The only reason I ask you is so that I can try and get inside his head, to see what he was thinking. It may give us a clue as to who this freak is." With a look from Nate, Dani moved closer and draped an arm around Edna Mae's shoulder.

Edna Mae visibly relaxed and allowed herself to sag against the younger woman. "I didn't want this."

"We know," Dani whispered to the battered woman.

Nate took a breath. "So, Edna Mae," he began again, "what happened next?"

Edna Mae looked at Gloria, who smiled encouragingly at her. "He thanked me. He said I was an excellent lover and that he was sorry for having to force me, but that I should be glad that he didn't—"

Gloria leaned forward. "That he didn't *hurt* you?" She looked up at Nate, who was again staring at her. "I know these things can be hard to say out loud, but we're here for you. We're going to go into the other room here in a minute, as soon as the detective finishes, and we're gonna do that exam I told you about, okay. We're gonna do everything we can to get this guy, okay, Edna Mae?"

Edna Mae nodded.

"I'm finished for now," Nate said. "It's getting late and she still needs to get home to see her kids tonight." He stood. This time Nate squeezed Edna Mae's shoulder. When she looked up, he met her desperate gaze. "We'll get this guy."

She touched his hand. "Thank you."

With that, Nate turned and left the room. Dani followed him out. "She's a touchy one," she said and tilted her head back toward the closed door.

"Yeah, that whole touching my knee thing was kind of weird." He chuckled.

She laughed too. "But then you go and grab her shoulder on the way out. What were you thinking?"

Nate grimaced. "Oops. I thought about that about half a second after I'd touched her. I didn't want to snatch my hand away, didn't want to make her think she was dirty or something."

Dani giggled again. "Oh, I don't think that's what she was thinking at all. Anyway, I'd better head back in there." She looked back toward the examination room.

Nate stared at her. "You don't think—she just got—no way."

"I'm just saying, she's hurt and vulnerable, and you're the big alpha male." Catching his grin, she corrected herself. "Don't let it go to your head. Almost any guy in a uniform or with a badge would make her feel safer now. Just be careful, you goofball."

He punched her playfully on the shoulder. "I will...and thanks." He shook his head as he watched her disappear back into the interview/exam room.

"Hey, come on," Murray called excitedly to Nate. "They got your guy at the station. Says he's ready to talk."

Nate snapped his attention toward the uniformed officer. "Who's got him?" He quickened his pace and headed for the door.

CHAPTER FIVE

(Present Day)

ASSISTANT CHIEF ZACHARY LAWRENCE LEANED BACK against the support of his overstuffed chair. The light was low and the evening had begun to grow cold. Certain that the building was now empty, he opened his lower desk drawer and retrieved the bottle he kept there. A bottle he kept for moments just like these.

Lifting the half-emptied flask of amber liquid, he poured two fingers worth into his coffee cup. Without hesitation, he lifted the dark porcelain and drained it.

"Bad day, huh?"

Startled, Lawrence slammed the cup onto his desktop and turned toward the open doorway. "Swift? What are you still doing here?" He didn't bother to stand or attempt to hide the bottle of Macallan Whiskey still on his desk.

Sergeant Swift's eyes darted first to the bottle and then back to the assistant chief's face. "I was just finishing up the paperwork on the Richards' I.A." He stepped through the open doorway. "You want some company?"

Lawrence stood and stretched. Coal black suspenders stretched taut over an ivory colored shirt. "No, don't think I'd be worth much company tonight. Think I'll head over to the gym and see if I can sweat out my old friend *Mr. Macallan.*" He lifted the bottle and dropped it back into the desk drawer with a distinct absence of ceremony.

Swift raised two fingers to the corner of his forehead in acknowledging the A.C. "I'll see ya later then, Zachary."

Zachary walked to the open door and leaned against the frame, slapping Swift on the shoulder. "Yeah, later." He watched as Swift made his way down the hall and out to the foyer. The thrumming hum of the elevator groaned through the building as the car first ascended and then lowered, taking Swift with him to the lobby.

Zachary Lawrence pulled on the collar of his shirt, loosening his necktie as he walked back to his desk. Looking down at the reflected light from the distinctively shaped bottle, he picked up his cup and reached for the decanter again. "I hate days like this."

***

Amber closed and locked the door of her egg-yolk yellow VW Bug. The vibration of the door caused the remaining clusters of ice and snow to slide in wet clumps from the black canvas roof. Pulling her coat tight around her, she hefted her back and then paused, noticing an unfamiliar gray late model sedan parked just inside the fire lane. Even from the short distance between herself and the car, she could hear the engine cracking and popping as it cooled in the afternoon chill.

Taking a moment to position her keys so that she could use them as a defensive weapon if the need arose, she walked forward with cautious steps, with a new awareness of her surroundings.

"Yeee-epp," came the slow protracted drawl from behind her and off to her right. "That'll just about make me think twice before assaulting you, pretty lady."

Amber spun toward the voice, dropped her bag, and brought her hands up in a defensive posture; the key positioned to gouge or rake and assailant's eyes.

"Almost." Lieutenant Donald Haynes stepped out of the gray shadow and smiled his best country-boy smile. "I see Nate taught you something. That's a good thing; a woman ought to be able to defend herself. You never know what a day might turn up."

Haynes walked over to where Amber stood, still with her hands and her weight settled so that she could run or just as easily deliver a quick kick. "Now, you not gonna kick me in my face if I bend down here to grab your bag, are ya?"

"Oh." She snatched her arms back to her sides. "Sorry, but you scared me." She heaved a sigh and brushed loose hair from her face. "What are you doing here?" She looked around again, wondering if Nate would suddenly jump out and yell surprise.

The thought startled her. She'd been thinking more and more about Nate lately. The sight of him standing protectively over Jackie at the party had not been missed by her; it played over and over in her mind, filling her with a sense of longing and loss. Ever since that night, she had forced herself to pray for Nate's happiness and God's will rather than focusing on what *might have been*. She shook her head to clear the thoughts and chanced one more look around the parking lot.

Haynes was standing in front of her now, her bag draped over his shoulder. "You gonna invite a fella in or leave me out here freezing?"

She smiled. "Come on; let's get something hot inside us." She turned and led the way to her first floor apartment. The small two-bedroom apartment was near the new Ten Mile Road exchange. The location afforded her a quick route downtown to the bank where she worked as a loan processor or just as easy to slip onto the I-84 west and go see Mother Richards as she had taken to calling Sherri, Nate's mother.

Inside the apartment, Amber went directly to her kitchen and began to run water for coffee. Turning back, she took the bag from Haynes outstretched hand and laid it on the counter. "You never told me why you're here? What are you guys up to now?" She spoke over her shoulder.

When Haynes didn't answer, she turned and looked at him. For once, the usual placid smile was gone, replaced by a look of worried concern. Haynes spread his hands toward her, his palms facing up. "Amber, Nate's in trouble."

***

Nate walked into his darkened one bedroom apartment and threw his keys on the kitchen counter, the metallic sound echoed across the tiled surface in the emptiness of the room. Muted sunlight cut through the gray darkness in slants, as it peaked through partially opened blinds. The silence of the mid-day apartment complex was almost tangible, heavy and stale.

Nate sighed and slammed the heels of his hands against his temples, as a low guttural sound dredged up from his core. He allowed himself to fall back against the solid surface of the closed door behind him. His stomach tightened and Nate groped reaching for the gun, his hand fumbling over the empty holster. Trailing his hand along his belt, he fingered the empty space where his badge had hung. He gasped. Forcing himself to breath, he leaned forward and dropped to the floor barely managing to catch himself on his hands and knees before crashing against the cold linoleum surface.

"Breathe," he said into the void and was startled by the sound of his voice.

He gave up on standing and rolled into a seated position, his hands draped between his knees, his chin resting on his chest.

"Why...? Why God? I didn't do this. You know I never touched that woman. So why? Why? WHY!?"

Time ceased to exist for Nate. When he looked up again, the shadows of early evening had linked themselves together, casting the room into a chalky darkness. A bone jarring chill crept through the room, and Nate realized his joints were stiff with cold and the lack of movement. Looking up at the ceiling, he moaned, his voice dry and cracking. "God, what are you doing to me?"

Silence.

He drifted into a gray nothingness that seemed without border or direction. He felt weightless and confused, angry and sad. Betrayed. Again, time passed.

A knock on the door stirred him, and he began to move toward his bedroom, not wanting to see or talk to anyone yet. Careful not to make any noise, he crawled toward the slit of darkness that was the doorway to his bedroom and the relative safety of his bed.

The knocking sounded again, this time hard and impatient. "Nate, it's Amber." The contralto voice sounded through the darkness. "Open up. I know you're in there. Come on. Open up. Haynes told me. I know what happened. Nate?"

Nate stood and stared at the closed door, a mixture of anger, shame, and unbelief warring inside him. He rubbed his face and felt, again, the emptiness where his gun had been. Loosening his belt, he pulled the holster off and threw it through the opened doorway of his bedroom.

"Nate, open the door," she called again. Nate didn't move. Part of him hoped she would leave, another wanted her to stay.

"Nate, I'm coming in. Your mom gave me her key. I—we need to make sure you're okay."

Nate shook his head not sure if he'd heard her correctly. He rubbed his face again, hoping to clear his thoughts. The sound of a key in the door brought him back to the moment. He started towards the door, reaching for it just as it opened.

Amber pushed open the door and, seeing Nate, rushed over to him. "Oh, Nate," she said, taking him into her arms. "I know you didn't do this. It will work itself out. God will make this better." Her thin, but quilted blue jacket had flung open as she reached out to embrace him. The silky material making a light chaffing sound as she moved.

Nate stood, defeated, allowing her to hold him, his arms hanging like dead weights at his sides. Bitterness swelled in him, chalky and suffocating; but then in sudden desperation, he grabbed her, held onto her anyway, crushing her against himself.

Relief washed through him. Nate couldn't believe how good it felt to have her in his arms or how long it had been since he'd held her. Gently, but firmly, he felt Amber push back away from him, breaking the hold. Looking into his face, she smiled. Then taking him by the hand, she led him to the sofa.

They sat in silence for a long while, neither wanting to be the first to speak. Nate looked at his fingers still intertwined with Amber's and wondered why she'd been the one to come and not his mother or father. He could see the concern in her eyes and the…. He didn't let himself finish the thought.

Leaning against the backrest, Nate raised, then dropped his hands into his lap. "Amber, they think I raped that woman."

"I know."

"I didn't do it!"

"I know that too."

***

"They put me on admin leave until the I.A. is complete. No contact. No explanation. No nothing. I feel like…like a crook or something."

Amber didn't interrupt him, she just let him talk. She simply listened. Pulling her hand free, she rested her face against her palm and watched as Nate exhaled and slumped back into the sofa. "Have you eaten anything?" She asked.

"What?" He looked at her as if he'd just remembered she was there. "What?" He asked again, his gaze barely brushing her face. The pain and lostness in his expression made her want to take him into her arms again. She resisted.

"Have you eaten," she asked getting up. She unfolded the leg she'd curled beneath herself when she sat and rose with a dancer's grace. "I'll make you something." She headed to the kitchen, after first stopping by the wall thermostat. She rubbed her upper arms and shivered then thumbed the temperature up a few degrees.

Familiar with the small kitchen from the days when hanging at the apartment with Nate was as common as being at her own place; Amber hummed a soft tune as she worked. After just a few minutes, the fragrance of scrambled eggs, melted cheese, and sautéed mushrooms wafted through the combined kitchen, dining and living room. Soon the gurgling breath of the coffeemaker added a nutty aroma to the cacophony of flavors and Nate's stomach growled. Amber smiled, acknowledging the low rumble.

"I didn't know I was hungry."

She smiled and sat the plate on the coffee table in front of him. "Eat." She lowered herself onto the sofa beside him, leaned back, and again, curled her leg beneath her. Propping an elbow on the backrest, she rested her face against her hand and playfully tossed the short curls at her neck. She pretended not to notice the longing in Nate's eyes as he first looked at her and then reached out to take a drink from the cup of coffee.

"Mmmm, that's good."

She smiled. "To think…all those years of making coffee at the bookstore kiosk paid off. Now eat your egg sandwich before it gets cold." She smiled at him and tossed her head, flinging loose strands of hair back from her face.

"Yes, ma'am." He took a bite from the sandwich and then without stopping or putting it back down, he finished it. Taking the paper napkin, he wiped at a dribble of melted cheese that clung to his chin. "Wow! That was good. I didn't realize how hungry I was. Thank you." He laid his hand on the sofa between them, his hand turned upward. She rested hers in his, their fingers locking naturally, easily. "Thank you," he said again, folding his much larger fingers around hers.

She smiled at him and squeezed his hand before pulling hers free and placed both her hands in the fold of her lap. She looked up at him. "I just needed to know that you were okay and to let you know that I'm here for you."

"Here for me, huh?" He said and clinched his hands into fists. A shadow seemed to drop like a curtain across his face. "Too bad my command wasn't here for me, huh?"

Amber didn't answer.

In one quick motion, Nate stood. Then collecting the empty plate and coffee cup, he started toward the kitchen. He'd just reached the sink and began to rinse his dishes when a knock sounded at the door. Frowning, he drew back his arm as if to crash the plate against the stainless steel surface. The florescent light gave Nate a sallow tinge to his skin, accenting the lines of weariness etched in his face. He looked tired.

Seeing this, Amber sprang up from the sofa. "I'll get it." She held his gaze for a moment longer, waiting for him to relax, and then headed toward the door. Opening it, she stepped back, a look of surprise on her face.

CHAPTER SIX

(Present Day)

"JACKIE, COME IN," Amber said, surprise and a feeling of embarrassment coloring her voice. Stepping back, she drew the open door, allowing it to swing free on the hinge. Biting her lip, Amber looked back over her shoulder. She watched Nate moving mechanically as if through a fog as he made his way through the kitchen. She looked back at Jackie, who still stood unsure, just outside the door.

The two women stood in silence, inspecting one another. Amber watched as Jackie's eyes traveled the length of her and then over her shoulder toward the sound of running water coming from the kitchen. A hesitation. "Come in, Jackie. I was just leaving," Amber said filling her tone with lightness.

Jackie looked back toward the stairs, a pensive gaze on her face, as if reconsidering her decision to stop by, but then with a sudden brusqueness, stalked passed Amber and into the apartment.

Amber sighed, rolled her eyes, and rested her face against the edge of the door. "Timing is everything," she whispered. Then straightening, she took a breath and turned to face the couple behind her.

Jackie had stopped just short of where Nate stood with his hands still under the running water. He hadn't turned, but stood staring at the stream splashing over his hands, watching as the water disappeared down the drain. Jackie laid a tentative hand on his shoulder, hesitated, and then wrapped her arms around Nate's waist, resting her face against his back.

Amber folded her arms across her chest and chewed the inside of her lip. Tilting her face and sighing before she spoke, she let her shoulders droop and went to retrieve her purse from the table. "Umm...Nate, I'll let your mom know you're okay, all right?"

Nate grunted.

Amber blew a lock of hair from her face that had fallen loose, her eyes tracing back and forth between Nate and Jackie. Shouldering her purse, she turned for the door. When neither Nate nor Jackie acknowledged her presence, Amber shrugged and left without speaking.

Moments passed. Nate finally turned, sliding within the circle of Jackie's embrace. They stood in protracted silence facing each other. Before long, Nate lowered his eyes to the floor. He studied the walls, the ceiling, shifting his gaze around the room, anywhere but into Jackie's eyes. Nate squeezed his eyes shut. For reasons he couldn't explain, he felt shame...embarrassed in her presence.

She reached up, placing her open palm on the side of his face. "Talk to me, Sweetheart. Tell me what's on your mind?" She managed to get him to look at her.

He shook his head and heaved a sigh, raising and lowering his shoulders. Grasping her by her wrist, he pulled her hands down to his waist. "Jackie," he said as if labored, "I didn't do this."

She didn't respond to him, but instead, led him to the sofa where he had recently been sitting with Amber.

He stared at her. "I said—"

This time it was Jackie that looked away. "I heard you…." She faltered.

Nate pulled his hands free and stood again. He walked over to the window and looked down on the darkened street. "I…didn't…do…this."

***

Assistant Police Chief Zachary Lawrence folded his rather large hands on top of the closed folder on his desk, the Treasure City symbol reflecting the low level light. The office was quiet and he was finally alone; he was alone. He kicked his desk drawer closed and pressed the pads of his fingers against his eyes, hoping that by massaging them the dull ache would go away.

He opened the file again and began to review its contents, hoping he would see something different. "Nate, Nate…how could you be so stupid. You don't pee in your own corner. Stupid, stupid mistake!" He stood and paced around his office.

The top sheet of the file contained written statements and one photocopy of what had been a crumpled sheet of paper. The folds and creases evident by the shadows created during the photocopying process. Even from where he stood, he could see the condemning words, words of invitation and acceptance. Descriptions of the things done, or to be done, using department issued tools, department granted authority. "Nate, how could you be so stupid," he said, cursing into the silence.

He paced again, stopping beneath the large portrait of John Wayne. Looking up, he muttered under his breath, "Sometimes, I hate my job."

CHAPTER SEVEN

(Seven Weeks Earlier)

A LIGHT DRIZZLE HAD REPLACED THE SNOW by the time Nate arrived back at the P.D. It was still cold, but the rain promised, maybe, that it might be warming up a bit. He turned the windshield wipers to the off position and sat in the quiet of the car listening to the soft droplets fall against the roof.

Nate sighed, grabbed his folder, and pulled his collar tight around his neck before opening the car door. Then with careful haste, he rushed through the steady but gentle rainfall, watchful, lest he slip on a hidden patch of ice and give the guys something else to laugh about.

Stopping by the security panel, he held up his ID card in front of the red beam, allowing the computer system to access his identification and register him entering the building. With a soft click, the locking mechanism released and Nate pulled the door open.

Nate stamped loose snow from his shoes and drew the scarf from around his neck. Now that he was inside the building the layers became almost too much, threatening to overheat him. *Just one more of the hassles of springtime in Idaho.* "Hey, Catz," Nate called to the uniformed officer that was passing. "Where'd they put the suspect from the rape?"

The older man answered without stopping, "Downstairs interview room A." He pushed open the door to the men's locker and disappeared inside. Nate looked at his wristwatch—0200 hours. *Swing shift was just getting off.* He wiped a hand across his face and headed upstairs to his desk before going in to confront the *would be* rapist.

Two hours later, Nate walked out of the interview room and grabbed the cup of bitter coffee being handed to him by Detective Durgins.

At thirty-one, Durgins appeared even greener than Nate had been when he was promoted to investigations. Although he looked the clean-shaven IBM type, Durgins had served as a Marine Corps sniper having done time on the ground in both Afghanistan and Fallujah since 9/11. The man had over twenty confirmed kills with at least one of them the result of hand-to-hand combat. "Knock that back," he said to Nate.

Nate lifted the cup and saluted Durgins with it before draining its contents. He immediately squeezed his eyes shut and fought to keep from gagging. "Wh-what is that?" He wiped his mouth with the back of his hand and winced.

"Your eyes will stop burning in a minute, but that'll wake you right up."

Nate coughed. "Yeah, but what was it?"

"Just a lil' sum-sum'n me and the boys cooked up one night while out on foot patrol in the Kush Mountains—"

"Kush?"

"Afghanistan near Kabul."

Nate rubbed his eyes again and had to admit he was feeling somewhat more awake than he had when he came out of the interview room. "Okay, that answers the where, but it still leaves the what. What is that stuff? I thought it was just black coffee."

He ran his tongue along the bottom canal between his cheek and jaw and tried to spit the chalky residue back into the cup he still held in his hand.

Brushing tears from his eyes, Durgins finally stopped laughing. "Well, it's like I said, just a lil' sum'n. The boys and I got tired of drinking that weak powered stuff that came in our K-rats. Besides, we usually didn't have the extra water to spare for mixing it up. So Brothers, a Jarhead from somewhere in the back woods of Tennessee, came up with the idea of not wasting perfectly good spit from the chaw of Red Man he kept in his cheek. So he'd spit it back in his cup, and when he had enough, he just mixed the coffee powder in and drank the whole concoction down. Oh Brothers thought he was just being green. You know, conserving, but found out by accident that it kept him awake too."

Nate jumped up from where he was starting to sit down by the huge conference table in the commons and rushed to the trash basket by the wall. Leaning over the open mouth of the gray plastic rectangle, he started to gag.

"Relax, old boy," Durgins said, slapping Nate on the back. "I didn't say I used tobacco spit, I said Brothers did. I found out it works just as good if you boil the leaves in just about a half cup of coffee. That's what you just drank." He smiled brightly. "Works, huh?"

Nate straightened his back and rubbed at his mouth. "Yeah, it works." He sighed and returned to the table to where he'd left the open manila folder. He wiped his mouth again. "That's not our guy."

"Figured as much. You know, you learn a little something about people when you fight alongside 'em and watch a few die. Now that guy in there, don't get me wrong, he's a freak, but he's not our rapist."

Durgins sat across from Nate and kicked booted feet onto the edge of the table. Interlocking his fingers, he cradled his head in his hands and leaned back. "That old boy," he indicated with a tilt of his chin, "is bad in a whole lot of ways, and since I did him the favor of running a records' check, he will be going to jail tonight. Thank you very much. But yeah, he is not our guy. He was just too eager, in a pathetic kind of way, to be the one we're looking for. But just in case, I thought it would be a great idea to do a DNA panel on him." He closed his eyes and smiled.

Nate rested both elbows on the table in front of him and chuckled. "That's pretty good leg work for a grunt."

"Oooo-raa," he said from behind closed eyelids.

Nate looked at his watch again and then back at Durgins. He was feeling wide awake. "Since I won't be going to sleep anytime in the near future, what-da-ya say we get this guy on his way to County and we grab a bite to eat?"

"I'll take a chew on that," Durgins said and dropped his feet to the floor. Let's go to the Sunrise in Old Town." Catching Nate's frown, he held up a hand. "Don't be frowning like that. It's nice since they cut the smoking out inside. I'll even buy."

Nate smiled. "I'll get my coat. You call patrol to get *Mr. Lucky* in there a ride to County," he said, making quotations gestures with his hands. He turned and headed for the CID office space. I'll talk you through the interview over breakfast."

Durgins didn't bother to answer, but kept dialing his cell phone and waved a hand in Nate's general direction.

***

"Hey there, let me get an order of hash browns—crispy and a side of bacon," Durgins said without opening the faded yellow menu. The restaurant, a survivor of the first era of Meridian's glory days, had been on the same corner for over thirty years.

Nate looked around the old building, remembering it the way it looked when he first visited. The aged walls had been dark and stained, sooty gray from the days when everyone smoked right along with their meals. Wood plank floors, polished to a subdued luster by years of foot traffic, and the repeated sweeping and mopping, endured through the years.

Cardstock-posters and pressed metal advertisements from a bygone era had advertised products long since out of production, still covered the walls, hanging in the place of honor beside rusted and out-of-date farming implements. Nate settled back in the vinyl-covered bench, closed his eyes, and thought about the old building.

A raspy voice broke in on Nate's reverie, "The old building has outlasted most what's been downtown. Use'ta be a work-bed for the Ada County Dairymen's Co-op Creamery."

Nate looked up at the owner of the voice standing above him. "It was back in 1929…oh, up until it folded in the 70's. Back before the creamery closed, it provided milk checks to members of the cooperative, enabling them to pay their taxes and provide food for their families," the leathery skin waitress continued her unsolicited narrative.

"Milk had been brought in from surrounding dairy farms to produce Challenge Butter. In its heyday, the creamery ran seven days a week, and in its last days it made SMA baby formula. Can you believe that?" She finished, a look of pride for the city's history on her face.

The old downtown movie theater, the depot, and blacksmith's shop and the creamery smokestack had all come and gone. But still, the restaurant on the corner continued. The interior was now bright with an inlaid patterned wood design covering the walls. Windows opened on three sides allowing the merging morning luminescence, but even with these upgrades in the building, the restaurant maintained its early time period feeling.

The waitress, a bottle blond on the backside of fifty, chewed her gum and pushed her wire-rimmed glasses back up her petite nose before making the note on her pad. She turned to Nate.

"What about you, hun?" When he didn't answer right away, she looked over her pad and down the slope of her tiny nose at him. He was studying the menu. "We don't have none of that health food stuff here, babe. We serve a big breakfast for a hardworking man." She smiled and braced her hip against the table, folding her arms across her small breast.

Nate smiled. "Very good. Let me get two eggs scrambled hard, sourdough toast, and a sausage patty."

Straightening, the woman smiled and finished scribbling on her pad, and then stuck her pen behind her ear. "You gonna be a'right, honey. We'll get you fed up right—put some meat on you." She reached out and squeezed his shoulder, then without asking, she refilled the two coffee cups. Turning, she yelled the order to the retired Navy cook busy in the kitchen.

"Hey—ah, add a side of waffles to my order, please," Durgins called as the woman began to turn away. She stopped and arched a brow at him as if adding the new line of script was a particular bother.

Durgins interlaced his fingers and rested his forearms on the table. "I love this place. It reminds me of one of the cookhouses from back when I rode cattle." He laughed at a private memory and lifted his cup, saluted an invisible comrade, and sipped from the hot black liquid.

Nate arched an eyebrow. "You worry me sometimes."

"Only sometimes? I've got to try harder, then. Naaa, it's just an old Frenchman; a cowboy I worked with on the Winecup, a ranch down in northeast Nevada. Well actually we called him Frenchie, but anyway he—"

Nate raised a hand showing Durgins his palm. "Is this gonna be one of those stories I'm gonna be sorry I let you tell me?"

Durgins leaned back, a mischievous smile creeping across his features, darkening his usually pale face by an increasing blush. He laughed. "Well, maybe I should save that particular story for another time. But trust me, it'll make you laugh." He looked at Nate waiting for his acquiescence.

"I'll pass. Besides, I still need to tell you about the interview."

"Back to work."

"Yeah. Anyway, old boy in there is a freak. You saw his history: drugs, theft, and some financial stuff, but no sex abuse. He didn't even have a DV on his rap sheet."

Durgins had become serious again, the playfulness pushed aside, though not far from the surface. "You'd think a guy like that would have at least one incident where he beat up his old lady or something. Not one count of domestic violence on his sheet. Hard to believe, huh?"

"Nope. He's a weasel all right, but the warrant will hold him in jail for at least the rest of this week. Don't worry though, he'll be back out robbing and breaking into cars soon enough." Nate laughed a mirthless laugh and took a drink of his coffee.

Nate sat forward and placed a file folder on the tabletop. "Okay, what do we know so far? Let's review the details. This is a mess. So where do we begin?" He lifted a yellow legal pad and began flipping through pages.

"Dude. You need to slow down. You asked about fifteen questions there and didn't pause long enough to take a breath." Durgins began laughing when Nate looked up from the notepad.

Before he could respond, the waitress returned with their food. "What did you do, grind up the whole pig? That's the largest sausage patty I've ever seen." A half-inch thick, the golden-brown patty covered three-quarters of the plate's surface. Crispy around the edges; the rich juices dripped off the side and pooled on the table. The fragrance of the piquant meat hinted of garlic, sage, and a number of other spices Nate couldn't identify before tasting.

Nate closed his eyes and savored the first bite of sausage. He chewed slowly and rested in a moment of pure culinary delight. "If you're through lusting after that shoat, maybe we can get back to work," Durgins said around a mouthful of syrup-drenched waffle.

With obvious effort, Nate pushed his plate aside and picked up the manila folder. He chanced one last bite of sausage, wiped his mouth with a napkin, and rolled his eyes before turning his attention back to the folder in his hand. "Okay, the perp attacked our victim just before the end of her shift...which was at—"

"Twenty-one hundred hours."

"Twenty-one hundred. That was about..." Nate said dragging a finger across the page, "a half hour before the attack. That's not a lot of time to case the scene, plan the robbery and execute the rape."

Durgins interlocked his fingers again, propping his elbows on the table. "He must have been in the coffee shop before. Didn't she say he moved around the store as if he knew how it was laid out?"

Nate dropped his notepad, meeting Durgins gaze with his own. "Do you think.... No it couldn't be that easy." He pushed the folder aside and pulled out the smaller notepad he kept in his breast pocket. Flipping through folded and tattered pages, Nate hummed to himself as he studied the notes and recorded messages stored there.

"You gonna let me in on this?"

Nate held up a solitary finger, stalling any further questions. "Bam! Look at that." He turned the notepad toward Durgins and slid it across the plastic table covering.

Durgins picked up the notepad and studied the writing. Dropping it back to the tabletop, he whistled. "Wow."

CHAPTER EIGHT

(Seven Weeks Earlier)

WANDA EDNA MAE FULLER STEPPED OUT of her shower and appraised her 45-year-old body in the floor to ceiling mirror. With shoulder length ash-blond hair and a stomach that showed little evidence of having carried and delivered two healthy babies, she smiled, still liking what she saw reflected in the mirror. Barely showing wrinkles at the corners of her eyes, Edna Mae's skin was smooth and her arms reasonably tight. She turned, looking at herself over her shoulder again and smiled.

Picking up the business card, she focused on the name and then tilted it slightly, allowing the light to reflect off the foil-embossed badge. With exaggerated tenderness, she ran her finger across the name and badge number. Extending her arm, she looked at her reflection just beyond the reach of her arm. Her eyes flickered between the business card to the image in the mirror. Back and forth, up and down, side to side.

"Mom," the voice of teenage a girl called from the hallway, just outside the master bedroom's door. "Pastor Luck is here."

Edna Mae looked for a dry spot and sat the card down softly. Then turning, she found her robe and wrapped it around herself, cinching it at the waist. "Thanks, hun. Be right out. Let Pastor know I just got out of the shower and will be a minute."

A few minutes later, Edna Mae joined her 17-year-old daughter, Machele, in the modest living room with their pastor from the nearby Nazarene Church. Both of Edna Mae's daughters, Machele and 15-year-old Jasmine, still had their father's last name and went by Hamilton. Each of the girls had their father's dark hair, with the advantage of their mother's length and athletic build.

Pastor Luck stood as Edna Mae entered the room. His dark slacks perfectly creased and his tie and dress shirt lay covered by the full-length wool coat he still wore. Edna Mae smiled and extended her hand to the pastor. "Girls, turn the heat up. You got the pastor sitting in here freezing." She invited him to take his seat again.

He smiled. "Oh, think nothing of it. I wear this thing out of habit more than necessity." He cut his eyes from Edna Mae to her daughters standing nearby.

"Jasmine, put on the teakettle and bring out a service for the pastor and I. Machele, bring us something to snack on, please." She sat back, but still managed to appear rigid; like she was afraid she might fall off the chair at any moment. The teenage girls sprang into action like a well-orchestrated military unit, no noise, no fuss, just quick efficient response. Then they both disappeared down the short hall into their respective bedrooms, doors closing behind them.

Reverend Luck looked around the living room. Studying the books lining the shelf, he took note of the authors posted there. Jane Austin, Lynn Austin, Terri Blackstock, Karen Kingsbury, Beverly Lewis, Robin Lee Hatcher, and Francine Rivers were just a few of the names listed in alphabetical order on the well-kept shelf. Paintings depicting springtime picnics and young lovers strolling hand in hand and children playing adorned the walls.

Cheap, but very clean, Victorian styled furniture completed the room's décor, bespeaking of a very definite female hand in its choosing. Pastor Luck cleared his throat. "Very nice," he said, lifting his cup to indicate the room before taking a sip of the tea." He arched his brows and looked down into his teacup.

"You like it?"

"Yes—I mean, I'm more of a coffee person, but this is really good. What is it?"

She smiled, obviously pleased with herself. "I knew you liked coffee, but I thought I'd take a chance to broaden your palate, so to speak. I make this blend myself; I call it Felicity."

Pastor Luck took another sip, savoring it.

Edna Mae scooted forward in her seat. "It's a blend of Arbor Black, Puerh, and Rishi. Of course, I add a little extra dried Jasmine in it to give it that extra sweetness you taste."

"There's no sugar in this?" He looked skeptical.

She smiled. "The Puerh is a Chinese tea and is a post-fermentation blend—"

He interrupted her with the lifting of a brow.

"That just means the tea leaves undergo a microbial fermentation process after they have already been dried and rolled. Then I add a Japanese tea, the Rishi, and it's naturally sweet, coming from the Jasmine family." She drank from her own cup before continuing. "Of course, well, Jasmine is Jasmine and it adds to the overall sweetness."

He took another sip, and after clearing his throat again, he sat his cup down. He looked down the hall to where the girls had gone.

"Oh, they won't be coming back out until you've gone. You can feel free to talk about whatever you need to," Edna Mae said.

Pastor Luck looked at the cup then back down the hall and shook his head slightly. He mumbled, hardly audible, "Like you could read my mind."

She giggled. "No, I just pay attention. I knew you would be coming by here this morning. I knew my mom would call you, and you always do your visits in the early morning, leaving your afternoons open for study and in-office appointments. So I told the girls that when you got here to have the tea ready and then to go to their rooms until we were done talking."

So, that's why the girls were buzzing back and forth before she came out. He smiled. "Yes. About last night…How are you?"

Edna Mae didn't answer at first, but turned her eyes away looking at the titles on her bookshelf. Her face clouded and tears threatened to spill from her eyes. Her gaze froze and she seemed to retreat into herself.

Pastor Luck followed her gaze and saw it come rest on the spine of a book by Elaine Landau, a biography on the life of Margaret Brown, better known, if perhaps irreverently, as the Unsinkable Molly Brown.

Then Edna Mae took a deep breath, squared her shoulders, and shifted her gaze back to the pastor. "I'm fine."

Pastor Luck started at her sudden and unexpected response. "Ah, you know, at times like these—I mean in the wake of such a terrible experience—I mean-"

She swallowed visibly and took a cleansing breath. "Pastor, I assure you I'm fine. I've had time to think about this. The scriptures tell us that the Lord is our Strong Tower and as one of His sheep, I can find safety in Him, in that tower. So, you see, I am all right. I have to be."

"Sister Fuller—Edna Mae, it doesn't work that way. You've suffered a trauma."

She reached forward, lifted the tea service, refilling his cup, and then poured more into her own. With careful purposed movements, she lifted a silver teaspoon and stirred both cups, then returned the pastor's cup to him.

He looked at her, puzzled.

"Pastor Luck, don't look at me like that. I'm not crazy. You teach us to take the word of God seriously and I have decided to do just that. You look at me as if I'm nuts or something. I'm not having an episode."

She stood and paced over to the sliding glass door. Moving the vertical blinds aside, she looked out at the shallow backyard. The morning sun was already beginning to melt away; the night's deposit of frost and water droplets beat out their steady staccato on the concrete patio and rock beds beneath the trees. She looked up at the sky and sighed again. "Looks like it might snow again."

Pastor Luck frowned and interlaced his fingers. "Well, you know what they say about the spring weather in Idaho."

"Yeah, if you don't like it, just wait a minute, it'll change. Just like everywhere else, huh?"

"And then a minute later, it'll change again. But, Edna Mae, we're not talking about the weather. Edna Mae, we're talking about your emotions and the potential damage to your soul. This was an awful thing that this man did to you." The pastor raised his brows and focused his stern, but compassionate gaze on the woman. He raked his long fingers through his salt and pepper hair, and looked at her with a father's disquiet etched in his familial expression.

She did not turn or face him, but instead, wrapped her arms around her waist, hugging herself. "I know."

He stood, but did not approach her. "You know, you don't have to try and do this—go through this alone."

"But, Pas—"

"I was there when Jack left you and the girls. I remember what happened. I know how that hurt you. Let us hel—"

She spun to face him, and for a moment, intense anger ruddied her face. Clinching and unclenching her fist, then just as quick, she spun back away to look out at the small garden again.

"Edna Mae, let the church help you."

She turned to face him again, her eyes shifting back to the spine of the biography once more. She relaxed then walked back to her seat. "I know you're just trying to help, Pastor. I do. And

I welcome it, especially for the girls." She lifted her eyes toward the hall. "But I know I am not Wonder Woman. I am trusting God and you." She reached out and patted the back of his hand.

"Edna Mae—" Pastor Luck began, but then didn't finish the statement. After a moment of condensed silence, he tried a different approach. "What are the police saying?"

She slipped her hand into her pocket and fingered the business card, rubbing the pads of her fingertips over the imprinted name and badge number. She relaxed. "They are being great. He is so fantastic."

"He?"

She locked her gaze onto his. "I mean the detective. He was really professional, and I just know he's gonna find the person that did this to me." She brought her hand from her pocket and folded them both in her lap.

He raised his eyebrows again and stared at her for what seemed a moment longer than necessary. "What was this detective's name?"

She looked away. "You know, I don't really remember; I met so many people last night. It's still kind of a blur to me."

"A blur, huh?"

She looked back at her pastor. She forced a smile that didn't quite reach her eyes. "I think it was Ricks or something like that."

Pastor Luck stood and adjusted his coat over his lanky frame. "Edna Mae, be careful. We don't want a repeat of what happened last time."

A quick flash of anger was quickly covered by a smile. "I'm all right, Pastor. This is not Jack. It's not four years ago. I'm a new—a different woman, and this is a completely different situation."

He finished his tea and sat the cup down, and then walked over to where she still sat with her hands folded in her lap. He leaned forward and kissed her gently on the corner of her forehead. "You know I love you like you were my own child,

Edna Mae. You can tell me if there's anything out of the ordinary going on here."

She smiled up at him, but did not look into his eyes. "I'm all right. I didn't spend all those years growing up with your daughters just to forget all you taught us. I'm all right."

He straightened and then brushed her hair back from her face. "I'll see your parents tonight. You know they are going to want to talk about this."

She stood and hugged him around his waist, resting her head on his shoulder. "Well, you know Dad, he's gonna want to find someone to beat up, as if he still could. And Mom, well, we'll just have to cross that bridge when we get there." This time she did look up at him meeting his eyes. "I *am* all right."

She watched him walk away from her house, hesitate before getting into his car and then disappear down the road. She lifted the card from her pocket and looked at the name again, and smiled. "Yes, he's fantastic."

CHAPTER NINE

(Present Day)

AMBER STOOD AND WATCHED as Sherri Richards laid her hand gently on the brow of the fragile old woman lying unconscious in a hospital styled bed. Known as Mother Lisa by the church congregation, the older woman had been disowned and abandoned by her family since becoming a believer at the ripe old age of eighty-three. Now, a year later, she was dying.

Sherri straightened and looked past the sleeping figure and out the window, watching as traffic hurried north and south on 12th Avenue. Folding her arms across her chest, she sighed and then brushed a tear from her cheek that had escaped and ran languorously down her face. Amber walked up to her and wrapped an arm around her, "Oh, mom, she's at peace now."

Sherri turned to look at the younger woman and offered a weak smile. "It's not that. The staff here at Sunny Ridge has been terrific. Mother Lisa has been made comfortable and her home going is not far off now."

"Then what?" Amber's eyebrows knitted themselves together in confusion. She grabbed one of Sherri's hands, squeezing it with soft, steady pressure. "Then why are you crying?"

Sherri pulled her hand free, shook her head, and waved off the question. "You know traffic sure has gotten worse down here since the Wal-Mart went in. Now the south side is almost as busy as the rest of the city." She turned and walked back to the bedside and brushed a wisp of gray hair from the sleeping woman's face. She watched as the elderly woman's chest slowly rose and fell again, shallow risings and shallow falls; a look of peace on the wizened face. "It's Nate."

Amber relaxed her brow, as the feelings of heaviness that she had, by great effort, pushed to the back of her mind, broke over her again and darkened her heart. "I've tried calling him," she confessed, "but he won't answer." She looked up sheepishly. "And since the last time Jackie caught me over there, and well, let's just say it was a bit uncomfortable for us both, I think."

"He has talked to his father about it. Once. But he won't talk to me. Says he's all right, but a mother knows." Sherri lifted the sleeping woman's hand into her own and rubbed the bluish veins, smoothing the paper-thin skin. "It's almost like Mother Lisa....They've all abandoned him too. No one has called him. No one texted him or even emailed. It's like he doesn't exist to them anymore." She looked up at Amber. "I know he's hurting, but he just won't talk to me."

"Maybe he's talking to Jackie—." She left the sentence unfinished after seeing the expression on Sherri's face.

"I like Jackie, but I have never believed she was the right woman for Nate, and now that he needs someone so desperately.... Oh, I don't know." She stared at Amber for a long moment then looked back to the sleeping woman.

Amber walked to the opposite side of the bed and lifted Mother Lisa's other hand. The knuckles, gnarled with aged, stood in stark contrast against the younger, smoother olive-tone of Amber's youthful skin. "But Mother Lisa has us now."

Sherri looked up and held Amber's gaze, this time with tears flowing freely. She lifted the aged hand and pressed it to her lips. "But who does Nate have? Who-who does Nate have?"

CHAPTER TEN

(Present Day)

THE SMELL OF BURNT COFFEE filled the small, dark apartment. A thin crust having formed on the bottom of the glass carafe; the coffee pot would need to be replaced. Nate sat on the floor across the open space that separated the living room from the kitchen. His bare back pressed against the wall, knees bent with his feet flat on the floor, his arms draped over his knees. In the bedroom the sound of the phone ringing screamed with an urgency that would remain unmet.

The answering machine clicked on. *The voicemail for this account is full. Please call back.* Silence.

Blessed silence.

The images from the past days rushed back into Nate's mind. *She passed. You failed.* The voices kept playing over and over in his mind. *You failed. You failed. Can you explain why you failed?* The failed polygraph hung over his head like a death sentence. A sentence he could not avoid.

Nate began to bounce his forearms against his knees, absentmindedly watching as his hands swung with the motion. Soft spring daylight flittered around the edge of the curtain. The diffused ambiance blended as it came through the beige window covering, and the too bright, yet dull, apartment color paint.

Lowering his eyes to the floor, he looked at the darken face of the cell phone lying next to him. Picking it up, he turned it in his hands, checking to see if it was still on. Shaking his head, he rubbed a hand across his chin and felt the three-day growth. Unlike his father's, Nate's beard filled in quickly, and in the half week since being escorted from the P.D., his beard was already full. The quiet he sought, had hoped for, now pressed in on him. Inhaling deeply, Nate filled his lungs trying to push back the weight of aloneness that threatened, crushing him beneath its heaviness.

Deciding he needed something, he did not know what, he drew his legs up and bounced up to his feet. Like a caged animal, he walked back and forth across the small space. Pacing. Stop. Turn, then repeat. Back and forth, back and forth across the room. Frustrated, he bent forward at the waist, he grabbed at the itchy beard, tempted to pull it from his face; he opted instead for a shave.

The steam rose from the sink and clouded the mirror like a heavy fog. Resting his hands on the edge of the bowl, Nate reached up with his left hand and cleared a swath across the surface of the glass with the palm of his hand. *I didn't do this. What can they be thinking? They can't believe I assaulted this woman.* "Ahhh...Lord, I'm going crazy! God, help me. I can't fight this. I don't know how."

With heavy hands, Nate lathered his face, massaging the shaving cream onto his face as if the vigorous application would ease his troubled mind. Looking up, he stared at the image that peered back at him. He looked bad even to himself. Dark circles hung beneath bloodshot eyes, and his usually clean face lay hidden beneath a curly beard. He hardly recognized himself.

Nate took a deep breath to steady his hand and then dragged the razor along the contour of his chin.

After a quick shower and shave, Nate headed for the hallway, which would lead him from his apartment to the street below. A soft tap of his right hip pocket, and feeling the empty place where he used to keep the keys to his Jeep—*their Jeep*—he corrected himself, brought back to mind the totality of his separation. He sighed and looked at the vacant parking space where his department-issued vehicle had been kept for the last two and half years.

Pushing his hands into his pockets, he turned, but not before watching as a carload of teens pulled into his spot and began to unload from their vehicle. Nate frowned and looked back toward the stairs that led up to his apartment and the keys to his personal car. Looking up at the gray sky and then checking his cell phone's caller I.D., just in case the sergeant had called or perhaps the L.T., Nate grunted and just started walking.

Early afternoon came with a soft shower that was quickly shifting toward snow, but for the time being, the weather was in that in-between phase more akin to slush. Nate continued walking unmindful of his direction, not caring. He just walked. The ache of betrayal hung heavy on him. Each breath felt as if it had been dragged across rough-hewn stones. He played the events over and over in his mind, and still, he could not see where the fault had come, where he had been wrong.

He remembered the investigation getting off to a promising start, in spite of the fact they hadn't had much to go on. The team had responded well. The lineup of the usual suspects had risen and had been winnowed through. He and Durgins had cut the list down to three viable options. *Where did I go wrong?* The question plagued him.

The sounds of playing children drew Nate from his reverie, and he looked up and jumped back just as a car sped past him. A heavy wash of gray water rose up like a hand trying to grab him.

With a gasp and hurried steps backwards, he moved just in time to avoid getting soaked with the icy spray.

Looking across the road, he saw the children; groups of boys throwing soggy snowballs at each other while all the time brushing wet detritus from their already soiled jackets. Turning from the scene he continued walking, the feelings of isolation, once again, his only companion.

Sometime later Nate found himself on the greenbelt near the campus of BSU not too far from the memorial stone for the murdered flight attendant, and he remembered the last time he was at the large cenotaph. The day then, unlike today, had been bright and sunny. It was his first homicide investigation, and again, he had been questioning God.

Nate looked up at the lowering vault of the sky, icy droplets stinging the exposed flesh of his upturned face. "You still listening to me, Father? I have no idea how to get out of this one. Everything I have worked for—fought for, seems to be turned against me. I can't fight them. They're too big for me."

Silence.

Frustrated, he turned toward the sound of the near frozen water as it splashed noisily over jetting rocks and around trees that grew on the river's edge. As the monument became clear through the newly growing foliage, Nate stopped, unsure why he felt a sudden urge just to stand still. Removing a glove, he wiped water from his face and looked around, his senses on high alert.

Still, silence.

Birds silhouetted against the sky, flew overhead in sudden burst of movement, and the sounds of traffic not far away added to the background noise that was to be downtown Boise. Nate turned in a slow circle until he was once again facing the stone.

Wait. As if on the breath of the air, the sound seemed to echo in Nate's mind. *Wait for what—for who?* He reached for his gun, only to remember that it, too, had been taken, confiscated along with his badge and I.D. card. His identity.

Who are you? The question had floated to him from the direction of the river. Slipping the glove back on, Nate flexed his fingers against the on setting chill. *Where are you going?*

Nate turned again, looking for the owner of the voice.

Grabbing the sides of his face, Nate groaned from deep within himself. *Who am I now, Lord? I don't know where I'm going. I don't know who I am anymore.*

"Mr.? You all right?" A twenty-something college student approached Nate with wary steps. His hands extended out in front of him. "Do you need some help? I could call someone for you."

Straightening, Nate waved him off. "Naaa...I'm okay. Just thinking out loud. Trying to clear my head." Nate pulled the collar of his jacket closer around his neck, embarrassed at having been caught in such a vulnerable moment.

"Who are you?"

Nate looked at the young man, startled at the boldness of his question. "Well—"

The youth raised a hand, cutting off Nate's response. "Where are you going?" He asked seemingly into the air. It was then that Nate noticed the Bluetooth attachment clipped to the young man's ear. "Can you at least tell me if I'm getting warmer or not?" He burst into laughter. "Marco!"

From somewhere beyond the bend in the path came a faint response. "Polo."

Nate arched an eyebrow.

The college student turned to face Nate fully. Reaching up, he unclipped the communication device and held it up for Nate to see. "It's a game we play. Some of us get dropped off in a strange part of town, and we have to find our way back. It's kind of a race against the clock and the other players," he said smiling.

"Okay."

"But I can still call you that help if you need it. There's no rule against me calling for help for someone else; just not for myself. Besides, I couldn't leave a wounded Samaritan on the side of the road now, could I?"

Nate studied the man again and then looked at the direction from which the youth had come and then to the opposite direction toward the river. A questioning scowl crawled over his face. "Were you just down by the river?"

The young man followed Nate's travelling gaze with his own. "Are you sure you're all right, man. It's no problem. I can call someone. I'll even wait with you until they get here."

Nate finally looked down at himself, his cloths were wet from the constant drizzle and his hands and feet felt as if they were freezing despite being seasonally dressed and gloved. He chuckled in spite of himself. "No thanks. I'm okay, really." Even as he said it, he wondered if it were true. *Am I okay?*

"Look, mister. I'm going to go catch up with my friends, but if you don't mind, can I pray for you before I go?"

Nate's head snapped up.

The young man raised both hands toward Nate, his palms facing him. "Nothing weird, I won't even touch you. I'll stay over here."

Nate didn't answer, but stared at the stranger, then let his eyes rise upward to the darkening sky. He noticed that the young man had removed his hat and had lifted one hand toward the sky. Without waiting for a response from him, the stranger had begun to pray.

"Father, I ask you to help this brother. I don't know who he is or where he's going, but I know You know. Show him the path You want him to follow. In spite of what he may be feeling, assure him that You are still in control. In Jesus name, amen." His pocket buzzed and he reconnected the ear-clip communicator. He smiled at Nate and then hurried down the path, disappearing around the curve.

Nate followed the young man with his eyes until all he could see was an empty path and growing darkness through the trees.

Suddenly cold, he wrapped his arms around his biceps and shivered. "What was that, Lord?" He asked of the sky.

Silence.

The sounds of the river continued and the afternoon traffic began to pick up. The sounds of the birds had died away with the growing gloom and the last of the evening light began to drift down toward darkness. Just up ahead, he could barely make out the rounded top of the stone that sat alongside the path. He remembered the Abyss case and just how close he had come to losing Amber. Then he remembered that was exactly what had happened. He'd lost her anyway. The feelings of heaviness returned.

CHAPTER ELEVEN

(Six Weeks Earlier)

NATE SAT AT HIS DESK reviewing the investigation notes. Chris MacGilvery stood over him, a sour look on his unshaven face. "Look," Mac said, picking up his briefcase, "there's nothing you can do until we get the lab reports back. So you might as well go home, get some sleep, and come back when you're fresh."

Nate looked up at him and smiled. "You're right." He rocked back in his seat, lifting his feet to his desk. He closed his eyes and interlocked his fingers behind his head. Taking a long moment, he rested in that position, his eyes closed before addressing Mac again, "So you guys will be gone for what, two weeks?"

"Three." Mac answered as he moved toward the door. "I'm so looking forward to getting away from this on again off again snow and just laying on the beach soaking up some sun."

Nate smiled, dropped his feet to the floor and rocked forward. "So-Cal, huh?"

"So-Cal, yep." He stuffed the final papers into his briefcase and snapped it shut. "I think Durgins will be all right on this. He's new but he's sharp."

Nate stood and put his own desk in order, moving papers and closing drawers before turning off his desk light. "Oh, I'm not worried about that. I just hate the fact that you'll be down there kicking it with Mickey and the boys, getting all tanned, and I'll be here freezing my behind off." The two men laughed and headed toward the door.

"Richards," a voice called out from the far side of the CID work pod.

Nate stopped and looked back to see who it was that had called him. Mac slapped him on the shoulder and kept walking. "Later."

Turning to look at his partner before the door closed between them, Nate called out, "See you in three weeks, partner."

The door swung shut and Nate turned back to see the chiseled face of Detective Durgins coming toward him. Nate wondered how the man always managed to look so clean-shaven no matter what time of day or night it was. "Hey, glad I caught you," the blond-haired Durgins said. "I was going over the file, just looking at who did what, and I noticed some details I wanted to run by you."

Nate sighed and leaned his back against the door that led out into the hallway. He smiled, taking note of Durgins exuberance. He wondered if he had come across so annoyingly excited when he had first transferred up to CID. "Is this something different than what we discussed at breakfast?"

"Well, yes and no." Durgins scratched his head, a quizzical look coloring his youthful face. "Well, anyway, the way I see it, it comes down to one of three possible suspects."

Nate was tired and wasn't in the mood to just hangout talking case facts. He wanted to go home, take a hot shower, and go see Amber—he frowned. No, not Amber! He needed to see Jackie. He scratched his head in confusion.

Seeing the frown on Nate's face, Durgins hurried forward with his explanation. Nate swung a hand toward his desk and invited Durgins to join him as he walked back and settled down behind his desk. Nate pressed the switch at the corner of his desk, and the lamp tucked beneath the hood of his desk flickered and came on.

Durgins sat in the seat at the corner of Nate's desk and leaned forward, resting his elbows on his knees, intense. "Look, we've got DNA from the scene and based on the witness statements from…" He looked through the stack of papers, shuffling them in his hands, "—from Kathy Kellerston-"

"Kellerston?"

"Oh, yeah, you haven't heard about her yet. Patrol ran into her putzing around the scene last night. She claims to have been involved in a relationship with a guy who fits the description of our bad guy."

Nate swiveled his seat around to face Durgins. "Really?"

Durgins arched his brows. "What? What do you mean?"

Nate chuckled. "More likely she's been dumped and is mad at the guy and sees this as a chance to hammer him." At Durgins confused expression, Nate added, "No doubt this guy is a dirtbag, but dimes to a dollar he won't be our guy. It's too easy."

"Well, be that as it may, I think we need to look at him. He's got to be worth a look."

Nate looked at his cell phone, checked the time, and then compared that to the clock on the wall. "But not tonight. I'm tired. Tired minds don't plan well."

Durgins stood. "Oh no, no. I hadn't planned on tonight. I called her and had her plan to come in tomorrow at 1500 hours. You good with that?"

Nate sighed and stood, flicking the desk light off as he did. "Doesn't matter. It's scheduled, I'll be here. Let's say we meet here at noon for prep." The two men started toward the door, Nate for the second time in the last half-hour. "Who needs a weekend anyway," he muttered under his breath.

Durgins stopped, bracing his arm across the doorway, blocking Nate. "Hey, I can do this solo if you're too tired."

Nate laughed. "Yeah, right. I can only imagine how much of my backside Brown would bite off if he even thought I'd considered it. Besides, we're a team now. In for a penny...?"

"In for a pound," Durgins finished. Dropping his arm, he slapped Nate on the back as he passed. "Ooo-rahhh, Marine!"

"Ooo-rahhh," Nate answered, and then added, "Can we go get some sleep now. Well, actually, I sort of got a date tonight."

Durgins got an aw-shucks smile on his face then held up the stack of papers. "I think I'm gonna hangout and go over these a bit more. Study some."

Nate snatched the papers. "Oh, no you're not. Get out of here. Go home. Go to the Sunrise, but get out of here and do something not cop related for the next few hours. I'm gonna need you fresh tomorrow. Not all dragged out and overly tired—and relax."

Durgins laughed. "I am relaxed. This is how I relax, either this or go to the gym." He reached up along the wall and turned off the lights, leaving the CID workstation dark. Nate pushed him in the back as the military minded Durgins filed past him. The men laughed as they made their way to the elevator and down to the lobby.

***

Nate reached across the small table and took a hold of Jackie's curled fingers. She'd stretched her hand toward him, her palm facing upward, inviting. He cleared his throat. "Ah, I'm sorry. I guess my mind is just on work."

"It seems like you've had a lot on your mind lately." She smiled weakly. The low light reflected in her green eyes, causing them to sparkle. She tilted her face forward and lowered her lashes, hiding their light for the moment. Withdrawing her hand, she rested her cheek in her open palm. A single tear fell from her lashes and streaked down her face. "Are we all right?"

"What? Why...of course. Why would you say that? We're having a few bumps is all." Nate got up and moved his chair around the table to sit beside her. Taking her in his arms, she rested her face against his chest. He took her right hand with his left and began stroking the back of her knuckles. He whispered into her hair. "I know things are tough right now, but we can get through this."

Jackie settled herself against him, accepting the comfort his nearness offered. She didn't speak. She couldn't, but a nagging sense of dread continued to grow in the pit of her stomach. She looked at their intertwined hands. Lifting her thumb, she brushed it against Nate's and sighed at the contact. She turned to look up into his face, watching as his chin worked as he spoke. "We're just fine." She heard him say. "We're fine," he said in a distant sounding voice.

Nate pushed her back to arm's length and stared into her eyes. "Look, I love you and nothing is going to change that."

She smiled, sad and unsure. "Yeah," she whispered, and pulled herself back against his chest. They sat together in silence; the restaurant was quiet around them. Waiters and busboys began cleaning tables as the last of the patrons began to empty out.

"This reminds me of our first date," Nate said as he held her against him continuing the interplay of their fingers. He could feel her stir against him. "It was winter then."

She shivered as if his words brought back the realization of that frigid evening. "Yes, but it's spring now; the time for growth and change." She pulled back from him and looked into his face. Now it was his turn to wonder at unspoken thoughts, the feelings which played behind the emerald fire captured in her eyes. Long moments passed and still she held his gaze. Not speaking, not moving, just looking and thinking.

The lights flickered and then came up to full, illuminating the dining room and the montage of Italian ballads came abruptly to an end. "Excuse me, sir." The voice had come from behind them. Nate turned and saw the manager standing with an apologetic look on his face. "I'm sorry, sir, but the restaurant is closing. Is there anything else I can get for you?"

Nate looked around and noticed the tired expressions and arch bow of the employees' shoulders as they moved with varying degrees of energy. Nate looked at the face of his cell phone and grimaced as he took note of the time. "Wow."

Jackie pulled away from Nate and grabbed her purse before she began moving to get up. "Oh, sorry." She brushed a tear from her cheek.

"If you need a few more minutes, I can—" The manager began.

"—No, no, we're leaving. I ah, lost track of the time," Nate said as if distracted. He stood and helped Jackie into her coat.

Once outside, the couple walked slowly together, his arm around her waist, her head against his shoulder. They stepped carefully around puddles as they continued their trek in silence. Nate checked the time again. "You got to be somewhere?" Jackie asked, noticing the movement.

Nate jostled her closer to him. "No."

"You just keep checking the time." Her voice was soft, inviting.

Nate smiled at her, although his smile was lost in the near darkness. He kissed the top of her head. "You know me. It's been a long day, and I was thinking about doing that interview tomorrow. Durgins' got enough energy for him and me both. I'd hoped to have the day with you tomorrow. I was going to hangout and bug you at the coffee shop all morning."

"That would have been nice. We could have got out of there around ten and gone downtown."

Above them, the night sky cleared and a cold wind swept across the parking lot. As they reached Nate's car, he turned her to face him. This time the parking lights did reflect in her eyes, and it warmed him. Tilting her face upward with the side on his index finger, he kissed her gently on the lips. He pulled her against him, holding her that way for several minutes.

The various stores, Best Buy Electronics, Sally's Beauty Supply and even Tully's Coffee, which shared the central parking lot, were all closed. Only the Target Super Store across the street still had lights on, its larger than life red and white icon shining beacon-like against the night. Nate leaned back, a mischievous grin pulling at the corners of his lips. "You know, we never did get our cup of coffee."

Jackie returned his smile, all her earlier misgivings forgotten temporarily. She squeezed his hand and snuggled closer to him. Together without speaking, they decided to run across the wide street rather than driving the relative short distance.

After a series of stops and starts, slipping, sliding, and laughing, they made their way into the foyer of the brightly lit box store. Continuing in and to the right they made their way toward the Starbuck's counter only to find that it, too, had closed. "What? No! It's a conspiracy," Nate said, throwing his arms up in mock disbelief.

"What now?" She held on to Nate's arm, fighting for control as a fit of the giggles threatened to overtake her.

Taking a deep breath, Nate settled himself. "I don't know. I didn't plan any further than run across street. Get coffee. Drink coffee." He laughed again. This time they drew quizzical stares from the late shift staff as they stood by in red frocks and blue pullovers watching the strange couple.

Growing serious, Jackie placed a hand on his chest. "We still haven't had coffee."

Sensing the change, Nate looked into her eyes. "You're right about that. Got any solutions?"

She stepped away from him, drawing him after her by the hand. "Come on, if there is one thing I can do, it's make coffee." She led him from the flat overhead florescent light out into the chilled darkness of the vaulted sky.

Twenty minutes later, Nate found himself sitting back on a light beige secondhand sofa in Jackie's living room. With a matching loveseat on the opposite side of the room and the black-facing of an inset fireplace, the room was warm and cozy, even without the low burning gas log with its blue and tallow-colored flame. Soft jazz filtered through the room from ebony-faced Sony SS-B1000 bookshelf speakers.

The muted mauve IKEA floor rug covered most of the old wooden floor, and with the track lighting set low, and the giant woven fans set like bookends mounted on the wall, all blended to give the apartment an easy feeling he had come to like so much about being here.

At the far end of the narrow room, Jackie had kicked off her shoes and stood barefooted at the counter. The single light over her head brought out the red highlights in her hair, and Nate leaned back appreciating the picture of femininity. She looked up, and he smiled warmly at her. Studying her form again, he prayed. *Lord help me.*

"So how do you afford all this on a barrister's salary?" He walked up behind her and hugged her around the waste, snuggling her at the neck.

She smiled, and pretended to shake him off, however her movement lacked conviction. "What? I told you the furniture was all secondhand, and the speakers—"

"Bose speakers."

"No," she smiled and brushed a strand of hair from her face, "Sony and they were only about $55.00 each, so not a great expense."

He laughed and hugged her tighter. "How about that computer console you use to make coffee," he said releasing one hand and reaching out to touch the control panel of the very expensive looking coffee maker on the counter.

She slapped his hand. This did have conviction.

"Hey, now." She rubbed the back of his hand. "But this is my baby." Even from behind her, he could feel the warmth and color that would be rising in her face as she began to describe her coffee maker. "This is no regular coffee maker here. This is the Clover Coffee Maker and cost almost $11,000.00." She burst into laughter as Nate pulled his hand back and stepped away from her.

"Eleven what?" He wiped his hand across his face, the surprise still very evident on his features.

Jackie turned to face him and continued laughing. "My uncle is a friend of one of three Stanford engineers who designed it. It's reported to be the world's best coffee maker."

He relaxed and reached a tentative hand forward again, this time almost reverently. "World's best, huh?"

She poked him playfully in his stomach. "Starbuck's seemed to think so. They bought it and now people like you and I can't even buy one...even if you had $11,000.00." She poked him again and turned back to the coffee maker. Lifting the chrome colored cup, she poured the premeasured coffee grounds into the boiler at the top of the machine. Like an elevator floor, the circular platform lowered automatically into the housing and steaming hot water poured from the built in piping.

Using a mini whisk, she stirred the mixture. Nate looked over her shoulder as the mixture quickly began to steam. The machine began to whir and the sounds of gears and lifts moving buzzed softly. A strong sucking sound filled the kitchen and the coffee mixture disappeared only to reappear from the bottom of the machine into Nate's waiting cup. "What just happened?"

She smiled like a proud parent a revealing surprise gift to her anxious child. "It combines the best aspects of the French Press and vacuum tube coffee makers. Once the water is heated up to the desired temp, the header there presses it down and then the chamber is sealed. Once that happens, the whole thing is sucked up and forced through a very fine filter into your waiting cup." She lifted the cup and passed it to him.

He reached for the creamer and she caught his hand. "Taste it first, and then add anything you want." She looked up at him and her eyes seemed to glow with excitement—emerald fire.

Nate held her gaze for a long moment and then raised the cup to his lips. He smiled.

"You like it?"

He nodded his head again, his smile broadening.

"What are you smiling about? Is it that good?" She moved to put the creamer and Splenda away, but he caught her hand. "What?"

"I still want my cream and sweetener—"

She frowned, confused. "But you said you like it."

He smiled and pulled her closer to him. "Yes, and you also said I could add anything I wanted."

She turned to retrieve the carton of creamer, but Nate caught her chin between his index finger and thumb. He pulled her face back to him and lowered his lips against hers.

Her breath caught.

He pulled back and looked into her eyes. They smiled and kissed again, this time with fervor on both sides.

After a long moment, she pulled away and stepped out of his embrace. She turned to put the creamer away again, desperate for something to do with her hands and get her mind off the track on which it had been traveling.

He reached for her again.

"Nate," her single word response stilled him. With a sharp inhalation of breath, Nate stepped back raising his hands up between them as if on guard. "Nate," she said again, this time imploring. She reached out, grabbing the tips of his fingers with hers. A soft, weakened smile pulled at the corners of her lips. Apologetic. "We can't…"

"No, no," he said and gathered her against himself. "No, babe, I'm sorry. It's my fault. I just seem to forget myself when I'm with you sometimes." He tossed her curls playfully and then brushed her cheek with his knuckle. Taking her by the hand, he led her to the sofa. "Maybe there's something on T.V. we can watch.

As the flat screen picture glared to life, Nate turned his attention to the remote control held in a lazy grasp in his fingers. She watched him as he flicked from channel to channel before stopping on the sports station. She knew he would.

Curling beside him with her knees tucked tight, she grasped his hand and played with his fingers, watching him while he watched TV. He turned and smiled at her briefly before turning his attention back to the screen. She smiled in return, but it failed to reach her eyes.

CHAPTER TWELVE

(Six Weeks Earlier)

NATE WALKED INTO THE OFFICE and wasn't surprised to see Durgins already seated at his desk, files open and the interview room prepped and ready to go. Looking up from the stack of papers and folders opened on his otherwise neat desk, he acknowledged Nate with a tilt of his head. Nate thought Durgins' boyish face looked as if it had never needed a razor. Shaking his head in brief movement, Nate smiled.

Durgins shifted his gaze first to his wristwatch then up to the wall clock. "You're early," he said around the wooden toothpick perched between his lips.

"Apparently, not. You beat me here. I thought an hour early would get me in with time to go over everything." Nate waved his hand to indicate the office and interview room.

Durgins stood up, pushing the chair away with a snap of his legs. "Oh well, that's all done now. What do you think we should use as theme with this woman? I know you said that you didn't have a good feeling about her, and I admit that she does have an angle—I mean, she has a reason to lie. And she does have a history of lying, but I think we can still use her for what we're trying to get done here. What do you think?"

Nate lowered his face to hide his smirk. "How much coffee have you had already?" He looked over to where the coffee pot sat almost empty.

Durgins followed his gaze and tipped his chin. "Get you a cup? You look like you need to catch up." Nate shook his head again, indicating that he did not. He sat at the table, pulled the file across to himself, and began leafing through the loose pages. Something Durgins had said bothered him on a different level.

He remembered his actions with Jackie from the night before and a feeling of shame nibbled at the corners of his conscience. The phrase, "...use her for what we're trying to get done..." kept niggling at his mind. Was that all she meant to him? He looked off into nothing and allowed his mind to replay the scene. He remembered them sitting together on the sofa, him talking and her smiling back at him. *Had her smile been missing something?* He could tell she wanted him, that she loved him, but at the same time, there was something sad about her.

Did he love her?

Nate grunted and adjusted himself in the chair trying to escape a sudden feeling of discomfiture. He looked back at Durgins who was now up pacing back and forth across the small room, smacking the side of his leg with a rolled tube of papers in cadence with each step. "Okay?" Durgins asked into the air. Nate watched him, knowing he was simply processing information out loud.

Durgins continued. "Kathy Kellerston, age twenty-six, two children. Been arrested several times. Mostly small stuff."

"Any 160's," Nate asked, interrupting him.

Durgins stopped pacing and flipped through the small sheaf of papers he'd been drumming against his thigh as he walked. He looked up. "Yeah...possession of a controlled substance and paraphernalia going back to her teens. One burg and a couple petit thefts." He returned to the table and sat across from Nate. "You think this is a waste of time?"

Nate leaned forward and massaged his eyes with the palms of his hands. He forced thoughts of Jackie from his mind. "No, not necessarily." His voice sounded tired, even to him.

"You all right?"

"Just tired. Long night."

"Must have been a good almost date." Durgins chuckled with a knowing tone.

Nate looked up, catching his meaning. "No. It's nothing like that. The date was nice and safe. I just got stuff on my mind. Things I need to figure out. As a Christian I just want to do it right. Besides, man, you know I'm into the whole sex after marriage thing."

Durgins smiled. "Hey, man, when it comes to women, I just love 'em. I don't try to figure them out. I'm not that smart."

Nate wadded a sheet of paper and threw at the slightly younger man, bouncing it off his shoulder. "What'd'ya say we get back to what we came here for?"

Durgins laughed and tossed the wad of paper back at Nate. "I'm good with that. It's like we say on the ranch: Whenever we have a particularly mean heifer to deal with, it's just best to deal with her head on. Those young females can be mean in ways a bull never would. They can seem all gentle and kind, and then at the last minute, will turn and gore ya. But a bull, well, he's all about letting you know right up front that he's in charge. Know what I mean?"

Nate scowled and then rubbed his temples. "You make my head hurt sometimes; you know that?"

"I'm just saying, this woman coming in may be, you know, might be like you were saying, trying to play us for her own purposes. We just need to watch and make sure she doesn't turn on us. That's all I'm saying."

Nate laughed. "Now, wasn't that easier?"

"Sure, but it lacked a certain bit of color. You gotta admit that the heifer story will kind of stick with you. Nothing like a good solid word picture to set a thing right in a fella's mind." He smiled, full of self-confidence.

Chuckling, Nate checked his watch again. "She's late." He was amazed at how easily time passed with Durgins. The man had a way of getting him to laugh and, before he knew it, an hour would pass by unnoticed.

"I'd better go check the front door just in case she forgot to use the callbox." He left the room, and Nate found himself alone in silence. And against his will, his mind returned to Jackie. He found himself wondering how easily his attentions had turned to the physical with her. In all the years he'd known Amber, and especially in that last year before she moved out of state, Nate had been carful never to go *there*.

Thoughts of his first date with Jackie, and how they had ended their evening with a lingering kiss, surfaced in his mind. He shivered with the recollection. He reveled in the remembered sensation, while at the same time, felt shame for the track on which his thoughts had been. Since then, the temptation to be physical was always there—never far from the surface.

He knew that Jackie was a devout believer, and his own faith was very important to him as well. But when they were together, it became easier and easier for him to go *there* and easier for her to give in. Something had to change. "Oh God," he breathed aloud and rubbed his hands roughly across his face, "What am I doing to this girl?"

Hearing the door open, he turned to see Durgins step through and stop, the door resting against his shoulder. Nate squared his shoulders and exhaled; composure back in place.

As Durgins held the door, a rather old looking 26-year-old Kathy Kellerston walked through. Entering the room, she looked around without stopping to do so. With a practiced ease, she surveyed the interior, taking note of the where, what, and who was present. She turned sultry dark-blue eyes onto Nate.

She wore her artificially colored black hair pulled back and held in place with a soiled white hair band. Her mascara looked as if it had been worn since the night before and was caked in the corners, while appearing faded at the edges, causing her eyes to look clumpy and tired. "Miss Kellerston," Nate said extending his hand.

"Kathy. Call me Kathy or I'll think you're talking to my mother." She smiled in a way Nate could only believe she intended to be alluring.

"All right...Kathy. Thank you for coming this afternoon. I know you must be busy. Can I get you anything?" Just then Durgins returned carrying two Styrofoam cups of water. He sat them on the table in front of the woman. She sat, assuming the seat where the waters had been placed.

Nate looked at his partner and nodded. Durgins smiled slightly, as if to say, I'm on it.

Kathy lifted the first cup and drank quickly, using a portion of the water to rinse her mouth, before finally swallowing. She smacked her lips slightly and then smiled. "I had a bad taste in my mouth from last night." She finished the first cup.

Nate exchanged a glance with Durgins, then pulled out his own seat and sat to the right of Kathy while Durgins sat opposite of her. Deciding it was better to handle this as Durgins had suggested, *"deal with her head on..."* Nate opened his file and pulled out the woman's written statement she had given to the patrol officers the night before. "You remember writing this?" He set it on the table in front of her.

Picking up the sheet of paper, Kathy dragged a chipped fingernail across its surface. Her lips moved as she appeared to read the thick lines of script. "Yeah, that looks like my writing. Although I'm surprised you can read it."

Nate smiled. "I was having a bit of trouble."

She giggled and the men snickered along with her in an attempt to help her relax. Durgins leaned back from the table, crossing his arms over his chest and Nate knew he had shifted into the mode of cover-officer, watching this woman's every move. Not only would he be Nate's backup in case she became violent, he would study her for the small signs of deception, *tells* as the poker players referred to them.

She picked up the second cup and ran a stubby finger along its rim before drinking from it. Sitting back in the nylon backed chair and bouncing nervous eyes between the two men, never really looking away from either of them entirely. "I suppose you want me to tell you about Brett."

Nate placed both hands on the table, palms down, in a gesture he hoped would seem none threatening and not overly interested. "Is this the man you told the patrol officers about?" He said casually.

"Yeah, Brett Torrie. Me and him had a thing for a while. He's my baby-daddy, but we don't see too much of each other anymore." Nate pretended to be writing this down, but looked up and arched a brow at Durgins. The younger detective got up from the table and opened the door that led into the interview room.

Having moved to the door of the interview room, Durgins waited for Nate's signal then spoke. Pulling the toothpick from between his lips and using it as a pointer, he directed Kathy's gaze toward the open door. "Hey, Kathy", he called, "why don't we move it all in here? That way we won't be bothered if someone comes through while we're talking."

Apparently, the fact that it was Sunday afternoon hadn't registered with Kathy or that the building had been locked when she arrived, and that she had not seen anyone else as she entered the building. She got up quickly and followed the detective into the smaller room.

Nate lagged behind her, feigning to collect and order the stack of papers, before going to the switch by the door and activating the digital-video-recording, DVR system before he, too, followed them into the room.

Checking to make sure the red record indicator was on, Nate settled in the faux leather chair at the corner of the small table and contemplated the lady sitting across from him. With a short intake of breath, he began, "So Ms—" He stopped, noting her raised brows and began again. "Kathy, tell me about Brett."

CHAPTER THIRTEEN

(Six Weeks Earlier)

THREE HOURS LATER, THE TWO DETECTIVES WATCHED as Kathy Kellerston walked out of the CID substation's lobby. As the heavy glass door's magnetic lock engaged with a dull click, Nate could not help but wonder at the information she had given them. If there was ever a situation where something had been too good to be true, this may very well be it. Nate unfolded the small fold of paper that Kathy slipped into his hand just before walking through the door. Without looking at it, he dropped it into the folder he carried.

"So what do you think?" Durgins asked with a slight eagerness in his voice.

"I don't know." Nate leaned his face against the coolness of the glass. Looking up, he noted the shifting colors of the late afternoon sky and knew it would be dark soon. Chancing a quick glance at his watch, he realized he had only a few hours left before he would be expected at his father's Sunday evening Bible study.

Lifting his face from the glass, he looked back at Durgins. "You can't deny she paints a pretty picture. This guy Brett is at least good for a hook even if he's not our man."

Durgins slapped his fist into an open palm. "Let's go get him. We can get him in here for questioning."

Turning fully and resting his back on the floor to ceiling window, Nate stuffed his hands into his pockets, the folder jammed between his bicep and chest. "Whoa, cowboy, let's think about what we've got first. Didn't you guys have a saying on the ranch about going slow and not rushing in?"

Durgins relaxed with obvious effort. Propping a foot on one of the tables in the lobby and resting his elbow on it, he asked, "So, what's your call?"

Nate remained reclined against the window, both hands stuffed in his pockets, his face downcast. "I don't know, partner. I think we need to assess what we have...see what it's telling us." With a bounce, he hefted himself from the glass and walked over to where Durgins stood. Pulling the folder from beneath his arm, he tossed it on one of the empty chairs and sat in one near it.

Turning his attention to the folder, Durgins removed the toothpick from between his teeth and pointed it at the collected sheets of paper inside. "What was that she gave you anyway?"

"What?" Nate opened his eyes, but without sitting up from his slouched position, he rolled his face toward his partner. "What was what?"

Durgins reached down and grabbed the folder. Opening it, he found the unfolded square of paper. Laughing, he dropped the folder back into the seat and walked around the U shaped formation of chairs to stand directly in front of Nate.

This time Nate did draw his legs in and sat upright in the chair. "What is it? What did she say on that? She better not had been stroking us—playing us for the fool." He reached for the paper Durgins held between his right index finger and thumb.

Laughing, Durgins snatched the paper away and danced back out of Nate's reach. "Come on, don't leave me hanging, what does it say?" Nate couldn't help but smile, knowing Durgins was about to bust his chops about something.

"Oh yeah," Durgins began, "she's got playing on her mind, but it ain't with us. She wants to play with *you*."

This time Nate did manage to grab the slip of paper from Durgins hands. He paced toward the front door, and standing in the fading light, he read the page.

"If black men could blush, I'd see a crawl of red flush up your neck now, partner." Durgins continued to laugh as he reflected on the very froward statement conveyed in the note. "She doesn't leave much to the imagination, does she? She already got your part scripted out." He burst into laughter again.

Nate waded up the paper and threw it at Durgins, who dodged it with ease. "Let's get out of here; at least one of us does have a life."

"I bet you do."

The two men moved together toward the elevator on the opposite side of the lobby. Pressing the call button, Nate rested his shoulder against the wall. When Durgins made kissy lips and smiled, Nate punched him on the shoulder. The men broke out in easy laughter as the doors slid apart.

Just as the elevator door slid shut, the last of the sun's light seemed to dim, and the lobby faded into the soft grayness that exists between sunset and nightfall. Behind them, neither man paid any attention to the small wad of paper that lay tucked beneath the wire-rack of pamphlets and free booklets attached to the south wall.

***

Lieutenant Brown leaned back, the chair creaking with his weight as he did. Lifting his shoes to the corner of the desk, he interlaced his fingers behind his head and smiled. "So you think this Brett Torrie is our guy, huh?"

Nate exchanged glances with Durgins. "He fits the M.O., and for right now, we just don't have a lot else to go on.

Whoever the perp is, he was clean." Nate leaned against the doorframe and looked down at his new partner. Durgins sat ramrod straight in one of the two chairs in front of the lieutenant's desk.

He kicked the leg of the chair and Durgins turned to look at him. Nate mouthed, "Relax." Durgins grinned and nodded, lifting one booted foot, propping it on the knee of the other. Bracing the familiar toothpick, he looked back and winked at Nate.

Brown dropped his feet to the floor with a dull thud and stood. Massaging his lower back, he arched and then stretched. "So, what's your next move? You want to bring this guy in for questioning or what?" He sat on the edge of his desk and rested an elbow on one knee.

Durgins sat forward then bounced up to his feet. "Now we're talking!"

Nate smiled and walked to the far side of the office and stared at the awards and plaques that adorned the lieutenant's wall. "It would be nice to execute a search warrant and interview him all at the same time. That way he won't get a chance to create a story," he said without facing either of the two men.

Brown sighed. "Who's gonna write it? You?" He pointed to Durgins.

Durgins rubbed his chin and then stepped forward. "I've never written one, but there's no time like now to learn how. I'm game."

Nate turned. He walked toward the desk, taking slow unmeasured steps. Something bothered him, but he couldn't quite wrap his mind around it. His focus softened as he replayed the interview and the events from the last forty-eight hours through his mind. The victim. The witness. The interview. Like an old time flipbook, the images flashed through his mind.

"Richards!"

Startled, Nate turned and faced the lieutenant. "Sirrr—I mean, yes, sir. I think we should write this up and coordinate the interview."

"What's wrong? Something not sitting well with you?" Brown asked. Durgins looked between the two of them, a look of anxious anticipation playing across his face."

Nate hesitated slightly before answering. "It's just that it's thin. All we have is the statements made by Kathy and she's not up for any awards for character of the year."

Brown reached back and picked up the file and began flipping through the report covering the interview. "Think she's lying?"

"Absolutely. The question is about what and why."

Durgins reached forward and tapped the corner of the file, causing it to dip in the lieutenant's grip. "Yeah, but she gave us details that she had no way of knowing. The dark clothing, the mask, the ropes, and even the green duct tape and weird accent. You have to admit that was a bit strange. Too coincidental."

Nate rubbed his face and then settled himself in the chair he'd vacated earlier. "That's what bothers me. It's almost too good—too well packaged. But I don't think we have a choice; we almost have to look at it. We need to bring this guy in, and I'll set up the interview." He leaned back, clasped his hands in his lap, and looked from Lieutenant Brown to Durgins. The sour feeling of unease still growing in his gut. He let out a long, slow breath.

Durgins turned and left the room, calling over his shoulder as he did, "I'm on the warrant."

Nate hadn't moved. Resting his head against the wall behind him, he closed his eyes. Brown stood and paced around the small office, first studying, then straightening the frames on the wall. "What's your theme?"

Nate answered without opening his eyes. "I was thinking pride. From what she says about this guy, he's a bit of a control freak; so if I can prick his pride, he might tell us something in spite of himself."

"It's a risk."

Nate opened his eyes and sat up. He raised a brow.

"If he calls your bluff, that same pride may cause him to lock down and say nothing." Brown walked back behind his desk and sat before placing the file back on the stack in front of him. "But I see you don't have any other choice."

Nate stood, sensing the meeting was coming to an end. "I could always just ask him to confess."

"Yeah, tell me how that works out for you." Brown slipped his glasses on and began reading through the files on his desk, leaving Nate to stare at the top of his balding head. After several seconds had passed, Brown spoke again without lifting his gaze. "Close the door behind you."

Nate opened his mouth and then closed it without speaking. He turned and slipped through the door, and as he did, he grabbed the handle, allowing it to swing behind him.

"If you don't think you can do the interview, I'd be glad to replace you on it." Brown said.

Nate looked back at his commanding officer. His head was still bowed over the folders, for all intentions not having moved from his earlier position. "Naaa, I got it, sir."

"Good. Close my door."

Nate closed the door.

CHAPTER FOURTEEN

(Six Weeks Earlier)

EDNA MAE ROLLED TO HER BACK and stared at the ceiling in the growing light. Pulling the covers up around her neck, she smiled at the memory of her dream. With a dreamy look on her face, she rested the back of her right hand against her forehead while playing with the lace bordering the edge of the bodice of her nightgown.

The beep-beep-beep of the alarm intruded on her reverie, and she rolled to her side, lowering her legs over the side of the bed. Checking the time, she smiled knowing she still had three hours before her scheduled meeting. Grabbing her robe, she made her way to the shower. As the tail of her robe swept off the bed, it caught the edge of the business card, pulling it from the corner of the bed near where her pillow still rested.

The small piece of pressed paper flipped end over end as it fell to the floor coming to rest face up near the nightstand. The pressed-foil badge, name and badge number, revealed that it belonged to Detective Nate Richards. Edna Mae hummed and sang softly as the spattering of the shower sounded through the open bathroom door.

***

Nate walked into the courthouse and immediately felt as if he'd forgotten something. Patting his pockets and checking his cell phone, he stopped just inside the revolving door and looked back at the bright sunshine reflecting off the wet street.

"What?" Durgins asked, looking between the guard check station and Nate. After a hesitant step forward, he turned and walked back to Nate. "Man, what's wrong, let's do this."

Nate smiled, shrugged his shoulders, and followed his partner in. "Ever get that feeling like you've forgotten something—left something undone?"

"Sure, but I typically find out that I was wrong and that I'd done it already." He smacked Nate on the shoulder and then pushed him playfully toward the guard station. Pulling their badges out so that they could be inspected, the two men walked through the checkpoint without stopping.

Nate pulled off his outer coat and draped it over his forearm. "Third floor. Let's find us a prosecutor and get this thing written."

Just behind the guard station, twin stairs wrapped upward from the first floor to the balcony on the second. Both plain clothed and uniformed bailiffs stood against the railing, keeping a watchful eye on the activity below. The two detectives headed down the short hall, which separated the main lobby of the Ada County Courthouse from the rear office where several tired and anxious customers stood in line waiting on everything from obtaining licenses to paying traffic citations and court fees.

The bell rang and the elevator door opened. Nate looked back at the sunshine through the floor to ceiling glass wall and, after the smallest of hesitation, joined Durgins in the elevator.

CHAPTER FIFTEEN

(Present Day)

As NATE CLOSED THE DOOR of his POV (personally owned vehicle) behind him, he stood listening to the music coming from inside the Greater Abundant Life Christian Church fellowship hall, his father's church. Closing his eyes, he savored the rich baritone of his father's voice rising above that of the choir, "*Jesus is mine, mine, mine.*" The drums and base providing a rich background for the Hammond B3 organ and piano as the choir continued singing:

"Everywhere I go..."
"Jesus is mine, mine, mine."
"No matter what I'm going through..."
"Jesus is mine, mine, mine."

Nate stopped in the foyer of the fellowship hall with his hand on the brass door handle. Taking a breath, he rested the side of his face against the cool surface of the wood, absorbing the vibrations. Nate steadied himself and prepared to walk into the brightly lit room. As he opened the door, his father had just turned his back to the congregation and stood singing. Facing the choir, his arms raised above his head like a fighter just having been declared the victor.

Nate, hoping to go unseen, tried to slip into the last row without drawing attention to himself.

"Richards."

The voice was familiar although out of place. Nate turned to see Lieutenant Donald Haynes staring at him. The man's dark skin and somber face should have fit in well with the multiethnic congregation, but the silver badge and the black handled gun bulging out of his waistband set him apart as other. Nate looked around nervously, catching his father's eye just as Lieutenant Haynes gently grabbed him by the elbow. "Nate," Haynes said soft but firm.

"Sir." Nate looked at his father and then to his mother and Amber sitting beside her. Then turning back to Haynes he said, "Sir, what are you doing here?"

Haynes chuckled, "I thought you wanted me to come to church. Let's walk." Without waiting, he stepped past Nate and disappeared through the double doors at the rear of the sanctuary.

For a moment Nate didn't move. He shifted his eyes toward his father and then caught the concerned look on his mother's face. She stood and made as if to come to him. He raised a hand stopping her mid-rise. Beside her, Amber chewed her bottom lip while staring into Nate's face.

The last thing he saw before turning toward the still opened door was his mother taking Amber's hand and looking down at the younger lady before sinking slowly back into her seat.

The exchange had taken only a few moments, a few heavy beats of his heart, to work itself out and gone unnoticed by the majority of the congregation. Nate stepped through the door and held it, allowing it to close softly behind him.

Haynes attempted a smile. It was weak, but genuine. "How are you doing?"

Nate looked at his friend and then shook his head. Without answering, he pushed past him and went back into the parking lot. Knowing Haynes would follow, he didn't stop until he had put several car lengths between himself and the building. "What is it? What are they doing now?"

Haynes continued walking until he had come around to face Nate. "How you doing? I really want to know."

Nate thrust his hands into his pockets and swallowed before attempting to answer the question. "How am I doing? I don't know. How am I supposed to be doing? My own command thinks I'm a liar, has placed me on suspension, cut me off from everybody and everything that made up my world. And to top it all off, they think I'm some kind of pervert." He pulled his hands from his pockets clenching them into fist.

Massaging his temples with trembling hands, he turned away from Haynes. Spinning back to face him, he rushed his hands back into his pockets. "Other than that...I'm fine. Just fine."

Haynes rubbed his face. "Nate." He reached out and grabbed Nate's shoulder, squeezing it. "Nate—ah..."

Nate looked into his friend's face. "Don...what? Wh-what is it now?" He was exhausted and spoke as if he were slowly deflating.

"Look, I shouldn't be telling you this, but—but, I don't agree with the way they're handling this whole thing. I think it stinks."

Nate stepped back toward his friend. "What? What now?"

"They started drawing up termination orders. They were talking to legal on Friday. The way I hear it, the whole thing could be over in another week or so."

Nate pinched the skin across the bridge of his nose. Frowning, he shook his head like he was trying to wake up. "But nobody's even talked to me. No interview. No follow-up. Nothing."

Above, the gray sky hung thick and heavy, like layer upon layer of storms were just waiting to break through with a deluge of fury. "Just like that?" It wasn't really a question to be answered and Haynes didn't try. Nate looked, unfocused on his friend, "Doesn't ten years of service mean anything?" Another rhetorical question.

"Look, Nate, I shouldn't even have told you about this, but look, us brothers got to stick together. Heck, there's only the two of us since Sabrina retired, right?" He laughed at the familiar joke, hoping it would break the morass of darkening emotions settling on his younger friend.

A fine rain began, soaking the men as they spoke.

Pulling his collar tighter, Haynes waited until he knew he had Nate's full attention. "Ever since that woman passed her poly, admin has amped things up. Moving fast, Nate. You need to find an attorney and quick. Have him contact the department for you. That way they will have to slow everything down, and you get to see everything they have against you."

Nate was lost and looked it.

"Are you listening to me?" Haynes asked. "Nate, if you don't stop them, they are going to fire you. Go talk to Sabrina. She went through a similar situation a few years back. Maybe she can turn you onto her lawyer."

Nate's arm hung by his side as rain ran in rivulets down his ashen face. The pain in his eyes drew Haynes toward him. Grabbing Nate by both shoulders, Haynes searched his face. "Nate, talk to Sabrina." He turned to walk away. "Get a lawyer, Nate."

The rain became harder, changing from the soft patter of droplets to the soft pellets of icy slush. Nate stood and watched his friend disappear into the early gloaming as the previous threatening storm clouds released its fury.

Turning back toward the sound of music, Nate froze. Standing on the porch of the church stood a lone figure. She did not speak and made no move to join him. But even though she stood well out of the icy rain, her face shone with wetness. Nate raised his arms and let them drop back to his sides.

Without hesitation, but with slow deliberate movements, Amber stepped off the porch and into the rain, going to stand with Nate in the downpour.

***

"I don't know Mother Richards; he doesn't really talk to me either. I'd hoped that maybe he and Jackie would have—" she interrupted herself and waved her hand as if erasing the thought. "I was just hoping there would be more time for me—for us," Amber said then dropped her spoon back into the bowl of cheeseburger soup. She sat back, rocked forward, and then standing briefly, curled her right leg beneath her. "Mom, I do love him. What should I do?" Amber stared into the bowl in front her, stirring it without really seeing.

Sitting across the small table in her modest kitchen, Sherri laid her hand gently on the back of Amber's. "Darling we just have to keep on loving him. He's in a bad place now…a real bad place."

Amber brushed away a tear that had escaped down her cheek. Lifting the spoon, she sighed and pushed the soup away. "It hurts me to see him in such pain, and he won't let me in. He won't let me help him."

Sherri looked at the woman she would have as a daughter and her heart ached for her. She caressed the hand she'd covered with her own. "We'll have to be like Deborah and Jael," she said, forcing a smile she did not feel.

When Amber lifted her face, a gray shadow of confusion darkened her features. Sherri continued, "Deborah stood in the gap for the nation of Israel when the men of the nation were M.I.A., so to speak, and Jael nailed the problem right on the head. If you get my meaning"

Both women chuckled at the biblical reference of Jael the wife of Heber and how she, during the time of the kings in

Israel's history, hammered a spike through the temple of Sisera the captain of the Canaan army, thus delivering Israel from the tyranny of their enemy. "Yeah, she pinned it down." Now both women broke out into warm giggles. The sorrow, while not gone, was for the moment, covered by a shared joy.

"Should I even ask," Gracie said coming in from the dining room. She looked at Amber's face and could see that she had been crying. "Nate again, huh?"

"Well I was just thinking, you know, about what I should do," Amber said, waving her hand as if it had been a matter of insignificant consequences.

Gracie sat down and pulled Amber's untouched bowl of soup in front of her. Without hesitation, she began eating from the bowl. "Well, you know what William James said, 'When you have to make a choice and don't make it, that is in itself a choice.'" Again, without looking up, she grabbed the basket of rolls, which had been set on the table, and began sopping her soup with it.

Both Amber and Sherri exchanged glances, each with their own fond memory of the young lady sitting with them. "Out of the mouths of babes," Sherri added.

"As long as we're dueling quotes," the 19-year-old looked up and smiled, "King David, Psalm 2."

"I was referring to Jesus, Matthew chapter 21, young lady." Sherri answered with a laugh.

"Touché." Gracie lifted her cup granting the score such as it was.

Amber sat forward and interlaced her fingers, resting her lips against her hands. "William James?"

"Oh, we've been doing philosophy around here lately. William James was a pioneer in American Psychology," Sherri stated in way of explanation.

"Actually," Gracie added, talking around a full mouth, "he was trained first as a doctor and was the first American educator to offer an actual course in psychology."

Amber nodded. "Well at least that much is decided," she stated matter of fact.

"Really?"

"What's that?"

Amber looked at the two women. "I know what I'm going to do."

CHAPTER SIXTEEN

(Present Day)

SABRINA JACKSON WALKED IN SHORT QUICK STEPS to reach the phone, rearranging the plastic Wal-Mart bags in her arms as she made her way. Picking up the handset, she trapped it between her ear and shoulder. "Hello." Nate was surprised at how good it felt to hear her voice, for a moment feeling like old times. "Sabrina, it's me."

She lowered the bags to the countertop and reached over, turning the front eye of the stove on, heating her water for tea. "I was wondering when you'd get around to calling me. Actually, I thought I would have seen you before now." She retrieved a cup and a saucer from the cupboard and took the cream and a bear-shaped squeeze jar of honey from the cupboard.

The retired officer had been Nate's first partner and mentor. A veteran of almost thirty years, she had finally called it quits after taking an assassin's bullet to the skull. When Nate hesitated to answer, she forged on. "I'll flick the switch on the Keurig. Green Mountain French Roast, okay?"

Nate cleared his throat. "Actually, I'm parked around the corner."

"Silver Chrysler 300 S8 with 2C plates parked on the south side of the street. I know. Just because I'm retired doesn't mean I've stopped watching my back. It'll be ready by the time you get here. I left the side door unlocked." She hung up.

Outside, Nate smiled at the cell phone in his hand before slipping it back into his pocket. Dropping the transmission into drive, the 3.5 liter V-6 engine barely purred as the sleek vehicle eased into the lane of traffic.

The two friends sat in companionable silence watching as blue and yellow flames danced along fluted logs in the natural gas fireplace. For a moment the only sounds heard were the airy breath of the fireplace and the steady ticking of the grandfather clock near the foot of the stairs in the front room.

Nate shifted forward in his seat and placed his cup on the small table to his right. Just to his left and across from him, Sabrina lifted her cup taking a tentative sip. She watched her friend over the rim of the mug.

"When did you get on the tea bandwagon?" Nate asked.

She lifted the cup and looked at it, then looked back at Nate before taking another sip. "Just a little something different. It's also easier on my stomach. After thirty years of drinking some of the worst coffee this city has to offer, it's a welcome relief. But I don't think that's why you're here—to talk about tea." She set her own cup down and leaned back in the smaller of the two easy chairs, the larger one belonging to her husband Karl.

Nate sobered. "They're trying to fire me."

Sabrina crossed her legs at the ankles.

"They still haven't called me in or interviewed me or anything. I still haven't written a report answering to the allegations."

She giggled a mirthless expression. "That's not how these things work, sweetie. You don't get called in until the decision has already been made. Got a lawyer yet?"

"No, not yet. Do I need one?"

Sabrina lowered her hands into her lap, folded her fingers and smiled. Nate chuckled, joining her. "Yeahhhh," he said, elongating the word, "that's really why I'm here. And just to talk to someone who might understand what I'm going through."

"Oh, yes child, I know what you're going through." Sabrina lifted the teapot and began to pour hot water into her cup. The steel-gray flower petals, briefly obscured by the wafting steam, seemed to dance in the off-white background. After adding a newly packed tea ball, she stirred the tea in her cup. "Sometimes I forget how young you are, Nate."

He smiled at her but did not speak.

"I'll just let that sit for a minute," she said setting her cup down and then looking back up at Nate. "Yeah, I've been there. Twice. And let me tell you, each time you go through an I.A. it feels worse than the time before." She sat back again, this time crossing her legs at the knee. Then closing her eyes as if remembering, she allowed her head to fall back against the headrest. A slight frown creased her face, and then in an unconscious motion, she lifted her fingers and gently touched the scar just within the borders of her hairline.

The scar was all that was left after the bullet, fired by a rogue cop, had creased rather than penetrating her skull. The difference made by the slightest of angles had been the difference between her being just another statistic of an in-the-line-of-duty death or a retired wife and grandmother.

She opened her eyes and smiled at Nate who had been watching her intently. "Yep, it's kind of like that." She dropped her hand back to her lap. For me it was an accusation of theft. Back in the day, back before we went metro, we use to use a special fleet pump down at the end of Bower Street, near the dead end on the west side of the city. Over a period of time, there were large amounts of gas that just came up missing. I mean hundreds of gallons. Somehow my name came up."

"What happened?"

She shook her head. "The then chief, Chief Huxley, called me in, asked for my badge and gun, and sent me home. Told me I was under investigation of theft and when, not if, he got the proof, he was going to personally drive me out of uniform and pursue criminal prosecution."

Nate sighed and looked back at the fire again. Taking advantage of the pause, he refilled his cup of coffee before bidding her to continue.

Sabrina stirred her tea and added honey to her cup, stirred it again and then tasted it with a satisfied smile. "The good news, Nate, is that this will all pass, and you will be where I am now one day, enjoying retirement."

"The bad news is," Nate said, turning to look back at his friend, "I'm the man down, and right now it feels like everybody has either turned their backs on me or—"

"They're taking a bite out of you. Yeah, we eat our own. Trust me, I know. This is a strange business. Don't let anyone else try and touch us, but given the right circumstances, we'll turn on one another, and then tear each other apart. That's the funny thing about us cops." She shook her head again, a slight motion from side to side, making a tisking sound between her teeth. "Yeah, you need a lawyer. I got a guy who can help you. He loves cops but is no friend of administration."

"Is that what we want? I mean, do we want to antagonize admin?" He turned his back to the fire and played with the coffee cup in his hands.

Sabrina rocked back in her chair then hefted herself to a standing position. "Baby-boy, we're way past being worried about how they feel. If they fire you behind this, not only will you be out of a job, you'll be out of a career."

Nate started. "A career? Why?"

"Come on, Nate, don't be dense. If they fire you for behavior unbecoming of an officer, coupled with a charge of dishonesty, the department will almost be forced to move for a

Brady ruling against you. They'll almost have no choice if they are going to protect their own backside."

CHAPTER SEVENTEEN

(Six Weeks Earlier)

PASTOR LUCK PULLED ANOTHER TISSUE from the box at the corner of his crowded desk, his hand trembling as he handed it to Edna Mae. He waited for her to stop crying and blow her nose. Her lips trembling, she looked over the wadded ball of soft pink paper and sniffled. "I'm just so stupid—I mean, I thought he cared. Not just using me." She blew her nose.

"Edna M—"

Edna Mae let her eyes travel over the walls of the small office, taking in the familiar images she has seen time and again. Pictures of the pastor's family covered the wall and desktop, he and his wife Libby and the girls when they were small. Edna Mae stopped and caught her breath when she saw herself in a picture with the Luck girls at the beach.

She reached out, touching the back of Pastor Luck's forearm. "I know what you're gonna say and you're right. You even tried to warn me. I just can't believe I allowed myself to go there again." She wadded the tissue and wiped her eyes with it before setting it on the table in front of her.

Sitting back, she covered her knees with her downturned hands. She wore her hair loose and it fell across her shoulders with a small bounce whenever she moved her face. Sighing, she stood and walked over to the window, looking out over the parking lot at the gray clouds. "Back when Jack left me…the-the girls and I—I wasn't in a good place back then. You know I wasn't really myself, a little unstable at best." She hugged herself around her waist and leaned her face against the coolness trapped in the pane.

Straightening, she turned to face Pastor Luck. "But not this time. It's been months, and my levels have been good. Constant." She shook herself as if chilled, and then with a sudden brightening, she walked with quick steps back to the pastor's desk and took her seat.

Pastor Luck pinched the area between his eyes and sighed. "Okay, okay, Edna Mae. I believe you. We'll make sure this comes out right. The church will stand with you."

He stood and Edna Mae understood that her time had come to an end. She picked up her purse. Looping one of the long straps over her arm, she opened the bag and took out a small package wrapped in seafoam-green colored tissue paper. When she saw him begin to object, she pushed the small box into his hands. "Oh, don't be silly, Pastor Luck. It's just a little something to thank you for believing me. It's nothing fancy, just another sampling of that tea I made for you at my house."

He smiled at the memory. "What was it called; happiness? joy?"

"Felicity." She smiled at his obvious delight. If you really enjoy it, I have a companion tea to go with that called Adorning. I make it from—well I'll let that be a surprise. But let's just say it'll get you going." Closing her purse, she smiled and moved toward the door.

Pastor Luck followed her out into the foyer where his assistant Mildred looked up from her computer screen. The older lady smiled and then turned her attention back to the lines of script on her screen.

Edna Mae waved at the older woman and returned the smile and then ducked out the heavy wooden door. Pastor Luck lifted the box to his nose and inhaled deeply. The excitement at tasting the tea again brought a delighted spark to his eyes.

"Really?" Mildred said, removing the headset from her ear. "Must be something special."

"You have no idea. This is the best blend of tea I've ever had. She makes it herself. I'll make us some." He turned and hurried to the little sink area and pouring two cups of water, set them in the microwave. He turned back to where Mildred still sat behind her desk, her chin resting on the backs of her hands. "You're gonna love this."

***

Outside in the parking lot, Edna Mae settled in the front seat of her Subaru wagon. She dropped her purse on the floorboard, and as it caught the edge of the seat, it fell open dumping the contents of her bag on the floor. Keys, a wallet, papers, and cosmetics rolled out, spreading across the mat. Frustrated, Edna Mae slammed the gearshift forward, putting the car back into park. Leaning across the center console, she began to gather her purse's contents.

One by one, she threw the objects back into her purse. The house keys, the wallet, the compact, and the papers. Picking up a small white bottle, she froze, focusing on the label.

Holding the small plastic container next to her face, she sat up in her seat, captivated by the person staring back at her from the rearview mirror. Screwing off the cap, she lifted one of the small white tablets to her lips. Dropping it on her tongue, she stared at the inscription, WW above the number 277, reversed image in the mirror.

Resealing the container, she dropped the almost empty bottle of LithiCarb extended release tablets back in her purse.

Taking a drink of stale tea left in the cup holder, she swallowed the pill.

***

Edna Mae smiled and watched as the man's hand traced the curve of her forearm and then came to rest on the flat of her stomach. The hand flexed and extended a single finger, which began to move in lazy circles, sending small tickling spasms across her abdomen and down the front of her legs.

Sitting up, she pushed the hand away while trying to catch her breath between gasps of laughter. "Come on, stop." She panted.

Rolling to her side, she looked over her shoulder as the coffee colored hand reached after her. She scooted away. "Nate, stop. Please, don't tickle me."

But when the hand reached her the grasp was not gentle as she had anticipated, but hard-painful. The hand began to fold itself into a knot of her hair and began to pull. "Nate, you're hurting me," Edna Mae complained.

This time when she turned, she screamed. The figure had changed. It was no longer Nate, but Jack, her ex-husband that stood over her. His face twisted in rage and eyes burning with hatred, the hand, now a fist, flew toward her head. She screamed and pulled her hands back to protect her face.

Edna Mae sat up in bed, still shaking from the lingering tendrils of the dream, the memory. With a trembling hand, she brushed tears from her face and turned on the small lamp next to her bed. Wrapping one hand around her waist, she began to double over. Bile rose to the back of her throat, filling her mouth, with its foul flavor, as strobing spots of light began to dance across her vision.

The bedroom door swung open and her daughters stood silhouetted by the hallway light. "You okay, Mom?" Jasmine, the older of the girls asked.

"We brought you some water and your pills," Machele added, coming over to the bed. She sat next to her mother and pushed the small glass of water and tablet into her mother's clawed hand. She looked up, her own face softening. "We heard you crying again."

CHAPTER EIGHTEEN

(Present Day)

"COME IN, COME IN," Sherri Richards said, stepping back so her son could walk through the open doorway. "I saw you walk out of church with that man, Lieutenant Haynes, yesterday. What was that all about? What did he want? We've been so worried."

Nate smiled at his mother's fastidiousness. Leaning forward, he kissed her cheek. "Hi, Mom." He knew she still sometimes thought of him as her *baby-boy* and you know what they say about mama bears and all. He chuckled at the thought. "Is Dad home?" Sherri turned and began making her way to the kitchen. "You want something to eat? Your dad ran to the store for me; he'll be back shortly. Let me get you a cup of coffee."

Nate ran his hand along the mantle and wasn't surprised to find it free of dust and lint. He looked at the now empty dining room table and remembered how cakes and other treats had covered it on the night of his father's birthday party. He shook his head at the memory. *Had it been that long since he'd been to his parent's house?* So much had happened.

He turned to call out to his mother and was startled when he found her standing behind him with a cup of coffee in each hand. "Oh, I didn't hear you come back in."

Sherri offered him a smile along with the cup. "It's no wonder; you've been so distracted lately." She motioned toward the easy chairs on either side of the floor lamp. After sitting in silence for a few minutes, Sherri broke in on the quiet. "I heard you and Jackie were having some problems."

Nate sputtered and looked over the brim of his cup. "What—what? She told you that? You've been talking to Jackie?" He set his cup on the mantel before rubbing his face with his hands.

"Nathaniel Richards, you get that cup off my mantel. You know better than that." She got up from her seat and in quick strides made her way to where Nate stood next to the mantle. Pulling a napkin from her pocket, she wiped the mantel. "You better not have stained my paint—"

"Sorry, Mommy," Nate said in a high-pitched voice and grabbing his mother around the waist began tickling her.

Sherri pulled against her son's playful antics, happy to see him laughing again. "You let me go, young man. You're gonna spill that coffee on my carpet."

"Or what?"

She swatted his arm and tried to pull away. "Oh, no you don't," Nate said and began his tickle-assault in earnest.

Just then the door leading in from the garage opened, and Reverend Richards came into the kitchen. "James…help…he's tickling me," Sherri managed between gasping breathes.

Reverend Richards stopped in the doorway and looked over the tops of his glasses. "You two leave me out of this. I just came to get a glass of milk, sit down, and enjoy a few of these here cookies." He began to laugh.

"What is going on down here?" Gracie asked as she made her way down the stairs. With her dark hair wrapped in a towel, Gracie made her way to the counter and, after collecting a handful of cookies, sat on the barstool to watch.

"You know," Reverend Richards said, leaning over toward Gracie, "sometimes I think my family is nuts."

Gracie laughed. "No, Dad, I know we are." With that, both Nate and Sherri, by silent consent, decided to call the match. No clear winner declared. The two of them joined the others at the cookie plate and continued laughing with an easy familiar air. Gracie, formally adopted by Reverend Richards and Sherri, eighteen months prior, had first come to live with the family as a ward of the state.

Just one of the many street kids, throw-away-youths, which had littered the heart of Old Town until she had helped Amber escape from a street gang. Having left that life behind her, Gracie had now become one of the Richards clan. Reformed, attending college, and a recent convert to the Christian faith.

Gracie smiled and the light of it lit up her face. Nate tousled a lock of the brown tresses that had escaped the towel. "What up, you?"

Gracie held his expression for just a moment before answering him. "How are you?"

Nate looked away. "Fine. Where did I leave my coffee?" He asked of no one in particular.

Gracie stood and walked past Nate. "It's on the table by the lamp, I'll get it." Returning to the kitchen, she put the cup in the microwave. "You know, 'God, when He makes the prophet, does not unmake the man.' "

Nate shook his head and looked from Gracie to his parents, then back to Gracie. "What?"

Gracie returned his smile. "John Locke."

Nate looked at his father, the confused expression still on his face. Reverend Richards chuckled. "She's been studying philosophy."

"It's one of John Locke's best arguments on the need for truth, and the true understanding of it," Gracie interjected.

"But what does tha-" Nate began, but was not able to finish.

"—God is working in you, Nate." She retrieved the coffee from the microwave and handed it to him. "And just because He is building up your spirit-man, doesn't mean that your brain has to stop functioning. As a matter of fact, it should be working better."

Nate frowned. "Did you just insult me?" He said gesturing toward Gracie with his mug. He smiled and turned to his parents. "Did she just insult me?"

Sherri rose, put an arm around Gracie's shoulders, and kissed the girl on her temple. "I think what Gracie is saying is that God is working in this whole ordeal, and He is working in you. He gave you a brilliant mind, use it to help yourself."

Reverend Richards took a bite from a raisin and oatmeal cookie and chased it with a drink of milk. He looked at his son and smiled. "You gotta love philosophy."

Nate chuck bumped Gracie on the shoulder before he placed his own kiss on her forehead. "Thanks, I think." And for the next moment everyone sobered and the room grew quiet.

Nate took a swallow from his cup and set it down on the bar surface. "Mom, you asked what Lieutenant Haynes wanted the other day. Well, he came to tell me that the command staff has drawn up termination orders. They plan to fire me."

"What?"

"They can't do that."

"How can they just fire you?" The conversation about Jackie forgotten now.

Nate raised both hands, palms facing his family, satisfied that his mother's attention had been diverted from the topic of Jackie. "They can and they have. Haynes wasn't supposed to tell me. Heck, he wasn't even supposed to know. He took a risk coming to the church, but felt it was safer than meeting me at my house or calling."

Reverend Richards, who had stood and walked over to where his son was, placed a hand on Nate's shoulder. "What are you going to do, Son?"

Nate took another drink from his cup and first looked at his mother before he answered. "I'm going to fight it. I've already talked to Sabrina about this, and she's getting me some information on a guy she used a few years back when she went through a similar situation."

Gracie chewed and swallowed her last bit of cookie. "Wow. There was a time when I would have said that is exactly what I expect cops to do. But since living here and getting to really know some of the guys, like you and Mac and Durgins, now I'm really…well surprised. And a little angry."

"That makes at least two of us, Sweetheart," Sherri added.

"So when are you supposed to meet this lawyer fellow?" Reverend Richards asked.

"By Wednesday," Nate answered. "This is a far cry from being over. It goes beyond me just being fired by Treasure City. If they do this, they'll file to have a Brady ruling against me."

"A what?" Sherri asked.

Nate turned toward his mother. "Basically, Mom, if they file a Brady ruling against me and it sticks, then I'm done as a cop. It becomes a brand, a tag that would require every prosecutor to disclose to the defense that I had been proven to be a liar. That nothing I say or do should be trusted."

"If they did that then you could never win a case. All the defense would have to do is tell the jury you're a liar and…." At the realization of what was being suggested, Sherri was unable to finish her statement.

"That's why I've got to fight it," Nate said.

The room fell back into silence as each contemplated their own thoughts. After several minutes, Reverend Richards broke the stillness. "Well, there's one thing we can do."

"What's that?" Nate asked staring at the last swallow of coffee in his cup.

Gracie stood and walked over to him. Grabbing his hand she wrapped both hers around it. She looked at Nate. "We can pray."

CHAPTER NINETEEN

(Six Weeks Earlier)

AFTER RETURNING TO THE POLICE STATION, search warrant in hand, the feeling that he had forgotten something continued to niggle at the back of Nate's mind. Durgins jumped from the car as soon as Nate had shifted into park and hurried excitedly toward the door. "Let's go buddy-boy. Let's get this thing rolling."

Nate didn't answer, but continued sitting behind the wheel of the Jeep, the motor idling. "Nate, come on, man. Let's do this," Durgins urged from the curb in front of the vehicle.

Nate finally made eye contact with the younger man. "Oh man, I finally remembered what I was supposed to do. I was supposed to meet our victim and review her statements with her. That was supposed to happen this morning. Dani was going to join me." He looked at his cell phone, checking the time.

"What you gonna do?" Durgins asked. He had moved closer and was now standing just outside the driver's side window. "You want me to get this up?" He held up the folder containing the search warrant. "I'll get this to the L.T.'s office and get the briefing started."

Nate shifted the vehicle into reverse. "Yes, please. I'll call Dani while en route and get her to meet me there."

Durgins looked at his wristwatch. "An hour?"

"If that," Nate said as he began backing up. "This won't take long at all. Thirty minutes tops. Let's just say, I'll meet you upstairs in an hour, just to be safe."

Nate pulled out into traffic on Locust Grove and headed north. Pulling his phone from his pocket, he dialed. "Hey, Dani—Oh man, stupid recording." He slapped the phone shut, frustrated at having only reached her voicemail.

Sighing, he opened the phone and pressed the redial. When the recorded message had finished, Nate took a shallow breath and spoke into the mouthpiece. "Hey, Dani, this is Nate. Sorry about this morning, but I got stuck at the prosecutor's office getting a search warrant." He looked at the clock on the dashboard and then continued speaking. "It's just past 1300 hours, and I'm on my way to Edna Mae Fuller's for that meeting. If you still can, why don't you meet me there."

Nate continued driving north until he reached Chinden Boulevard, known as 20/26 to the locals and headed west. Pulling into the subdivision to the north of the highway, he stopped and looked down the tree-lined street, taking in the early spring colors that were beginning their annual struggle against the ice-like grip of winter. Sighting the house near the far end of the street, he was hoping he would see Dani's brown 2006 Ford Taurus parked out front.

Nothing.

Against his better judgment, Nate pulled up in front of the house, and after taking a breath, he got out and walked up to the front door. Just as he reached to ring the bell, two things happened: He was startled by the deep barrel-chested bark of what sounded like a very large dog; and secondly, the metal screen door opened and two teenaged girls rushed out.

The older of the two girls stopped short of crashing into Nate's chest. With a furtive brush of her hand, she pushed long reddish brown hair back from her face. She greeted him with a shy smile. "Oops, sorry. Didn't see you."

Nate cut his eyes quickly from the face of the girl to the snarling mouth and gray mask of the Great Pyrenees being held by the collar by the younger of the two girls. Judging from the size of the dog, Nate was glad that it really wasn't trying to get away from its master and onto him.

Relaxing, the dog seemed to consider Nate with its large wise eyes. It tilted its head to one side then the other and dropped its face before stepping toward Nate and licking the back of his hand. Nate released a breath, he was only mildly aware he had been holding. The girls giggled.

"Sheba likes you," said the younger girl.

Nate smiled. "I'm just glad she's accepted me into her company." The teens looked at each other and then back to the detective, scrunching their noses. They giggled again.

"Mom, the detective's here. We got to go. See ya later." They called out as they ran from the doorway to the car in the driveway. Nate jumped slightly when he felt the warm large tongue caress his hand again, suddenly not as comfortable with the dog as he had been when the girls stood with him. *Okay, Lord, please keep this dog calm.* Nate prayed silently.

As if she'd heard him, she nudged Nate's hand with her nose, demanding that he rub her again. Relaxing somewhat, Nate stooped and began to rub the dog's neck and scratch her back and shoulders.

He jumped again when he heard a sultry voice above and behind him. He stood and looked through the mesh of the screen and saw Edna Mae leaning against the doorjamb. She had on a pair of jeans that seemed to have been picked out to accentuate her full hips, and a cream-colored cowl neck sweater. Her long ash-blond hair was worn down and cascaded over one shoulder.

She smiled.

Nate turned and looked back at his Jeep parked along the curb then pulled out his phone hoping to see that Dani had called to say she was on her way. When he looked back again at the doorway, it was empty. He looked into the void, trying to come up with a plausible reason for a quick departure.

"Well, come on in," Edna Mae called from inside. She added, "Sheba." At the command, the dog nudged Nate with her huge head. Nate shrugged, pulled the door open, and walked in.

"I thought you had stood me up." She came back into the small sitting room off the side of the living room carrying a tea service. "I took the liberty of making us something to drink while we talked. I hope you like tea."

Nate smiled flashing the warmth of his usual charm and gesturing with his hand, said, "Sure."

Studying him, she returned his smile and in similar fashion as her daughter had earlier, brushed hair back from her face. "Don't tell me you're a coffee kind of guy: a coffee in the morning, coffee at noon, and then coffee before bed kind of guy?" She laughed, not affording him a chance to answer. "Never mind, you'll love this. I blend it myself."

Still standing, Nate looked back at the open doorway. He slapped the file folder against his thigh and then opened it. "May I sit?" he asked attempting to get control of this meeting.

She looked up at him, tilting her face upward slightly. Her hair fell forward again, hiding her face. "I was hoping you would."

Nate sat on the opposite side of the coffee table and spread open the folder between them. Resting his elbows on his knees, he pulled his recorder from his pocket and placed it on the table near the folder. "Okay, in your message you said there were some other details you remembered from the assault."

When she didn't answer, he looked up at her. She was sitting back, her legs crossed at the knees, her hands folded on her lap. Nate cleared his throat. "If you'd rather wait until we can get together with Dani that would be okay. I don't want you to feel uncomfortable."

She still didn't answer, but studied him. She smiled again.

Nate lifted the cup and sipped the tea. Holding it back from his face, he looked into the dark liquid. He addressed her with it. "This is good." He stood.

"Wanda," he corrected himself at the look on her face. "Edna Mae, why don't we reschedule this? I know you have a busy day and my mess up shouldn't be a cause for you having to redo your entire day." He took another sip of the tea and then set it back on the saucer, collected his folder, and turned toward the front door.

As he reached the entryway, he saw that Edna Mae was starting to rise from her seat. "You don't have to leave, Nate—I mean, Detective Richards. Really, this is a good time for me."

Nate looked at his recorder to make sure the red light was still glowing. "No, I don't think so. I'll check with Dani and we'll reschedule. That will be best, I think."

He looked at her face and, for the briefest moment, thought he saw disappointment before she covered it. Then her usual bright smile was back in place. Just then, his phone rang and vibrated in his pocket. Checking the caller I.D., he saw that it was Dani. "Hey there, where are you?"

Dani chuckled. "Well, good afternoon to you too. I'm in my car right now, but I'm still downtown. You still wanna go out to see Edna Mae today."

Nate looked at Edna Mae and smiled, then mouthed, "Excuse me." She smiled softly and began gathering the tea service.

Nate turned his shoulder to her and spoke into the phone. "Well, about that…"

"Tell me you didn't go out there by yourself."

"Well, her daughters were here when I first arrived."

"Nathanial Richards, you saw the way she was at FACES. You be careful." She sighed, but her voice held a smile.

Nate returned the lighthearted jibe. "Yeah, I'm leaving now."

Edna Mae walked up beside him and leaned against the far wall. She arched a brow. "Is that Dani?" she asked.

Nate nodded, but continued talking into the phone. "No, I'll be back at 19 before that. We have that meeting with L.T. Durgins is waiting for me now."

"Should I just meet you back at the station then?" Dani asked.

"Affirm; see you at 19 in let's say...10 minutes." He closed his phone and turned his attention back to Wanda. "As you figured, that was Dani. Like you, she went on with the rest of her day when I missed the appointment this morning." He offered her an apologetic expression and extended his hand.

A few minutes later, Nate found himself back in his car feeling he had just barely missed something bad. He pressed the stop button on his digital recorder, turning the machine off. Patting his pocket, he shifted the car into first gear and pulled slowly away from the curb.

***

From just inside the shadow of the screen door, Edna Mae watched as Nate sat still in his car, not moving. Seeing him pat his chest, she smiled. Pulling the business card from her pocket, she lifted it up until the light reflected on the foil-embossed badge. "Nate Richards," she said softly, and then stepped back from the doorway and pushed the heavy wooden front door closed.

CHAPTER TWENTY

(Six Weeks Earlier)

NATE WALKED INTO THE UPSTAIRS BRIEFING ROOM. Several uniformed officers sat around the horseshoe pattern of tables along with four detectives plus the lieutenant and a patrol sergeant. "What did I miss?" He sat down beside Durgins, who was studying a copy of a county assessor's map, determining the best lanes of ingress and egress to the targeted property.

He looked up at Nate. "L.T. wants uniforms to go in first, but I thought I would go with the entry team. You okay with that?"

"Yes, he's okay with it." It was Lieutenant Brown. "Aren't you, Richards?"

"Absolutely, sir." Nate pulled his own folder over in front of him and began leafing through the pages. "Who's gonna place the call?" When no one answered, Nate said, "I guess I will."

"That's awfully nice of you, Richards," Brown said. "I want this guy distracted and otherwise obligated when the welcoming party goes in the door." He turned back to the group in general. "Okay ladies, we gonna do this or not?"

Sergeant Higgins stroked his mustache with meaty fingers. The large man had been a professional football player before a freak accident ended his career. He brought the same tenacity and never-say-die attitude that helped him win college accolades and put him in position to do great things as a down lineman in the NFL, into being a front-line-supervisor. "I got Jackson and Smitty on the key; and Torres and Campbell on long gun cover with Bell and Stanz on shields at the door. My team's ready to go." Jackson, almost as large as Higgins, was an excellent choice to be on the key, a weighted tube of metal, reinforced in Teflon rubber used to break open doors if the occupants either refused or were too slow in compliance.

Higgins cleared his throat. "Somebody want to read the warrant to us, so we know what we're looking for?"

Nate pulled a copy of the warrant from his folder and began reading the list of items authorized to be seized: "Brett Torrie, male, white, age 31. We know he has a past affiliation with the Aryans but nothing recently. Mostly 160's, low level drugs mostly, and his last conviction was for sexual assault, but the charge was dropped to a simple battery during plea bargain. Questions?"

After several minutes more of discussion, the team rose and exited the briefing room. Once the teams were in position, Nate lifted the phone, hit the record button and began dialing. After two rings someone answered the phone. "Brett Torrie?" Nate asked.

"Yeah, who's this?" answered a gruff, tired sounding voice.

Nate gave the thumbs up to Lieutenant Brown and then turned back to the conversation. "Brett, this is Detective Richards with the Treasure City Police Department. There will be someone knocking at your door in a minute. When that happens, I want you to do exactly as they say, okay? That way no one gets hurt."

"Well, I tell ya what. I don't know who you are or what you're planning, but if even one comes up in my house they better bring their A game, cause I'm gonna bust a cap in the—"

Just then, a loud crash sounded in the background. Nate could hear banging and then someone yelling "Police. Police. Police." Muffled sounds filtered through the receiver. Then someone cursed and screamed as if the air was being forced from them.

Higgins' deep resonant voice, sounding like Sam Elliot, floated up from the speaker, "Police one, bad guy zero." Then the phone line went dead.

Nate turned to look at Lieutenant Brown. "The house is secure, sir. Brown stared at him, but didn't say anything. Instead he turned and headed toward his office.

Without looking back, Brown said, "I'll be in my office; call me when he's in the building. I want to watch the interview."

"Yes, sir." Nate stood and walked over to the interview room. Checking the desk and placing his props, an overstuffed folder and blanks CD's, where he wanted them. He sat in his designated chair and dragged his hands through his hair. He sighed. "Lord, this is thin, at best." He stood and stretched. "But right now it's all we got."

He sat back down and wondered if Brown was sitting at his desk watching him on closed circuit. He thought to himself that Brown would make an issue of his praying, but then laughed, knowing it wouldn't make a difference if he got a confession.

Three and a half hours later, Nate escorted Brett Torrie out of the interview room. "Thank you, Mr. Torrie, for coming in."

Torrie frowned, pulled his jeans up on his narrow hips and shook a disfigured cigarette from a compressed pack he carried in his back pocket. "Well, I didn't have much of a choice about that, did I?"

Nate stopped and looked at Torrie, reading the man's intentions. "It's a no smoking campus. I'd have to write you a ticket if you light that." Nate smiled. "Actually, you did have a choice. I think Detective Durgins explained that to you when you were in the backseat of the patrol car. He explained then that while you did not have a choice about having your home searched, you did not have to come here to be interviewed." He stepped around in front of Torrie, forcing the man to stop and look up at him. "Is that not how you remember it happening, or are you telling me my brothers forced you to come down here against your will?"

Torrie waved his hands in front of him dismissing the question. "No, no. No one forced me, except that big bear of guy who rammed his knee in my back." Torrie slipped his hand behind him and massaged his lower back.

"Well, I did tell you to cooperate and you wouldn't get hurt." Nate tried to hide a smile.

Torrie resumed walking, stepping past Nate. "Yeah, yeah, yeah. I just know I'm gonna have to see my chiropractor after all this."

Nate followed Torrie to the rear elevator, and pushing the button, took the car to the lobby. When the doors opened, at least six uniformed and two plain-clothes officers greeted them. The five men and one woman looked at Nate and nodded, then as one, turned their attention to Torrie.

Torrie cleared his throat. "There's too many Pi—I mean cops in this place for my liking. I think I'll be leaving now."

The officers stepped to either side forming a narrow alley, forcing Torrie to walk through the middle gap. Straightening, he made his way to the double glass doors, stopped, straightened his back, and pushed through the doors, making it a point to look back at Nate. Torrie put a cigarette between his lips and pulled out his lighter then continued toward the sidewalk.

Outside, the traffic had slowed significantly, and Nate watched as the man looked first north and then south before he hurried across the street. It wasn't long before the growing shadows had reached out and engulfed him and Torrie disappeared around the corner, lost from view.

A voice spoke from just behind him. "Why didn't we hook him?"

"Not enough." Recognizing the voice as Durgins, Nate spoke without turning. "Oh, he's dirty and I wouldn't trust him to play with a broken toy, but I don't see him doing this one. I got his prints, including the new one for his right hand, which shows the scars from the machine shop injury and a DNA sample. We'll have the lab rush a comparison test and see what we see."

Durgins sighed. "He was squirming in the interview." Durgins slammed one hand into the other. "It just feels wrong watching him walk away like that."

"Yeahhh," Nate said making it sound like a sigh.

Durgins dropped his hand on his partner's shoulder. "This job makes you tired."

At this, Nate turned and smiled. "Now you see why I drink so much coffee. He looked at the giant clock high up on the lobby wall. "It's late. It's been a long day. I'm tired and I'm hungry. Let's get a bite to eat."

Durgins, who always got excited when it came to eating, perked up. "Let me set my desk and we can get out of here."

As the two men came off the elevator, Lieutenant Brown stood waiting for them, his arms folded across his paunch. "Well, where's the gifted silver tongue of yours on this one, Richards?" He had not spoken unkindly, but a long habit of bantering had made the comment sound like a jab.

Nate looked at Durgins and both men looked back at the lieutenant "Well, sir, I just don't think he's our rapist. First, we checked his alibi and he was nowhere near Nampa on the night of the assault." Nate sat on the edge of one of the nearby desks, massaging his eyes with both hands.

"We went over that garage—" Durgins began.

"—Vintage Coffee Shop," Nate interrupted, with a tired sounding smile.

Durgins smirked. "Hey, I remember as a kid working on cars and bikes in that shop."

"Yeah," added Brown, "and I remember this all being cow pastures. Now what about our dirt-bag we just let walk out the front door."

Nate dropped his hands and let them dangle between his knees. "It brings us back to square one unless the lab gets a hit."

Brown cursed and slapped the wall. He cursed again, this time looking at his palm. "I was hoping this would be one of those quick ones." He turned and began walking, and Nate and Durgins followed. "I still have a few contacts at the lab from my Narc days; maybe I can pull a few strings. Get ahead of the six week waiting period."

Durgins whooped. "That's what I'm talking about."

"Whoa there, cowboy," Brown said. "All I said is that I would try." He looked at Nate. "Better slow this one down before he burns himself out." Brown gave the men a two fingered salute and walked into his office leaving them staring after him.

"How about that dinner," Nate suggested. Durgins brightened and hurried to his desk. Standing, Nate leaned a shoulder against a nearby wall and folded his arms across his chest. Closing his eyes, he prayed quietly. "Father, you're going to have to show me this one, cause I got nothing. You showed Elisha what was going on in the King of Syria's mind; I know You can help me."

"Talking to yourself?"

Nate startled, surprised at Durgins' voice. "Not to myself, my friend. Not to myself." He smiled, slapped him on the shoulder and headed for the door.

Durgins hesitated for a second then started after his friend. "What'd'ya say we get a steak? A nice thick juicy one."

"Long as I don't have to listen to country music while I eat."

"Ah com'n, you know as well as I do that the best steak is grilled by cowboys, and I know just the right place. Let's do it, partner."

CHAPTER TWENTY- ONE

(Five Weeks Earlier)

NATE ARRIVED AT JACKIE'S APARTMENT promptly at seven. He had been determined not to be late again. He hadn't seen her since the dinner and coffee and he knew she was beginning to feel overlooked. He rang the bell and then remembering, quickly slipped a mint in his mouth.

The door opened. "Hey, beautiful," he said and handed her the bouquet of mix flowers: peonies, parrot tulips, lilacs, sweet peas and forget-me-nots."

She lifted the spring-bunch of reds, vibrant oranges, purple and blue to her face and inhaled the sweet fragrance. He took the first moment just to appreciate looking at her. Highlighted from behind, the red in her chestnut colored hair was dazzling. She smiled and her entire face seemed to glow with the delight of the moment.

"Hey, stranger. I was beginning to think you'd forgotten where I lived." She offered him her cheek, and he placed a soft kiss against it before wrapping her in his embrace.

After a moment, she pulled back and invited him in. As he entered the smallish apartment, the aroma of braised onions, garlic and celery greeted him, making his mouth water. "What is that?"

She giggled. "It's the soffritto."

He frowned. "Suffi—what?"

She turned and walked toward the kitchen and selected a vase to put the flowers in. "Soffritto. It's for the Stracotto di Manzo alla Fiorentina." Holding the tips of her fingers together she brought them to her lips and kissed them with a loud smack. "Or for you '*nessuno di lingua italiana*' The Braised Beef of Florence."

Nate hurried to the kitchen behind her. "Are you kidding me? You're making Italian Pot Roast?"

She straightened and looked back at him and arched a brow in question. "I watch the cooking channel," Nate answered her unasked question.

She smiled. "Then you won't mind the red wine."

Nate assumed a serious natured expression. "Well, as long as it's red and not a white wine, because that would just be wrong."

She turned her back to him and, lifting the potholders, removed the top allowing the fullness of the fragrance to fill the room. "You'll be pleased to know I used an Italian medium bodied wine to bring out the Mediterranean countryside flavor. The veggies are simmered in the soffritto as well, so we should be totally submerged in Italy once we begin our culinary experience."

Coming up behind her, Nate hugged her around the waist. "Really? What's for dessert, shaved ice?"

She lifted the stone dish and carried it to the table. Nate watched her as she finished setting the table. "As a matter of fact, Mr. Nosey, we're having biscotti with a new blended dessert coffee, special for this occasion." She pulled his chair and waved him to his seat.

Nate shook his head. "There are just some things a man has to do." He walked around to the opposite side of the table, pulled her chair, and then returned to where she was standing and took her hand in his. "My lady, I think this seat has been reserved for you." She sat and he adjusted her seat for her at the table.

Taking his own seat, Nate sat and they prayed over the meal. He smiled at her across the table and lifted a fork of meat to his mouth. "Oh my goodness," he said in between bites, "this is delicious."

"You know what they say about a man's stomach." After this, they ate in relative silence. She looked at him over the flowers, which she had set in the center of the table and smiled at his obvious enjoyment with the meal. She rested her chin on the backs of her hands and watched him. It had been over a week, and this was the first time she's really had his attention, and other than the greeting and the discussion about the meal, there really hadn't been any meaningful conversation between them.

He looked up and smiled at her. "So how's the Library these days?"

"It's fine."

Nate put another fork of roast into his mouth and turned his attention back to the meal.

Jackie watched him again, returning to silence. She waited until he finished eating and sat back, beginning to relax; she ventured to speak again. "How's the investigation going?"

Nate wiped his mouth with his napkin, and for the first time since sitting down, he stopped and really looked at her. "I did it again, didn't I?"

She nodded, determined to be honest with him.

"I'm sorry." He dropped his napkin on the table then lifted his chair and moved it around to sit next to her. She raised her eyes, watching him move but didn't speak.

When he was settled, he noticed that she'd hardly eaten. He lifted her fork and cut a small piece of the meat, noting again how tender it was, and placed it in her mouth. She chewed and a single tear trekked down her cheek. "Oh come on...don't.

Please don't cry." Moving his chair closer, he pulled her against his chest and held her there.

She didn't resist.

"Hey," Nate said, speaking into her hair. "It's not you. It's this stupid case. This should be an easy fix, but I'm missing something and it's kicking me square in the seat."

She still said nothing but, taking her hand in his, played her fingers across the backs of his knuckles. After a moment, she snuggled her face against his chest. She hated the draw she felt to him. She could sense him pulling away, drifting from her, but she just wasn't ready to let go...to let him go.

Nate lifted her face so he could see her eyes. "We'll fix this. When this case is over, we'll take some time just to be together. Would you like that?"

She nodded.

"I'll take a couple of days off and we can go up to the mountains or just spend a few days here in the valley doing whatever," he said hopefully.

She sat up. "I'd like that. How about I get the dessert or would you rather start with coffee?" She went into the kitchen, flicking the overhead light on and flooding the small area with the yellow florescent light. As she busied herself in the kitchen, she watched Nate and wondered at the almost bored expression he tried so hard to hide whenever he saw her watching him.

***

Sherri Richards opened the door and welcomed Amber inside. "I hope you don't mind my just dropping by like this," Amber said as she hugged the older lady.

"Don't be silly. If I had it my way, you'd still be living here instead of in that apartment by yourself." She ushered her young friend in and closed the door behind her.

The ladies settled in the living room and fell into easy conversation. "Not that it matters," Sherri began, "but what brings you out here? It's not exactly on your way home." She smiled knowingly.

"Mother Richards you never stop do you?"

She laughed. "Why should I? It's not over yet and I may still get my way." This time they laughed together.

"Speaking of Nate," Amber segued, "how is he these days?"

Sherri pressed her hand to her breast. "Oh, were we speaking of Nate?"

Amber frowned and swatted at Sherri's knee, then looked up as a soft thump, thump, swooshing sound drifted through the ceiling. "You're so bad."

Sherri giggled at Amber's slight reddening in her cheeks. She followed Amber's gaze to the ceiling. "Oh, that's just James on that treadmill of his."

Amber nodded and then turned her attention back to the topic of conversation. "But seriously, Mom, I usually at least see him every once in a while, but since the night of Reverend Richards' party, I haven't seen or heard from him...other than one afternoon at church." She then quickly added, "Not that I expect him to check in with me or anything."

Turning serious she added, "Mother Richards, I feel like there's something wrong. Like Nate is heading for trouble. Or something." She waved her hand at Sherri's worried expression. "Oh, I don't know. Maybe it's nothing."

Sherri took Amber's hands into her own. "We shouldn't dismiss your feelings so easily. It may be the Lord trying to tell us to pray. I've had a bad feeling in the pit of my stomach, like a knot, for the last few days myself. I've been asking the Lord to show me what's going on. Maybe you coming here is my answer to prayer."

Finally giving herself permission to experience the sense of worry that had plagued her, Amber grabbed a firm hold of the older woman's hands. "Oh Mom, what can we do? What should we do? Should we call Nate and check on him?"

Sherri looked at the woman sitting next to her, smiled, and took a brief moment to whisper a silent prayer. *Father, thank you for not allowing the love she has for my son to die. Thank you for giving him someone who will truly love him.* Then out loud, she said, "Well, before we do that, we're gonna pray.

They lowered their heads until their foreheads almost touched. Then in soft whispered tones, together, they lifted their voices in earnest prayer. It was sometime later that they looked up, their faces wet with tears, but whether from concern about Nate, or the assurance that the Lord had heard their prayers, it was uncertain.

"You know there are not very many things that look as good to me as women with their heads bowed in prayer." Reverend Richards stood at the base of the stairs, a limp towel draped around his neck. He looked hot and his black T-shirt stuck to his still firm chest.

Both ladies sat up and with short quick motions, wiped tears from their faces. "Oh, James, I've told you about sneaking around the house like that. You gonna send me on to heaven before you—you keep that up." Sherri rose and went to her husband. She kissed his face then slapped his shoulder. "You're all wet."

Reverend Richards grabbed her and kissed her firmly on her forehead. "That's good healthy sweat, woman. How do you think I keep this youthful frame," he said as he raised his arms in a mock bodybuilder's pose.

Sherri turned to Amber. "Don't pay him no mind. He's getting old. You know he just recently had another birthday."

"As long as I keep you smiling," he said as he winked at her. Letting her go, he continued toward the kitchen and swatted her bottom as he passed.

Sherri gave a little bounce as the swat landed. "Don't forget your Altoprev." She looked back at Amber, the love and respect she felt for this man, caused her to flush slightly. She rested her hand on her face and smiled.

Amber laughed out loud. "I love you guys."

"You wouldn't know he was going on sixty-five years old…." She smiled at the man she'd been married to for over four decades. Just as the door began to swing shut, Reverend Richards turned and struck a Hulk pose, bowed slightly forward from the waist, arms curled and flexing his biceps and chest. The doors closed shielding him from their sight, but they could hear him laughing at himself in the kitchen.

"Altoprev?" Amber asked, a slight furrow in her brow.

Sherri turned back to face her, "Oh it's just a statin…Lovastatin, a cholesterol medicine. He still tries to eat as if he's twenty-five as well."

Amber relaxed. "It's nothing serious then?"

"It could be if he doesn't eat well. At least he's always exercising and is in pretty good shape." She looked back at the door and just for a moment, her vision drifted into the unseen. Shaking herself, she turned back to Amber. "So, who's gonna call, you or me?"

CHAPTER TWENTY- TWO

(Four Weeks Earlier)

TWO DAYS LATER LIEUTENANT BROWN WALKED into Nate's cubicle and dropped a manila folder on his desk. Nate looked up, putting his phone call on hold. The look on Brown's face told Nate everything he needed to know about what was in the folder. "That bad, huh?"

"Well at least my contacts still work. This is not the official report, but it's clear from this that Torrie is not our rapist."

Nate opened the file and began going over the numbers and reading the brief summary. He traced the print with his finger as he read. "Hey-"

"Yeah, that is at least interesting. We don't know who our man is, but we did get a positive on the sample. If he's been arrested anywhere in the U.S. we'll get a match sooner or later."

Nate rested his elbows on his desk and rubbed his eyes, pressing his fingertips against his closed eyelids. Just then, Durgins came into the small space. "Is that the lab report? Is it a match for Torrie?" He asked in his rapid-fire fashion.

Nate lifted the file and handed to him. Brown took a half step backward, rested his elbow on top of the file cabinet, and looked down at the two men, Durgins having sat on the edge of

Nate's desk. Durgins exhaled a long and deliberate sound. "You gotta be kidding me. I thought for sure he was our guy."

Nate looked over at Durgins. "Even though his alibi put him here in Meridian on the night of the rape?"

"People lie."

Nate sat back. "Yeah, it wouldn't be the first time, huh?"

Lieutenant Brown harrumphed and turned to walk away. "I'll leave you ladies to your work. Don't waste that favor, it took me a long time to get that much juice at the state lab."

"Hey, thanks L.T.," Nate called toward the supervisor's retreating back. Brown did not respond nor slow his egress, but simply raised a hand and waved it in the general direction of where the two detectives still sat.

"So what's next?"

Nate lifted his feet to the desk and clasped his hands behind his head. "I don't know. I guess we start over. Hit the streets, canvas the neighbors and see if there is anything we missed. A car, a person on foot...anything that might give us somewhere or something else to look at."

"That bad, huh?"

Nate dropped his feet to the floor. "Yep, that seems to be the anthem of this case." He accepted the file from Durgins and stood.

Durgins stood as well and began to collect his coat and file folder. "How so?"

Nate shook his head, more from frustration with the *go-nowhere* investigation than from being questioned by Durgins. "It just seems like every time we take one step forward we wind up going three steps back. We spent all day at the prosecutor's office getting that stupid warrant and got nothing out of it."

Durgins nodded, but didn't say anything. Nate grabbed his partner by the shoulder and squeezed. "You ready to go knock on some doors?"

Thirty minutes later the two men walked on opposite sides of 2nd Street South in downtown Nampa. Nate looked around the familiar street, although he worked out of the Meridian Office, there was something he liked about the small-town-feel of the Nampa area.

Even though the counties of valley had decided to adopt the metro policing model, the cities and towns still managed to maintain their sense of uniqueness. Boise, Meridian, and Nampa, being the largest cities in the valley, seem to set the pace for everything else, which still had its rural agrarian feel. Boise was the capital city and center of entertainment; and Meridian like the little brother of the star student-athlete, was fast making a name for itself as a fantastic place to live, work, and play.

On the other hand, Nampa was somewhere in between. Here in the downtown area, Nate observed, it still held on to its turn of the century small town feel, but as you traveled to the south and west of the city, you would see the beginning of the suburban sprawl.

Walking on the opposite side of North 12th, Nate watched as his partner came near the open doorway of Tina's bar. In contrast to the brightness of the early afternoon sun, the mouth of the bar looked like a cave leading into darkness. Boasting itself as a hardcore drinking hole, the bar had become more of a dive for inner city regulars, a long way from a once elegant refreshing station along a main stop of the Oregon Short Line Railway.

A couple of Tina's typical patrons stood just outside the door. Two men wearing faded and dirty jeans, one wearing a very used cowboy hat and the other a soiled red bandana tied over what looked to be greasy hair. Durgins stopped to talk to the men.

The two men stepped to either side of Durgins, flanking him. Judging from the posturing, Nate could tell things were not going to go well; at least not for the *good old boys*. Nate started across the street. Waving his hand, he made his way through the light traffic.

Just as Nate reached the curb, he saw the knife. The all too familiar snap-click of the blade resounded off the stonewall.

Durgins snapped his face toward the sound.

Before he could move, cowboy hat guy began a low arching swipe that would have disemboweled Durgins, had the blade made connection.

As the glinting metal careened across his waist, Durgins stepped back just outside the arc of the swing. The tip of the blade sliced through Durgins' shirt, leaving the gap flapping in its wake.

As the knife passed his gut, Durgins then stepped in, closing the distance between the assailant and himself. Before cowboy-hat-guy could begin his back swing, Durgins trapped the wrist of the hand holding the knife.

A forward rotation on the man's arm exposed and locked the elbow in place. With a violent stroke, Durgins brought a crushing forearm strike against the joint, reversing the angle of the arm. Cartilage ripped. The sinew snapped. The joint collapsed in on itself, causing the man's arm to bend backwards.

Without hesitating, Durgins snatched the man's disfigured arm behind his back and, with all due force, drove him face first onto the sidewalk.

Running, Nate was within three yards of his partner when the bandana guy started his move, targeting the exposed back of Durgins.

On the ground, Durgins grabbed his assailant's other arm behind and pulling out his cuffs, began snapping the steel bracelets in place. He looked up just in time to see bandana man stepping forward like an NFL kickoff specialist and prepared to plant a booted foot into his face.

In one continuous movement from the handcuffing, Durgins released the cuffs, pulled his Glock .40 from its holster, and pointed it in the face of bandana guy. "You might wanna reconsider that, partner."

Bandana guy froze, his nose inches from the barrel. From the focus of his eyes, even from behind him, Nate could tell he was staring at the 155 Grain Speer Gold Dot Hollow Point round, chambered and ready to launch. "Now, why don't ya put that foot back on the ground before I spread your face over Main Street." He rose slowly, keeping the gun leveled in the man's face. "I can't think of one good reason to mess up this pretty sidewalk," Durgins finished with a smile, which made the smoothness and ease of his actions seem all the more intense.

"Mind cuffing that one for me, boss?" Durgins called out. It was then that bandana guy noticed Nate was standing behind him. His shoulders slumped just before he locked his fingers together and placed his hands on his head. "Ahh, look, he's assuming the position," Durgins said, still pointing the gun at the man's face.

A moment later the scream of sirens began echoing off the buildings and through the alleyways. "The cavalry is coming," Nate said. "Let me get this guy cuffed so they know who the bad guys are. Who is the cowboy with the broken arm?"

Durgins stood and moved to his left, eliminating any cross-fire situation. "Oh it's not broken, I just dislocated it. Of course it's gonna be sore for a while." Then he directed his comments to cowboy guy, "But those are the kind of things you need to consider before going and trying to cut the police, it'n' it, Jake?"

Snapping the last cuff into place, Nate assisted bandana guy to a seated position next to his partner in crime. "Jake Cook? Then this must be Arniston Beliczynska. Nice, great grab." Nate pulled out his phone. "What set him off, anyway?"

Lifting his face from the pavement, Jake turned to look at the detective standing over him. Directing several racial and otherwise derogatory comments at Nate, Jake began cursing and threatening to sue for police brutality. Durgins grabbed Jake in the crook of his injured elbow and pulled. "Look here, Jake, let me help you sit up."

The man screamed in pain.

Three marked units pulled in, screeching their tires as they stopped. Lights still going, but the sirens quieted, uniformed officers leapt from the cars, guns drawn, ready to enter the fight. Nate raised his badge and identified himself and Durgins.

One of the uniformed officers stepped forward. "Nate...what are you doing out here? I thought you were riding a desk over in Meridian." But before Nate could answer, the man turned to see who had been handcuffed and began to laugh. Jake Cook. Don't tell me—that guy has to be Aniston Beliczynska. We've been looking for these guys for two weeks for that bank robbery over on the boulevard, and you two knuckle heads stumble right into them. Go figure."

Nate laughed. "You can thank Durgins for that, Judson. He has a nose for finding trouble." A few minutes later, both men were seat belted in the rear seat of patrol units and on their way to county, with Cook making a brief stop at the E.R. for medical clearance first.

"Who's got the paperwork on these two?" Judson asked.

"Book them on the warrants, that will hold them until we can get in and do the paper for the ADW and RO," Durgins answered.

"Let me guess," Judson said, "Jake pulled a knife, that would be your assault with a deadly weapon, and old Anniston just had to jump in and help his buddy? And that would be the resisting an officer. Good thing these guys are stupid."

"Very good; hey, why don't you write the report, and we can finish our canvas of the businesses down here," Nate said.

"You wish."

The last of the patrol cars pulled away from the curb and the small crowd had begun to disburse. Soon Nate and Durgins were alone on the sidewalk and the afternoon flow continued as if nothing ever happened. "Just another day in the valley, huh?" Nate asked.

"Just another day."

"By the way, that was way cool back there. High speed, low drag all the way."

"You like that, huh? You should have seen some of the stuff we had to put up with in Fallujah, it would make that look like a walk in the park. Ooo-rah!" The men bumped knuckles and began back down the way they had come. "What-da-ya say we finish this up and get a bite to eat?"

"Sounds like a winner to me. My treat."

"Now how can I argue with that?"

A half hour later, the detectives started down Second Street, the same street where the rape had occurred. For now, Nate walked into restaurants, flower shops, printers offices, and varied other small businesses asking the same questions over and over: Did you hear anything? Did you see anything strange or unusual? Coming back into the sunshine, leaving the last of the small shops behind, he locked eyes with Durgins, who walked on the north side of one-way street. Nate pointed to his wristwatch and then held up both hands and flashed the ten minutes sign twice.

Durgins acknowledged Nate with a dip of his chin and then pointed at another converted gas station. This time the old business had been transformed into a small Mexican bakery and convenience store, Rosarita's Bakery. Remembering fresh sweet bread and the hot jalapeño rolls, Nate shook his head wishing he had said ten minutes instead of twenty. Catching the fragrance of baking bread in the air, he shook his head again and pulled on the handle of the huge sandstone building, the Nampa Christian Center.

The pastor, a young man in his mid-thirties, met him in the foyer. Four sets of stairs greeted him, one on either side heading down, presumably into the basements and two more leading up into the sanctuary. Nate could see a kaleidoscope of colors reflected through the giant stained glass window, which was set high in the rear wall beneath the vaulted ceiling. Dusting his hands on his jeans, the pastor extended his hand. "Hi there, can I help you?"

Nate focused his attention on the man. He pulled a business card from his breast pocket and offered it to him as he introduced himself. "Hi, I'm Detective Nate Richards with the Treasure Valley Metro Police Department. May I speak with you for a few minutes, please?"

The pastor looked at the card, appearing to be reading each line of text. Then he looked back up at Nate. "Meridian office? Yes, my name is George Mann and I'm the pastor of this fine establishment. What can I do for you?"

Nate smiled, liking this young pastor almost immediately. "Pastor Mann—"

"Oh just call me George. I grew up hearing my dad called Pastor Mann and it makes me feel old. Can I get you a cup of coffee? Come on up to my office and we can talk. That way I can still answer the phone if it rings." Pastor George turned and headed up the stairs to his right. As he reached the landing, he turned to his right again. Nate paused, having expected to go into the sanctuary and then to an office just off the pulpit area.

Instead, he watched as the pastor continued up the stairs that wound in a tight spiral in a very steep ascent. Reaching an open doorway, Nate assumed he was finished climbing only to discover he had one more short flight to master before it opened out onto a loft-like room that served as the church's business offices. A small table held a coffeepot and a series of sweeteners and creamer. Above that was a smaller stained glass window, round and only about three feet in diameter. Pastor George poured two cups of coffee and offered one to Nate.

Nate accepted the cup of coffee and decided to taste it first before adding any condiments. He sipped and smiled, then inhaled the fragrance. "Hazelnut...mmm."

George smiled. "Creamer and sugar on the table." He sat on the edge of the slightly cluttered desk.

Nate ladled in two teaspoons of sugar and then added powdered creamer. He tasted it and smiled, then sat in a folding chair directly across from where the pastor perched on the desk. "Is this about the rape that happened a few weeks ago?" Pastor George asked.

Nate swallowed the mouthful of coffee he'd just taken then nodded. "Yeah, my partner and I are just out talking to the neighbors, so to speak."

"I didn't know the girl that worked there. I've spoken to her on occasion, a real friendly type. I think she attends a fellowship over in your neck of the woods. One of the traditional denominations, if I remember correctly. But how can I help you?"

Nate sat forward, and casually activated his digital recorder as he did. "On the night that this happened, did you guys have services or anything going on here at the church?"

Pastor George kicked his feet once then leaned back and grabbed a scheduling book off the desktop. He studied it for a few seconds then looked back at Nate. "No, no services. We usually try to keep Friday nights open for the cell-groups to meet at the members' homes." Then he seemed to focus on something written into the margins of the book.

Nate raised a brow and studied the pastor. "Find something?"

Pastor George looked up. "Just a note here. Looks like one of the associate pastors had a counseling session here that night."

Nate leaned a little further forward. "Do you think I can get that pastor's name?"

Pastor George wasn't paying attention; he was already writing. "Here you go…Pastor Jensen. Albert Jensen," he said without looking up, "I added his cell number as well. He works at the sugar beet factory, a swing shift foreman."

Nate looked at his cell phone and checked the time. He noted the time, 1330 and figured he had at least two hours before the swing shift started. He also noted that the 20 minutes had also passed and stood. "Thanks for your time, Pastor George." Nate extended his hand to the pastor.

George jumped from the edge of the desk and walked over to where Nate was standing. He grasped the detective's hand and gave it a firm shake. He started toward the staircase and Nate followed him down the twisty flight of steps.

A few minutes later, Nate had crossed the street and stood just outside the front door of Rosarita's and watched as Durgins slipped the last bite of a jalapeño roll into his mouth. Nate looked at his partner and raised his hands to his side, as if to say really, you couldn't wait?

"Hey, you said 20 minutes, that was two minutes ago." He smiled.

Nate reached for the aluminum framed and glass door, chuckling as he did. "Did you find out anything?" The small bells jangled as the door swung open and then banged shut behind them.

"Por la tarde," the middle-aged Hispanic man greeted them as they came into the small shop.

"Hola, mi amigo," Nate answered while waving.

The man's face brightened as he wiped his hands on the faded and slightly stained apron he wore. Coming around the corner of the counter, he extended a hand to Nate. "Usted habla español?"

Nate raised both hands, "No, no, muy poco. I'm afraid that's all my Spanish, my friend." The men shook hands and an easy laughter filled the room.

"Welcome to my store." He winked and looked around conspiratorially, and added, "Well, actually it's my wife's store; I just do all the work."

"Hey, I heard that." A female voice rang out from the small kitchen off to the right of the main room. A rather tall and beautiful Hispanic woman came into the room carrying a tray of fresh baked rolls. A fine sheen of sweat caused her honey-brown skin to glow in warm contrast against her dark hair. "Yeah, he does all the work, the baking, the mixing, and the cleaning." She smiled as she walked near her husband, leaning toward him; she accepted a firm kiss on her cheek.

The two smiled at each other and started placing the new rolls into the display case. The affection between the two was easy and abundant. Nate looked at Durgins. "You got anybody who loves you that much?"

"Just my dogs—and my horse come in a close second." The blond haired detective waved off Nate's next comment and headed to the back of the small store.

Nate could hear him humming to himself as he looked through the various cases. First a jellyroll and then a couple of brightly colored sweet rolls; Nate wondered how Durgins ate so poorly and still managed to stay so fit. He looked down at his own waistline, lamented the miles ran and hours spent in the gym, and decided to settle on only one treat instead of the three he imagined.

"Ah, you must be Rosarita," he said as the woman came back around the counter. Wiping her hands on the end of her apron, she came to stand next to her husband.

She laughed. "Actually, I'm Catalina and you've met husband Jorge." The shop owner smiled again, his face visibly brightening for the effort. "Rosarita was my grandmother. The shop was hers first then my mother's and now it's mine."

"Ours," Jorge said hugging his wife around the shoulders.

She nudged her husband in his ribs and smiled up at him. "So what brings you officers into our humble store?"

"I bet it's about that rape that happened at the coffee shop down the street," Jorge said as he accepted the rolls in clear plastic baggies from each of the detectives. After securing them in a larger bag, he handed them back, first to Nate then to Durgins. "No charge," he said when the men began to object.

Nate pulled a five dollar bill from his pocket. "There's no need—"

"You're gonna turn down my generosity and insult me in my own store?"

Nate shrugged. Durgins took a bite of sweet roll. "Well, if you put it that way...." Nate left the sentence hanging and took a bite of his own jalapeño roll. "So what can you tell me about the rape?"

At this, the couple became serious. Jorge pulled his wife a little closer against himself, and they exchanged a look between each other. "Well, for one thing, I don't leave her here at the shop alone anymore. And I don't let her walk out to the car after dark."

Catalina smiled up at her husband appreciatively, but bumped him with her hip, "Like I was a child that needed protecting." Then she lowered her head against his shoulder.

Jorge continued. "There was nothing weird that we saw. That was a Friday, right? We closed late that night, and I remember the church was all lit up, but I didn't see anybody that looked weird."

"Did you talk to them across the street at the church?" Durgins asked.

"That pastor...we don't go to that church, but I hear he's a pretty decent fellow," Catalina added.

"Yeah, I already stopped in there," Nate said. "I guess the question is whether you saw anything or anyone. You can never tell sometimes what might be important. So just do me a favor and think about that night and tell me what you do remember."

The couple looked at each other again and then back at the detectives. "There was that guy on the motorcycle." They said together.

"Motorcycle?" Nate asked.

CHAPTER TWENTY- THREE

(Four Weeks Earlier)

THE SICK-SWEET ODOR that was unmistakably the sugar beet factory hung heavy in the moist air. The Amalgamated Sugar Company stood like a sentinel on the horizon; twin plumes of steam were rising against the blue-gray sky. Stopping at the main gate, Nate lowered his window, and he and Durgins showed their I.D. to the guard. "Personnel?" Nate asked.

The gate guard nodded and pointed to a small door set in the side of the main building. "Go inside and just follow the corridor to the main office. You'll see the signs."

Nate tipped his head, touched the corner of his forehead and waved as he drove through the opened gate. The odor was stronger here, overwhelmingly so.

Stepping inside the building, Nate closed the door behind him as Durgins stepped past. The first thing they noticed was the warmth compared to the chill that still hung on the early spring afternoon. The second thing was that the air was decidedly fresher. He greeted the college aged female sitting at the receptionist desk. Judging from the abundance of cheerfulness and the crisp attitude, Nate reckoned her an intern. "Hi there, I'm Detective Nate Richards with Treasure Valley

Metro. This is my partner, Detective Durgins. We need to see one of your employees."

The young lady stood, her back straight, and extended her hand. "Welcome to Amalgamated Sugar, gentlemen. If you'll have a seat in the chairs against the far wall, I'll get someone to help you right away."

Tapping Nate on the elbow, Durgins led the way to the dull gray molded chairs along the corridor wall. "You feel that?"

Nate leaned forward. "Now that you mention it, you can kind of feel the vibrations coming through the walls. That's weird," he said. Like energy from a subwoofer, a low grinding vibration moved through the walls and floors causing the windows and hanging lights to move with slight tremors.

Just as Nate grabbed the several months old Field & Stream magazine, the receptionist returned. "Gentlemen, Mrs. Goeins will see you in her office. This way please." Without waiting, she turned and began down the hall. The soft thud of her sensible soled shoes was almost swallowed up by the cavernous hall.

"In here, please." She opened the door allowing the men to enter the small office. "Mrs. Goeins, this is Detectives Richards and Durgins." She turned away and returned to her workstation.

"She's a little spitfire, isn't she," Durgins said.

"Top of her class," Mrs. Goeins said. "She has been a real boost to us here. Crosses all her T's and dots her I's, if you know what I mean." They all chuckled. "So," she spread her hands, palms facing forward, "what can I do for you?"

Nate extended his hand, followed by Durgins. "Yes, we just need to speak with one of your employees. A Mr. Albert Jensen."

She raised a brow and pushed the door closed. "Our policy dictates that any employee that is questioned concerning company business or on company property be allowed to have a company representative present during that questioning."

Nate swung his hand in a low sweeping motion across his waist. "No, it's nothing like that. We think he may have seen something related to the rape that happened in the downtown area a couple of weeks ago. He's not a suspect, but he might be a witness."

Sitting up, Goeins acknowledged Nate and then leaned forward and spoke into her desk intercom. After a few minutes wait, Albert Jensen joined them in the small office. "Mr. Jensen, this is Detectives Richards and Durgins with Metro. They want to talk to you about an incident that happened in town. But since you're on company property and if you wish it, I will remain with you during any questioning."

"Oh no, ma'am, these good gentlemen can ask me anything they like. Since the work of the Holy Ghost in me, there's no secrets worth keeping."

Mrs. Goeins smiled at Jensen's exuberance, shook her head, and sighed as she left the men in the office.

"Wow, is it the sugar or what? Between you and that receptionist, you guys are giving Disneyland a run for their money," Durgins said.

"So how can I help you?" Jensen asked.

Nate turned to face Jensen and then pointed at the chairs. The men sat.

Nate opened the manila folder he had tucked beneath his arm. "I'm sure you heard about the sexual assault that happened down at the Motor Head Coffee and Tea Shop. I was told that you had a counseling or a meeting there at the church that same night. What I'd like to know is if you saw anything or anyone that might have been or at least looked out of place?"

Jensen tilted his head back and straining in concentration. Looking up, he began muttering. "We were in the back of the church and then exited out the rear. Traffic had all but died away that time of night. The bakery was still open, but I remember the Fuentes' were out front sweeping up."

Nate exchanged glances with Durgins. "Anything else?" He asked interrupting Jensen.

Jensen looked back at Nate, like he'd forgotten the detectives were in the room. "Ah, I remember it was cold, but dry. It was one of those still evenings when the winds not blowing but just still and cold. You know?"

Durgins cleared his throat. "Do you—"

"Oh yeah, there was this guy parked on a motorcycle in the alley behind the machine shop. I didn't think anything of it, thought maybe he was hanging out with the guys at the house on the other side of the fence. I see a lot of those types there...bikers, motor-heads, and grease junkies. You know the type."

Nate leaned forward. "Can you remember anything about the person on the bike? Anything at all?"

"Why? Is it important?"

"We don't know yet," Durgins said. "We're just checking all leads, Pastor Jensen."

Jensen looked from Nate to Durgins then closed his eyes again. "Well, from the looks and size, I think it was a guy. Mind you he was sitting, but I think if he had been standing he would have been at least six feet. He had rather broad shoulders and long hair. I couldn't see the color...it was too dark for that. But he did have on a long coat, like those cattlemen jackets that hangs down past the knees—oh yes, and he was in all black."

***

At just before noon the next day, Edna Mae sat on the edge of her bed and studied her reflection in the mirrored closet door. She smiled as she saw the way her hair fell over her shoulders enjoying the classic lines of her neck and cheekbones. Lifting her hair with the back of her hand, she watched as the light played on it as she allowed it to drift through her fingers. "I wonder if he likes dark hair?" She wondered aloud to her reflection.

She stood and, taking a quarter turn, admired the figure reflected. She smiled and then pulled on her light green robe, tying the silky covering closed at her waist. She lifted the business card and smiled then kissed it. Placing the card back on her nightstand, she turned and opened the bedroom door.

"Girls, I'm going to be heading downtown. I have a meeting with Detective Richards. I'll be back before dinner." The teenage girls didn't so much as lift their eyes from the TV in acknowledging their mother; instead, they continued playing Super Mario Galaxy on the Wii gaming system. The beeps and twittering chimes filled the air as the door closed with a soft click behind her.

After dressing, Edna Mae made her way out to her late model Volvo station wagon. Sitting behind the steering wheel, she enjoyed the accumulated warmth that filtered in through the glass. The sun won its labored battle with the heavy gray clouds that had hung low over the valley. The grass and street surfaces still glistened with the accumulated frost that had at last given way to the burgeoning spring heat.

Pulling into the angled parking on 14th Street, she sat and watched the customers going in and out of the coffee shop. For a brief moment, the terror she'd experienced came back to her. The loss of control, the helplessness, all of it came rushing back, breaking through her mental defenses as if they did not exist.

Gripping the steering wheel until her hands strained with the effort, she fought just to breath. Her breaths were labored. Dropping her hand from the steering wheel, she grabbed the gearshift, squeezing the ball-shaped handle; she prepared to shift the car into reverse.

A soft tapping on her window startled her, breaking her reverie. Looking up, she saw Detective Richards standing just outside her car, a worried look on his face. She observed how his brown eyes seemed to deepen as he studied her. His smile was warm and did little to hide the concern he was feeling: concern for her.

Taking a deep breath, she chanced a quick look into the mirror, brushed her hair back with her hand, and opened the door. "Detective Richards, how are you?" Her voice was bright— too bright.

Nate extended his hand and grasped hers in his. Helping her from the car, he stepped back, inviting her to join him on the sidewalk. "You okay? Looked there for a moment like you were having a hard time."

She looked away, frustrated that he had seen her moment of weakness. "No," she said shaking her head, "just too many things on my mind at once. How are you?" She asked again.

Nate smiled and nodded, but didn't push her on it. "I'm well, thanks for asking. I'm sorry but Dani won't be able to meet with us. Another call came up. We can do this lat—"

"No, no, we're both here and it's such a lovely day; I'd hate to waste it." She touched his forearm as she spoke. Gathering herself, she stepped past him and headed toward the double glass doors of the converted gas station.

Nate hesitated and, for the hundredth time, wished he called and canceled the appointment. Lately, Dani's warning had been replaying itself in his mind. *Any strong masculine role is attractive to her now.* He sighed and turned to follow after the puzzling woman. Reasoning that the area was public and the middle of the day, he set forebodings aside.

As Edna Mae walked in, she hesitated just for a moment before continuing inside. Waving, she called out to the manager and walked briskly to embrace the middle-aged woman.

"Edna," the woman said, stretching the word over several syllables. "How are you, sweetie?" Then without waiting for an answer, she looked over her shoulder toward the small kitchen. "Glendon! Glen-n-n-don! Glen, look who's here."

The coffee shop was basically a huge L-shaped building. The main lobby is what use to serve as the waiting room and customer contact area. The short hall, which led down the right side of the counter, connected the front and back rooms through an even shorter corridor where the bathrooms were located.

What used to operate as the service bay was now the lodge, with a stage for live performances and a loft, for those who wanted to be above it all and several booths with outlets and wall jacks for the internet minded. Along the walls and floor remained remnants of the shop's days as an automotive repair shop. Signs and posters advertised services, goods, and parts. The pit was where the cars were driven over and the oil drained and changed, and, of course, the lift that now served as an elevated stage.

"What is it, Tildie? Can't you see a body's trying to work?" The fifty-something redhead called as he came through the swinging doors. "Matilda, how many times have I told you not to just scream out like that in the store.... You're gonna scare off the customers," the slightest hint of his Irish brogue sneaking through.

"Don't be a git." Tildie wiped her hands on a towel and threw it at her husband. Glendon or Glen, as he was known by his friends, rushed out and enveloped Edna Mae in a bear hug of an embrace. "Don't go breaking the girl," Tildie chided, a smile in her voice.

"Well, I'll be gob smacked," he said. "I am so sorry that the ugly happened to you here at my own store. If I ever lay my hands on the manky—"

"Watch your mouth, Glendon O'Hare."

He smiled at his wife even as he released Edna Mae from the embrace. Turning to face Nate, who had been forgotten in brief reacquainting, Glen stuck out a meaty hand. Nate grasped the hand and shook it.

"Nate Richards, Treasure Valley Metro. I'm working the case for Miss Fuller."

"Come on in and have a seat. Tildie, get the man a cup of coffee. Edna Mae?"

Edna Mae smiled, enjoying the familiar atmosphere and kind hearted jabs the couple took with each other. "No, none for me, but I'll have a cup of tea if you have something worth drinking."

Tildie smiled and picked up the discarded towel. Draping it over one shoulder, she turned toward the counter. "Well, don't you go worrying yourself about that lass, I've got something you'll like well enough."

Edna Mae laughed. Nate laughed too, although he wasn't exactly sure what was being teased in the light hearted banter. "So I'm a lass again, now? So much for being the *bean phósta*, huh?"

Nate took the opportunity to look around the shop. Several free standing racks held cards, souvenirs, and trinkets for sale. The concrete floors had been sealed and polished to a high sheen and speakers hanging from the ceiling pumped soft Gaelic tunes throughout.

"Don't you mind her, Luv," Glen said, "you're always the perfect lady to me." He kissed Edna Mae's cheek and then headed after his wife to help with the coffee and a small plate of treats they had set aside for the visit.

Nate leaned back in the vintage fifties styled chair and watched the old friends enjoying each other. Opening the manila folder he carried, he laid it across his lap and began studying the papers, diagrams, and photos from the night of the assault.

Soon a cup of coffee and a small plate was placed before him, and the fragrance of the fresh roasted beans and hot soda bread and scones filled the room. Several small jars of jellies and jams as well as cubes of cheese were set out with the coffee and tea. Lifting the small biscuit-like scone, Nate took a bite and smiled, as the flaky treat seemed to melt on his tongue.

"You know most people add butter and jam to those," Edna Mae teased.

"Leave the man alone...don't you see he's eat'ng," Glen said with his own mouth half stuffed with buttered bread.

"Thank you," Nate managed between bites. Then after taking a drink from his coffee cup, he lifted it and looked inside. "This is good."

"What were you expecting...that assembly line stuff you get at the other places? This is real down-home coffee, Detective. Nothing fancy, just good beans, clean water, and lots of love in that cup," Tildie said. "We know you didn't come here to just visit, so we'll head to the back and get started on the inventory. Just yell at us when you're done."

Glen stood. "I've already put the closed for lunch sign out, so just ignore anyone who comes to the door. I'll apologize to them later." He began laughing as he followed his wife out of the main floor and out through the rear door. Even after the door sealed shut, his booming laughter still rang through the hollow structure.

"You ready?" Nate asked.

Edna Mae swallowed. She nodded her head. "I guess."

Nate paused again, second-guessing his going through this without Dani present. "We can do this another time, if—"

She shook her head again. "No. Like I said earlier, we're already here. So we might as well do it." She let out a long breath and flinched as if she surprised herself by it.

Nate stood. "Okay then. Show me where you were when you first became aware of the suspect in the store."

Edna Mae stood with slow deliberate measures. With leaden steps she walked through the swinging doors and stood by the sink as if washing dishes. "Okay, I was here. I was cleaning up the last of the plates, getting ready to shut down for the night."

Nate stood by the main door. "So what did you notice first?"

For a brief moment there was no answer, only silence met him in response. "Edna...you okay?"

She cleared her throat. "I was standing here washing the dishes when I heard the bell over the door ring. I remember it because it was just about closing, and I was mad that I hadn't already locked the door. Would have saved myself a lot of trouble if I had, huh?"

Nate looked at the pass-through window, but could not see her from where he stood. He looked at his file again then started toward the swinging door. "What happened next?"

"Well at first I didn't see anyone."

"Really?"

"Yeah, when I came out the back, I walked this way and came up to the register." Edna Mae had come out of the kitchen and turned to her left following the curve of the walk to where the counter met at the point of the ninety-degree bend that led to the back sitting room. "I was surprised and a bit happy because I thought whoever had come had left and I decided to lock the door before anyone else came in."

Nate had paralleled her and was standing on the opposite side of the counter, his back to the front door. "Was this when you noticed the perp?"

Edna Mae's expression had gone blank, her face flaccid. "Not at first. I was just starting to get happy that I could still get out of here on time. And when I turned he was standing behind me. He was just standing there staring at me. His eyes…"

Nate stepped closer; he was only about four feet away although separated by the counter. "You're safe Edna…I'm here. It's just a memory, it can't hurt you." He watched as she first inhaled then released a ragged breath. "Tell me what happened next."

She breathed in again and let her shoulder relax. "His eyes…he had such hungry eyes. When I first saw him, the mask and big over coat, I thought he was going to rob me, but when I looked into his eyes, I knew what he wanted. He wanted me." She shook her head again, small indistinct movements; just a furrowing of her brow and a tilt of her head.

Nate had moved around to where he could face her, but still with the counter between them. "What did he say? Did he do anything in particular?"

"He touched me."

"He what? How?" Nate began flipping through his notes from the initial interview. There had been no mention of touching during the first stage of the contact.

Although her eyes were open, she was unfocused on the scene before her, but seemed rather to be seeing, experiencing the images from a week or so prior. "He brushed my cheek with the back of his fingers. The gloves smelled like pine, like he had used Pine-Sol to wash oil or gas off his hands."

Nate nodded and made notes. "Then what happened?" When she hesitated, he added, "Remember, we only go as far as you're comfortable. We can stop any time."

"Then he lifted my hair and smelled it. He said I had beautiful hair. I remember I had to look up to see his eyes. They were two different colors."

Nate checked his notes again and nodded.

"I was so scared, I couldn't move. He grabbed my face with both his hands and then kissed my cheeks, first one then the other."

Nate looked up. "Did the nurse swab your cheeks during the exam?" She nodded and Nate noticed her face was wet with tears.

"He kissed me. He kissed me and I just stood there like an idiot and did nothing."

Nate walked around the counter and stood a few feet from her. "Edna Mae."

She didn't answer.

"Edna, you were not an idiot. You were in shock. Your mind had slowed down, trying to find a way for you to survive. You had to survive for your girls."

Reaching up, she brushed her cheeks. "For my girls," she muttered.

"Yes," Nate encouraged her, "for your girls." He reached a hand out to her and she walked toward him with small, slow steps. He escorted her back to the table where they had been sitting earlier.

Lifting the ceramic teapot, Nate poured Edna Mae a cup of the amber liquid and slid the mug over in front of her. "Drink this, it'll make you feel better," he said infusing his voice with confidence. He was afraid he'd pushed her too hard.

Lifting the cup, it trembled in her hands. The steam wafted past her face and she leaned forward, her elbows resting on the table. "Barry's Red Loose Leaf."

"What?"

She smiled. "The tea, its Barry's Red Loose Leaf; it's a mild blend. Most people drink it early morning, but it's one of those rare blends that's good any time of day. Thanks."

Nate returned her smile. "Glad I could help." He pushed the plate of goodies to her. When she shook her head, he dragged it back across the table to himself and lifted a scone from the plate. "That looked pretty tough. You sure you're okay?"

She nodded again and took another sip of her tea. "I'm fine, Nate. I just need a minute."

Nate looked up at her use of his name. He remembered again that they were alone and again he wondered at his decision to go forward without Dani present.

Edna Mae looked over the top of her cup at Nate. He had told her she was safe because he was here with her, that he would not let anything happen to her. She smiled at the memory. She liked the way he watched over her, like her own personal knight in shining armor.

"Thanks again for the tea, Nate; I'll be fine in a minute." *Did he start at the use of his name?* She cautioned herself. *She would have to slow down; he had to be professional. He was probably afraid that he was going too fast for her.* The thought warmed her.

"That's all we'll do for now," Nate said. "Let me go over what I got here and then we can come back if we need to." He stood as if he intended to leave.

Edna Mae reclined in her seat and continued drinking her tea. The tea he had poured for her. She looked up at him and studied his features. She liked the way his eyes sparkled when the light hit them just right. It reminded her of a cup of black tea. Although he wore his hair relatively short, she could still see the curls as they played around the edges of his face. She longed to touch them, to run her fingers through them and see how they felt against her skin.

Nate cleared his throat. "Did you hear what I said?"

She sat forward. "Ah, no, sorry. I was lost in thought for a minute. Would you mind repeating that for me?"

Nate continued stacking his papers and ordering his folder. "No, not at all. I was just saying, I didn't think it would be necessary for us to get together again until we get this thing into court. But if you need me for any reason you could always reach me through Dani."

Need you? Of course I need you. What? Are you thinking of abandoning me? "Sure. I can see that. If I need anything, I just call Dani, and if you need me, you can either reach me here or at home. You have my cell number, right?" She had to sound happy, confident. She didn't want him avoiding her because he thought it was too hard for her.

Just as Nate extended his hand to Edna Mae, Glen and Tildie came back into the room. "Hey, done already," Glen called out, carrying a case of various flavored coffee beans.

"You didn't even finish the scones. You have to take them with you," Tildie said. She pushed her long black hair back from her face, the fine strands of gray and silver working as natural highlights added to her regal appearance.

With quick practiced strides, Tildie gathered the remaining scones and soda bread and wrapped them, placing the packet in a small box. "You'll have to get your own jelly, but you can have the cheese." She wrapped the various cheese cubes in a separate sheet of wax paper and dropped them atop the breads.

Nate stood and turned back to Edna Mae, "I'll be in touch."

Glen dropped a heavy hand onto Nate's shoulder, causing him to stumble forward. "You're welcome here any time, Detective Richards. Anybody helping my Edna will always be welcome in my place. I just wish I could find the Ma—"

"Glendon," Tildie called.

"I mean—the person that did this in my place. I would show him what we do to the men who hurt women back home."

"Calm down my Irish warrior, we've battles enough to fight right here in this shop." Tildie stretched up and kissed her husband's cheek. The two slipped their arms around each other and stood together in comfortable silence. Edna Mae joined them and leaned her head on Glen's shoulder, and from where Nate stood watching, they looked like any mother and father and adult daughter.

He thanked them again and turned to walk away. Just as he did, his phone rang. It was Dani. "Richards."

"Hey, I just got clear of court. You want me to meet you there at the shop?"

"Actually, I'm just leaving." He rubbed his face, knowing what she would say next. Using the keyless remote, he unlocked the car door and settled in behind the steering wheel.

"Nate, you didn't put her through that alone, did you?" When he didn't answer she began, "Didn't I tell you she was fragile? Nate this woman is going to think she's falling in love with you, and it will be your own fault. Did anything happen?"

Nate sighed and looked at his reflection in the rearview mirror. After starting the car and pulling out into traffic, he answered her. "Not really."

"Not really! Nate, what does 'not really' mean? Was there any touching? I told you absolutely no touching, remember?" She was frustrated; Nate could hear it in her voice.

"No, no touching. Ah, darn…"

"What?"

He checked the traffic crossing on 12th and decided to turn right instead of waiting for the green light to turn. Now heading north on 12th, he watched the pedestrians moving idly by, some walking, others on bikes. A few passed in an obvious hurry, going where he did not know. "Well, when I first arrived and was telling her that you could not make it, she touched my arm. It was just a brief contact; I didn't really think anything of it at the time."

"Didn't you? You should have. Nate, if you're not careful not only will you blow this case, you're gonna get yourself into trouble. What else happened? I can tell there's something by the way you're not talking."

Nate turned onto 1st and then after making the light at 11th, followed it around past Lake View Park until it connected with the I-84. "She called me Nate."

Over the phone, Nate could hear Dani sigh—long and deep. "Did you correct her and remind her that yours was a professional relationship?"

"I was going to but she had been crying and—"

"Crying? And you had to be the hero. Nate, I told you—"

"I know and I kept my distance. I never came within four feet of her. No comforting, just encouraging her that she could get through this. I did tell her that I would not be able to meet with her again until we get to court, but she should feel free to contact you if she had a need."

She laughed. "At least you did that part right. What am I going to do with you." It was a rhetorical question and Nate did not feel compelled to answer.

"I'm on the freeway now, just passing Black Cat, want to meet for a Ho-ho? My treat."

Dani sighed and then giggled. "If I keep hanging out with you, I'll be as big as Lieutenant Brown. Besides, those things are made with hydrogenated oils and refined sugars. It'll kill you."

Nate smiled. "One won't kill you. Besides, it's been almost a week since we had one. Come on, I'll even spring for milk."

"Oh, okay, I'll meet you at the Eddy's on Locust Grove and Fairview. But this doesn't make up for you being stupid today."

"I know."

"And you'd better make notes indicating everything that happened there today. You know what *they* say."

They both laughed and then said together, "If it's not written down, it didn't happen." Then they laughed again before sobering.

"I'm serious, Nate, protect yourself. Make good notes and don't put yourself in a bad situation again. The job's bad enough without you being stupid."

"Ouch. I got you. I won't do it again." He paused as he activated his signal to exit at Meridian Road. "Thanks for caring Dani."

"Yeah, no problem. See you in about ten minutes."

Nate pulled out his notepad and put his pen between his teeth intending to make some quick notes about the afternoon as soon as he stopped at the light at the end of the off ramp. As he pulled up to the light, the signal went from red to green and he continued into the intersection.

Just as the nose of the Jeep entered the traffic lanes, a red Volkswagen Golf screamed past, southbound, and just barely missed hitting Nate. Startled, Nate dropped the pen and then threw the notepad on the floorboard. He reached down and activated his emergency lights and sirens.

Nate accelerated out into the southbound lanes and followed the speeding vehicle through the Overland intersection. As the siren continued to wail, Nate pulled in behind the vehicle. The driver, a teenaged girl, looked up, her eyes meeting Nate's in the mirror, and he saw her mouth a series of curse words into the receiver of the cell phone before she dropped it into her lap.

Once the vehicles had pulled along the side of the road on Meridian just north of Calderwood, Nate made contact at the driver's side window of the red car. He recognized the driver. "Christina Casabaum, we've been looking for you. Why don't you go ahead and turn your car off. I don't think you're gonna be needing it anymore tonight."

The teen lowered her head to the backs of her hands, which were resting on the steering wheel. "If I'd known you were a cop I would have stopped for that light. Sorry."

Nate looked at the eighteen year old and shook his head. He opened his mouth as if to speak, changed his mind, and closed it again. He held out his hand and Christina dropped the car keys into his palm.

Going back to his car, Nate lifted the mouthpiece for the radio. "TV9018. 10-99 check."

Coming through the vehicle's speakers, Dispatch responded to Nate's query, "TV9018 go ahead for 10-99 check."

"I have one female subject last of Casabaum, C-A-S-A-B-A-U-M, first of Christina, common spelling; middle initial T. DOB is 11-02-93. She should have a FTA, and PV warrant. Can you confirm if both those are still in the system and if so, confirm for validity?"

"Copy. Standby."

A few minutes later, a marked police unit arrived on scene. Shortly after that, Christina was handcuffed and in the rear seat of the patrol car, on her way to the Ada County Jail. The young rebel was under arrest for the two warrants plus two new misdemeanor citations for reckless driving and DWP, driving without privileges. Relaxing into the seat of the Jeep, Nate checked his cell phone and found that he had two missed calls from Dani. Shaking his head, he vowed to make it up to her.

CHAPTER TWENTY- FOUR

(The Present)

AMBER TOYED WITH HER KEYCHAIN as it dangled from the steering column. She had been sitting in her car, parked along the curb of Second Street near the Carlton Street intersection, for almost half an hour. From there she could see the main entrance to the Library Coffeehouse. She watched as patrons went in and out, escaping the cold and wet in exchange for a hot cup of comfort. She also knew Jackie was on duty.

Her breathing quickened, keeping time with the rapid back and forth rhythm rapped out by the swish of the wiper blades. She prayed silently and reached within herself, looking for the courage to do what she knew needed to be done. Opening the car door, she sighed in resignation. "Amber, you can't lose what you don't have." She headed toward the door.

Coming up the short set of steps, Amber pulled open the door and stepped inside. The warmth and gentle hominess of the place brought a sense of comfort to her. She inhaled the various flavors of fresh roasting coffee beans mixed with exotic teas and fresh baked pastries. She smiled as memories of times shared here came flooding back to her mind. She well understood why this place had been a favorite of Nate's.

Looking around, she felt it before she saw Jackie staring at her. Their eyes met and Jackie smiled at Amber, but it had not reached her eyes.

Amber took another deep breath and crossed the last few steps to the counter. She smiled. "Can we talk?"

Jackie didn't answer, but instead reached over and grabbed a porcelain mug from a stack. The mug was cream colored and had full grapes on the vine, raised on its surface. Below, in a soft flowing script, were the words, "This is the day the Lord has made…". She filled the cup with coffee, poured creamer in it, and indicated the Splenda on the counter behind Amber and to her right. "Pick a table; I'll meet you there in a few minutes."

Amber lifted the cup. "Thank you. How much for the coffee?" she asked reaching for her wallet.

Jackie dropped her gaze for a moment, then lifted it back to reach Amber's face. "It's on me."

Amber thanked her and dropped two dollars into the tip jar before turning to her left heading for the back room to find an empty table.

Selecting a spot in the furthest corner of the large room, Amber settled down and began to examine the room. Bookshelves lined the outside wall and paintings of jazz musicians adorned the back wall. On the short wall to her left were plastered images of the good times celebrated at the coffeehouse. Various parties and summer songfests depicted smiling employees and patrons all enjoying the warmth of this room and good friends.

She looked up when she noticed Jackie approaching. She was quite beautiful, Amber thought. She watched as the soft lighting from the overhead tracks reflected off the red highlights in the woman's brunette hair. It was long and full of curves and body, the way Nate liked it.

Even wearing the smock and simple trousers, Amber could see the full womanly contours that made Jackie so appealing to the men who came into the coffee shop…and to Nate. Meeting her gaze, Amber invited Jackie to sit with her.

The woman's greenish eyes flickered over Amber's face as the two women, again, studied each other's features. Amber spoke first. "Thanks for meeting with me."

Jackie cleared her throat. "I figured this would have to happen sooner or later."

Catching her accusing tone, Amber leaned forward. "No…it's not like that."

"Like what?" Jackie asked as she smiled with sad, glowing eyes. "That you're not here because you're still in love with Nate?"

Amber sat back, her mouth open.

Jackie smiled. This time her eyes warmed a little. "It's okay. I've known from the beginning that he was still in love with you. Although, I don't think he knows it. I thought I could replace you in his life." She lowered her eyes and wiped the table surface with absent-minded strokes.

Amber closed her mouth and leaned forward again, shaking her head in short quick motions. "Th-that is not why I am here. I came to ask you to go to him. Jackie, he needs you, and he's cut the rest of us off. He won't even take calls from his mother."

"And you think he's talking to me?" She stared at Amber.

"Well, isn't he?"

"No."

The two women sat in silence for a long while, neither daring to speak. The sounds of soft vocal jazz floated down around them from overhead speakers and the breathy roar of the gas fireplace hummed behind it all. Customers could be heard coming in, and the muffled conversations of sales and easy banter rose and fell in comfortable swells. Jackie turned and waved at Victor, the co-owner, raising three fingers in his direction and then pointing at her wristwatch. "Look-"

"I just thought…" Amber began, cutting off whatever it was Jackie was about to say. "…I just thought he was turning to you since he had turned away from everyone else."

Jackie continued from where she'd left off. "Look I don't know where he's going. I just know he doesn't come to me. I haven't seen him since the night I ran into you at his place."

"But that's been over a week ago," Amber said, her concern beginning to overshadow her curiosity. "I just thought—I hoped that if I spoke with you, you could at least tell me how he was doing and ask him to call his mom."

Jackie stood and looked down into Amber's upturned face. She reached across the small table and touched Amber's shoulder in a gesture of girlish familiarity. "Look, I don't know what to tell you, but if I could have held on to him, I would have." She smiled, pursed her lips, and began to shake her head in slow thoughtful movements. "Just like he's had to pretend he was over you." She looked away, back toward the counter. "Well, I guess it's my time to try and get over him now." She smiled sadly, turned and began walking back toward the counter.

Amber took a sip from the coffee Jackie had given her. Lost in thought and muttering in a low voice, she whispered, "This is good." Watching Jackie's retreating back, Amber wasn't sure if her comments had been directed to the coffee or about what Jackie had said.

Jackie stopped a short distance away. "If you see Nate, tell him I said good-bye. Tell him I'm leaving." Then she laughed a mirthless laugh. "First you, then me, huh? This guy has a way of running people out of this valley, doesn't he?" Without looking back, she continued walking and Amber found herself sitting alone.

Amber took another drink of her coffee and played the conversation over in her mind. One phrase kept popping out to her that Jackie had used; "…*he was still in love with you. Although, I don't think he knows it.*"

Nate was still in love with her. She took another drink of the coffee. In spite of herself, she smiled, and this time she knew exactly why.

***

Nate sat back and exhaled, sinking deep against the sofa. *What else could go wrong?* He pressed the playback for a second time and listened as Jackie's voice filled the hollowness that had become his life. Closing his eyes, he listened and covered his face with his hands as the recording played. "Nate, I-I'm sorry I couldn't tell you this in person, but I needed to do this for me." Jackie's voice slammed into Nate like hammer blows to his gut. He could hear the pain, pain he'd caused her. She was crying. "Nate, you don't love me....rather you are not in love with me. I know this and I can't stay here, seeing you and knowing that you don't love me the same way I love you. So, I'm leaving. By the time you get this, I'll be gone. I'm going back to Seattle. I just wanted to say thank you for the good times and Nate, know that I really did...I really do love you. Good-bye."

Nate slumped deeper in the cushions of the sofa and sank into the morass of guilt and depression that had torn and ripped at the edges of his mind. He sat looking at nothing and seeing even less.

The phone rang and Nate, startled from a mid-afternoon doze, reached out for it, picked it up, dropped it and grabbed it again. "Yeah." He rubbed his face and looked at his wall clock: *one-thirty,* He groaned. Judging from where the light fell against the flat screen TV, Nate knew time had passed. The empty plate from his breakfast still sat on the table; the remaining scrambled eggs looked stiff and pale in the afternoon light. Thankfully, it was still too early in the season for flies.

"Detective Richards."

Nate sat up, his mind alert now; all traces of fuzziness gone. "Yes, this is Richards. Who is this?" He rubbed the remaining sleep from his eyes. The plate, its contents, and missing flies, all were forgotten now.

The male voice on the phone paused for a brief moment before responding. "Man, I guess the rumors are true. You're in a bad way."

Nate stood. Arching, he stretched the kink out of his lower back. He sighed. "Butch." It was Butch Jensen, the local reporter for News Six, a local branch for one of the national corporations. He was not necessarily one of Nate's favorite people. "Butch, why are you calling me here at home?"

"Hey, I didn't know this was your private cell, it's the only number I have for you. But I didn't call to chat about cell phones."

Nate looked at the phone in his hand and realized he was using his department issued phone; his own cell still lay quiet where he'd left it on the table beside the TV remote. "Speaking of that…" He had no intention of supplying Butch with any information.

Butch cleared his throat. "The word on the street is that you've been canned."

Nate swallowed but did not respond. He looked around the small apartment, and although it was clean, it had a feeling of having been ignored. Dishes on the coffee table; a coffee cup on the counter, and a half-filled pot of very old coffee sat idle near the sink.

"Now I know you're probably still on the department's pay role, but according to my information, they're planning on ending that little arrangement and cutting you lose all together. It seems the little lady has claimed some inappropriate activity on your part while you were on duty and on the city's dime."

Nate still didn't answer, but he noticed that his breathing had become deeper, more labored. He worked to control it.

"Nate…?"

"What do you want, Jensen, some kind of a statement or something?"

"That would be nice."

Nate drew his arm back as if to crush the phone against the wall, thought better of it, and brought the receiver back to his ear. "Look Jensen, I don't know what you've heard or who you heard it from, but I did nothing wrong. I did not violate department policy and am innocent of any wrong doing whatsoever."

"Can I quote you on th—"

"Quote this. Don't call me."

"Hey, hey, Nat—"

Nate slapped the phone shut, and with determined, careful purpose, placed it on the table beside his own. He dropped back into the chair he had just vacated. Leaning forwarded, he rested his elbows on his knees and his face in his hands. "Oh God, oh God, I can't take this." *Lord, I just can't handle—*

A sudden knock on the door interrupted his thoughts. Nate rocked back into his chair but did not move to get up. The wrapping sounded again. With effort, Nate stood and made his way toward the sound. For some unknown reason, dread began to grow in the pit of his stomach. He looked back at the phone on the table.

Taking a breath, he opened the door. Assistant Chief Zachary—Zack Lawrence along with Lieutenant Haynes stood in the hallway. "May we come in," the A.C. said in his matter of fact way.

Nate didn't answer, but locked eyes with Haynes for a brief moment before stepping aside and swinging the door wider. With a sweep of his hand, he indicated the living room and followed the two men over. Suddenly self-conscious, he picked up the plate and started toward the kitchen. "Can I get you something to drink?"

"No, I'm fine."

"I'll take a glass of water, Nate," Haynes called from where he was beginning to take a seat.

Nate returned with two glasses of water and set one in front of each of the men. "So, sir, what brings you out to my apartment? I can't remember you being one to make house calls unless someone's been shot or killed. So…" he left the sentence unfinished.

Looking from the A.C. to Lt. Haynes, Nate thought he saw the slightest of nods from Haynes. The A.C. cleared his throat. "Nate this hurts me to do this, son, but I'm here to ask for your resignation. The administration has looked over the case and has decided that your behavior was not something that the department agrees with or can support. We do not want you representing our agency any longer."

"To be fair, the entire administration does not feel this way," Haynes added, but did not meet the A.C.'s gaze.

Nate stood and paced away from the men. "So, just like that? The ten years mean nothing? No formal hearing? No chance to answer the charges? Nothing? You just want me gone?"

The A.C. crossed his legs, lifting his left over his right. "It's just that we felt this would be easier. Cleaner. We don't want to drag your name through the mud on this thing; and we certainly don't want the department set up as joke to the community."

"But I didn't do it. Does that count for anything? Sir," all familiarity aside, "this is me speaking as just one of your troops. We wouldn't treat a common criminal like this. At least he would get his day in court; his chance to answer to the charges leveled against him."

Assistant Chief Lawrence stood. "Think about what I've said, Nate. We don't want this to get ugly."

"Ugly? Sir, if this goes down like you're suggesting, it would set me up for a Brady ruling and I'd be done as a cop in this state—in this country. This is already ugly." Nate walked back over to where his assistant chief stood, waiting for his response. "I can't admit to doing something I didn't do, sir."

"Well...okay," the A.C. said. "I'd hoped that by my coming out here in person we could avoid this getting any worse."

Nate nodded, but refused to give a verbal response. After a moment of weighted silence had passed, the A.C. turned toward the door. "I'll see you back at the station Lieutenant Haynes."

Haynes nodded, still seated where he had been. Lifting the glass, he took a small drink. "I should be back within the hour, sir."

Lawrence, with his back stiff and shoulders squared, made his way toward the door. Nate followed him. "What's next, sir?"

The A.C. did not turn or look at Nate, but continued walking. "You'll be hearing from us."

Nate closed the door and rested his back against it, facing back to see his friend now standing. "Did you talk to Sabrina like I told you?" Haynes said, spreading his hands out in front of him.

Nate swallowed, blinked once then again. "Ah-ah, yeah."

Haynes closed the distance between them. "Nate, do you see now that they are serious? They are going burn you, man. You'd better get busy if you're gonna have any chance at saving your career. At all."

Nate looked at his friend. A part of his brain understood what Haynes was saying. He could feel the threat, sense the heightened degree of danger. But the other side, the rational side, was telling him that this was not—could not be true. He saw his friend was still talking; Nate forced himself to focus on Haynes. "Nate, get a lawyer and no matter what you think you feel, don't talk to anybody at the station without your lawyer present."

"Does that include you?"

"Wha—", Haynes interrupted himself, shook his head and smiled ruefully. "Yeah...I guess under the circumstances that should include me too. If they question me, I'll tell them that I advised you to get legal counsel." Haynes set the empty glass on the edge of the counter. "See ya around, Nate."

Nate moved toward his friend and grasped his outstretched hand with his right hand while grabbing Haynes' right shoulder with his left. "Look L.T.—Don, thanks for everything, but it's probably best anyway if you're not seen with me much until this is over. I understand."

Donald Haynes looked down at the two hands clasped and then pulled Nate into a brief hug. Releasing him, he stepped back, swung his arms apart, and inhaled as if to speak. His elbow clipped the drinking glass that he had just sat down, sending it careening into the sink. The resulting crash seemed to fill the entire apartment with the sound of shattering glass. Both men froze where they stood, their attention drawn to the mess in the sink.

"Bad omen, huh?

Nate shook his head and forced a smile. "Nah, just another mess to clean up. You know I don't do luck. Good or bad." But even as he said it, a feeling of darkness, like a dull blade, began to pound its way into his gut. He shook his head again. "Nope, no bad omens here. I'm sure the Lord will see me through this one too."

Haynes held his gaze, and for a moment, neither man spoke. Then with an uneasy laugh, Haynes slapped Nate on the shoulder. "Yeah…" Although he had smiled, the light of it failed to meet his eyes. Turning from the sink, Haynes led the way out into the hallway. They froze.

"What's going on, Don?"

Two uniformed officers stood by just outside the apartment door, each holding a plastic container about the size of a box of file folders.

Haynes stopped and looked back at his friend. "The department will need you to turn in all your issued gear."

It was then that Nate noticed one of the boxes appeared already filled. He looked at Haynes for an explanation. "I was ordered to empty your locker. That's your gear." Haynes added, sounding apologetic.

The two officers, their eyes forward and faces down, not wanting to make eye contact with their former colleague. Haynes waved them forward. "I'll take those."

"But, sir," one officer objected, "we were told to ge—"

"Son, don't you think I know what your orders are? Now give me those boxes and consider your duties fulfilled. Head on back to the station." He took the full box and handed it to Nate first, and then turning back, he took the empty one from the remaining officer.

Throughout the exchange, Nate stood unmoving, his throat constricted. Closing his eyes, he swallowed. *God help me.*

After the two uniformed officers had gone, Haynes placed the empty container on top of the one already in Nate's arms. "I didn't see any reason to have anybody else packing up your stuff. Get packed and give me a call when you're ready, or I can wait if you—"

Nate cleared his throat. "Yeah. You think maybe I could…ah, just—"

"Oh yeah, no problem. I'll have someone come by and pick it up later." He reached up and squeezed one of Nate shoulders. "See you around, son."

Nate nodded, but did not respond. He simply watched as his only ally in administration walked away and Nate steadied himself against the renewed feelings of abandonment he knew would come. For long moments he stood in silence and looked down the empty hallway. The door to his apartment stood open and the gentle hum of the central heating unit was the only sound that disturbed the awkward quiet. Turning his face toward the doorway, Nate willed himself to move, but found himself still frozen to the spot where he'd been left standing.

Inside the apartment, his phone rang again.

CHAPTER TWENTY- FIVE

(The Present)

STILL HOLDING THE BOXES IN HIS ARMS, Nate kicked the door closed behind him. The silence of the apartment seemed to reverberate with the jangling intrusion of the phone as it vibrated against the tabletop. He stared at it unmoving.

Ring-ring-ring. Silence. The pattern repeated.

The ringing continued and still Nate stood just inside the door. With a sudden shrug of acquiescence, he dropped the boxes on the floor beside him and made for the phone. Just as he picked it up, the ringing stopped. Looking at the caller I.D., Nate frowned, not having recognized the number.

Placing the phone back onto the table, Nate started toward the kitchen. He had just flipped open the lid to the coffee maker when a knock sounded at the door, and at the same moment, the phone began to ring again. Grabbing the phone, he pressed it to his ear, "Richards," he clipped as he pulled open the door.

"May I come in?" Amber asked.

"Hi, Nate. This is Thomas Meir. I'm the attorney-friend Sabrina Jackson told you about."

Nate closed his mouth, then opened it again. "Mr. Richards, is this a bad time? I can call back if that would be better." The voice on the phone continued. He stepped back from the door and clipping his heel on the edge of one of the boxes stumbled before catching himself against the sofa.

"No, this is fine," he said into the receiver.

Still standing at the door, Amber frowned. "You want me to leave?"

Nate stood holding a finger up to pause Amber, then turned his attention back to the phone. Amber smiled, and for a moment, Nate felt the warmth of it inside him. He turned his attention back to the phone.

"Mr. Meer?"

"Close," the voice said with a thick Jewish accent, "but it's pronounced Meir; M-E-I-R, Meir. A name is like good food or a fine wine; you must savor it on the tongue."

Nate tried again and did a little better in capturing the ethnic sound of the name. "Look, can I just call you Thomas?" Nate looked up and smiled at Amber, watching her as she made her way around the living room. She had taken off her coat, laid it across the back of the stuffed chair, and allowed her hand to drag aimlessly across the seat back as she walked in short casual steps around the small room.

Nate was glad she had removed her coat; it meant she intended to stay awhile. The thought made him feel better somehow. He looked back to the phone. "So, Thomas, how can I help you?"

Meir laughed. "Oh, no my young friend, it is not I in want of help, but you. Don't worry. You come down to my office tomorrow at one, and we can discuss your case."

"But I—"

"—I know, I know. I told you, Sabrina has told me all about it. I will see you tomorrow, and we can talk about how to get you your job back and maybe make them pay you for the time you are sitting at home."

Nate looked at Amber and arched a brow. "Who is this guy?" he mouthed. Then speaking into the phone, he said,

"Okay, tomorrow…. Hey!" Nate waved his hand as if to gain the speaker's attention.

"Yes, Nate."

"Where's your office? It's gonna be kind of hard to meet you if I don't know where *there* is," he finished.

"Oh yes, that would be good. You will find me on Warm Springs. Can't miss it. Large sandstone building, converted from one of the old homes: 311 Warm Springs. I'll see you at one."

Nate pressed the red button on the phone and ended the call. He looked at Amber, and taking advantage of the moment before she looked up to meet his gaze, stared at her. He'd forgotten just how much he enjoyed looking at her. He noticed again how the soft afternoon light brought out the glow of her olive tone skin. She brushed loose strands of hair back from her face, red highlights reflecting, and then looked up.

She smiled. "What?" She asked, teasingly.

Nate returned the smile before looking away. "So, what brings you by? Can I get you something?" He began making his way toward the kitchen, picking up dishes as he went. "Cup of coffee, maybe?"

"Nate." She had followed him into the kitchen.

He turned and found her staring at him. "Ah, yeah…about that." He fumbled with his words before finally settling into silence.

"What are you doing? We have been going crazy worrying about you. You don't take my calls, your mom says you haven't been by there, and since Sunday, you haven't even been at Bible study." She closed the distance between them, laying a hand on his forearm.

He tried to turn away, but she gripped his arm. "Nate Richards," she said, then softened her tone. "Nate, don't shut me out. I want to be here for you."

He stepped back and looked into her eyes, then focused on her lips. He took a deep breath, then opening his mouth as if to speak, he looked away.

"Talk to me, Nate."

He sighed. "What do you want me to say? The A.C. and Haynes just left here." He pointed at the two plastic boxes sitting on the floor just inside the living room door. Amber followed the motion of his hand with her eyes.

"I was wondering about that."

Nate harrumphed. "Lawrence asked for my resignation."

"What?!"

Nate pulled away, his arm slipping from her grasp. "They want me to walk away." He began placing dishes into the sink, squeezing the bottle of liquid detergent, and ran hot water over them. "They took my badge and now they want my job—my career." He stuffed his hands into the rising mountain of foam. "Ouch." He jerked his hands free and began shaking the stinging liquid from his hands and arms.

Amber handed him a towel. "That was not bright." She smiled, hoping she could get through to him. Reaching past him, she shut off the water. "You know, most people save the insta-hot water for things like tea and coffee."

Nate smirked and looked back at the sink. "Yeah, well, I was in a hurry."

She took his hand and led him back to the sofa. "Come sit with me. Let's talk...let's pray about this."

It was only the smallest of hesitations, but Nate knew she felt it when she looked back at him. He smiled and tried to laugh it off. How many times had they sat together on this very sofa, talked, laughed, and even prayed together? He exhaled and she looked up at him with inquisitive eyes. "So, about this lawyer..." She left the sentence hanging unfinished.

CHAPTER TWENTY- SIX

(The Present)

JUST PAST 12:30 THE FOLLOWING AFTERNOON, Nate parked his Chrysler 300 along the tree-lined streets on Boise's north side. He walked around the front of his car and opened the passenger side door. Offering his hand, he helped Amber from the car. "Thanks for coming with me."

She smiled. "I told you I was with you. Now, let's go find out what this lawyer friend of Sabrina is all about."

The trees were green with new leaves, and along the concrete walk, the bolder of the plants had already put forth their blooms, enjoying the late spring sun. Looking forward to the bungalow styled home turned office space, Nate counted nine stone steps that led up to a deep-set porch.

He couldn't help imagining children of a past generation sitting, playing, fighting, and dreaming on these very same steps. Walking up onto the porch, the interlaced lumber boards gilded with gray veined granite slabs were solid, adding an overall sense of foundation.

"Solid, huh?" The Jewish accented voice of a sixty-something man came from just inside in the doorway. His round spectacles sat low on his nose, which made his forehead seem large coupled with the receding hairline of curly brownish-gray hair.

Both Nate and Amber looked from the floor to the man standing in the doorway, Nate nodded, "Yeah, I love these old houses."

"You must be Nate and this lovely young lady with you must be Amber Coles." He shook each of their hands in turn.

"Yes, and you must be Mr. Me-" he paused, seemed to think better of it and then said, "Thomas."

Thomas laughed and clapped Nate on the shoulder.

"But how did you—" Amber began, but was cut off.

Thomas turned to her. "How did I know you were Amber and not Jackie?"

Nate and Amber looked at each other, shocked into momentary silence. "Oh, I did not mean to embarrass you or make you uncomfortable. He pushed wired framed glasses back atop his prominent nose. Now, how could I do my job if I did not know who my clients were and what they were about?" He raised and dropped his shoulders and spread large soft hands in supplication before him.

"As for Jackie, let's just say I agree with Sabrina, I think you are a better match for him anyway." Smiling, he waved a hand in the space between them as if erasing a whiteboard.

Nate started.

Amber pulled her hand from Nate's.

They both cleared their throats. "Ahh, I see…I have your attention now. Shall we go inside?" He stepped back and swung his arm in a low arc toward the open doorway.

Just inside the French provincial-styled door, inlaid wood floors spread out in every direction. Accented by exposed stone and wood trim, the office had a decided masculine feel. A young dark haired woman stood and extended her hand, first to Nate and then to Amber. "Good afternoon, Detective Richards and to you as well, Ms. Coles. May I have the pleasure of getting you something to drink? Something warm perhaps?"

Nate nodded at the overtly warm greeting. "Thank you, Ms. Walker," he said reading the engraved name placard on her desk.

She turned and walked to the small coffee station and prepared two cups of coffee, and to their surprise placed several packets of Splenda with the cup and saucer she prepared for Amber before returning to join them.

Offering them the beverages, she turned, led them deeper into the office and directed them to have a seat in the conference room on the north-west side of the building.

Nate had been in several lawyer's offices over the course of his career, but never had he been in one quite like this. The table had one large section of a dark blue stone, with streaks of bright reds, oranges, and brilliant yellows, like lightning streaking a night sky. With scalloped edges arranged at regular intervals, the table had carved areas where plush leather seats had been arranged around the circumference.

"Zimbabwe Black, but an exceptionally rare piece." Thomas entered the room, showing an obvious admiration for the granite table. He carried with him an accordion file that was held closed by an elastic cord pulled taunt over the flap. "The Zimbabwe Black is a highly sought after piece of stone. Those who are supposed to know such things say it was formed in the Proterozoic age." He smiled and waved his hand again. "So they say."

Amber ran her hand over the smooth stone. "It's warm."

"Yes," Thomas said and pointed toward the ceiling. Situated directly above center of the table hung an elaborate molded brass fixture, a warm red glow emanating from the center light position. "It's a heat lamp. It also brings out the color in the veins."

Amber's lips formed a small O, but she did not speak. From beside her, Nate found himself focusing on the supple texture of her lips for the briefest of moments, before turning his attention back to Thomas who had sat across from them watching.

Caught staring at Amber, Nate sought to gain some sense of control. "So how do you know Sabrina?"

Thomas smirked and readjusted his glasses. Settling back in his chair, he pulled the black cord with an elaborate flourish and opened the folder. It was obvious; he did not intend to answer Nate's question.

Ms. Walker returned to the room and placed a leather folder on the table, one in front of Nate and the other in front of Amber. Nate looked at the folder laying closed on the table in front of him and saw his name on an embossed tag in the lower right hand corner.

Looking up, he saw Amber running her fingers across a similar tag of her own. She looked up, arched a brow and gave a silent whistle through pursed lips.

"These folders contain the basic information gathered from the case so far," Ms. Walker said. "Over the course of the investigation, I will occasionally have new paperwork to add to these. But I will simply email those to you to include at your convenience."

Then turning to face Thomas, she said, "I have spoken to Doctor Norman and he has the following dates available." She slid an open appointment book across the smooth surface of the stone table until it came to a rest in front of him. "Will there be anything else?"

When no one answered, she backed out of the office pulling the heavy wooden doors closed on silent hinges. "Worth her weight in gold, that one," Thomas said.

Again, Nate and Amber exchanged glances. Then with a slight intake of breath, Nate said, "This is a bit much...I'm not sure I can afford your services, Mr. Meer."

Thomas sat forward and dropped interlaced fingers on the table in front of him. "I thought we agreed you would call me Thomas. Besides my father would be greatly offended at the way you are slaughtering his name. It is pronounced Meir...it's Hebrew."

Nate stood and walked over to the large picture window that was behind him. He watched as the afternoon traffic poured in and out of the St. Luke's parking structure. After a long moment, his eyes drifted to the foothills in the distance, and he allowed his shoulders to sag. "Thomas, you obviously are very good at what you do, but even on full pay I don't think I could afford you."

Amber swiveled in her chair, turning to face Nate as he stood with his back to the room. When Nate fell silent, she rose, rested her hand on his shoulder, and cleared her throat. "Thomas, no offence...I mean this is a very nice office and your staff is over the top nice, but don't you think your rates might be a little bit more than we can afford?"

Nate smiled at her use of *we*. He turned back to face Thomas. He swept Amber's face with his eyes as he turned. "Thomas, you see—"

Thomas raised a hand, cutting off Nate's answer. "Sabrina said you could be slow at times. You are a member of FOP, correct?"

Nate nodded, having forgotten about the FOP membership. The Fraternal Order of Police Officer's, with more than 325,000 members in over 2100 lodges spread over the nation, is the largest arbitrator for police officers in the world. For years now, he had paid for the legal defense services, but this was the first time he would ever need to use it.

Nate exhaled and began to relax. "So what's our next step?"

"The first thing you need to do is sign the top sheet in your folder which will authorize me to act as your legal representative. Then, Nate, you need to read those files so you can see the case the department has built against you. Amber, you will need to read along as well; you should be able to catch the subtle details that might slip past our super sleuth here." Both Amber and Nate chuckled.

"The first thing I will do is call your command and let them know I have been officially retained and I am now representing you. That way I can get a complete copy of everything they have and not just the scraps I have now."

Nate lifted the front cover to the folder with his name on it and took note of the several pages already assembled. He wondered what Thomas considered a full file if this stack was just a scrap.

A soft rap sounded at the door and Ms. Walker made her way back into the conference room. She smiled warmly and placed a single sheet of paper in front of Nate. "If you sign and date here and initial there," she said pointing with a manicured fingernail, "we will have everything we need to have an official beginning."

She straightened and watched as Nate signed the paper. She left the room but soon returned with two copies and gave one each to Nate and Amber. "For your folders," she said.

"Okay, let's have some fun," Thomas said, rubbing his hands together.

CHAPTER TWENTY- SEVEN

(The Present)

SERGEANT SWIFT CAME INTO THE ASSISTANT CHIEF'S OFFICE and stood dutifully until the older man finished the call he was on. Although he had been in this office more times than he could count, he still found himself studying the plaques, trophies, and myriad of awards that adorned the A.C.'s walls.

"Yes, next Tuesday would be fine. That gives us just five days, counting the weekend. I'm ready for this to be over." The A.C. said into the phone. The voice on the other end was nothing more than a low mumble from where Swift stood looking on.

The A.C. stood. "Yes, one way or the other. Yes, over." He hung up and turned his withering glare onto Swift. Holding his hand, he snapped his finger impatiently. "That the file?"

"Yes, sir, the rap sheet included. It's not pretty, sir."

Assistant Chief Lawrence grabbed the file and began pacing around his office. Studying the sheets of paper, he flipped from one to another, then another, all in rapid succession.

Gripping the folder with his right hand, he slapped it against the palm of his left. He jerked his face toward Swift; he pointed the folder at him. "This could be a problem."

"Well, sir—"

"Who else has seen this?

Swift frowned.

"I mean, have you reviewed this file with—in its entirety, with anyone else?"

Swift swallowed shallow in the back of his throat and shook his head as he spoke, "No, sir. I brought it straight in to you. Is there a problem?"

"Wha-what? No, no problem. Just leave this here with me, and I'll take care of it from here. Sergeant, I mean Marcus, thanks."

Sergeant Swift turned and left the office and walked with quick steps down the echoing hall. Just as he exited into the brightly lit vestibule that separated the assistant and chief of police's offices, he locked eyes with Lieutenant Haynes.

Haynes, who just happened to be sitting in one of the richly appointed chairs, stood and greeted him. The administrative secretary looked up from her computer and frowned. "Lieutenant Haynes, the A.C. just put up a do not disturb light. Sorry, but I can't bother him until he says it's clear. I'm sorry." She smiled.

"Oh it's okay, Marilyn. I'll just catch up with him later." He turned his attention back to Swift.

"Shall I leave a note for him that you came up to see him?"

Haynes waved her off with a lazy arc of his hand. "Don't worry yourself, I was just gonna shoot the breeze. You know, catch up on old times." He smiled and clapped Swift on the shoulder as the man passed him.

Marilyn leaned forward and lowered her voice. "Too bad about Nate, isn't it? He was such a nice fellow."

Haynes smiled at the older woman. "Yeah, too bad, but it ain't over yet."

She smiled a sad smile and shook her head. "Seems like it always happens to the nice ones." She turned back to her computer, dismissing the men by the action.

Marcus Swift had just settled into the elevator and doors began to shut when Haynes stuck his arm through the narrow gap stopping them. "Whew, almost missed ya," he said in a lazy drawl.

"Yes, lucky me."

"Now, now, Marcus, what kind of attitude is that for you to have?"

"I know what you want, Don, and the answer is no. I am not authorized to discuss with you what the A.C. and I spoke about."

The door closed and the elevator jerked as it began its downward trip.

"I didn't ask you."

"But I know you, and—"

Haynes turned on Marcus and in one quick move stood face to face with the other officer. "Then you should know that all I want is what's right. We do not turn on our own. Not while I'm wearing these bars. If Richards is dirty, then I'll kick him out myself." Cursing, he stepped back from Sergeant Swift. "But before we burn a darn good officer, we had better have done our part right."

The elevator doors slid apart and another officer stepped onboard. "Afternoon, L.T.—Sergeant."

"Afternoon, son," Haynes said, the slow drawl back in place. "What'd'ya know, this is my floor." He smiled at the young officer and reached up, grasping Swift's shoulder in a casual familiar grip. "See ya around, Marcus. Think about what we talked about."

The doors closed and Sergeant Swift sagged against the back wall. He thought again about the file he'd given the A.C. and wondered about the assistant chief's reaction. *What is going on around here?* The elevator car jerked again and continued its downward trek.

CHAPTER TWENTY- EIGHT

(The Present)

"LET'S WALK FOR A WHILE, DO YOU MIND?" Amber asked looking up into Nate's face. She tilted her head back, closing her eyes, soaking up the warmth from the late afternoon sun.

Nate stopped and looked at her and couldn't help the tugging growing at the corner of his lips. He looked across the street to where his car was parked, and then with an ease born of years, he slipped his hand into Amber's and pulled her away in the opposite direction.

For long moments neither one spoke, but they simply walked in silence, each in the private arena of their thoughts. Above them, the not so long ago barren trees were spreading with new growth. Greens, reds, and bright pinks pushed out all around them. Flocks of birds seemed to swim through azure skies and billowing clouds hung in silent witness above it all.

"You know, this feels so right, so natural," Nate said, not looking at her.

"How so?"

They continued walking. "Your hand in mine. You and me together."

"Oh, really?"

Nate stopped and pulled her around to face him. "Amber," he stuttered and fell silent. He tried again. "Amber, this is not a good time for me right now. Seems like my life is one big series of something bad going on." He chuckled at himself.

Amber held his gaze.

"What I'm trying to say is…I like this." He held up their intertwined fingers.

She smiled, matching the one on Nate's face. "Me too."

He turned and started walking again. "Now that we have agreed on that, what's next?"

Amber slipped her fingers free of Nate's and wrapped her arm around his, hugging his bicep, laying her head against his shoulder. They walked. "Nate, I told you last year where I stood. I haven't changed my mind. I screwed up once; I don't intend on doing that again. I have known since I left here the first time, Nate. I love you."

"Amber I—"

"No, just wait. I have been trying for a while to say this and now just seems like the right time. So let me before I lose my nerve.

"When I came back and you were with Jackie, I told you then that I knew I was in love with you, and that I intended to win you back. But I did not try to interfere with you and Jackie. I figured the Lord knew what was best for you, and I…well…that I would just pray and see where things went."

Nate walked in silence as she spoke, his heart pounding with each word she uttered. He knew he had loved her once—had once truly loved her. Did he still? Or was he using her to fill the emptiness he felt inside due to the I.A., not to mention Jackie leaving? He was confused.

All he knew for sure was that he didn't want to feel that way any longer. He looked at Amber, watched her lips moving. If she was willing to fill the void in his life, Nate decided, he would let her. He could always answer the question of love later.

She was still talking. "…so now you know as much as I dare to say. What do you think?" She started slightly when she felt Nate bring them to a stop. Her breathing increased.

Nate could see the fear in her eyes; fear that he might reject her. She had taken a chance by putting all her cards on the table. The question was: What would he do?

She turned her face away. "Lord, did I move to fast? Is he not ready for what comes next," she muttered under her breath.

When Nate still didn't say anything, she chanced a look up into his face, but his features were shadowed with the sun at his back. "Nate, say something, please."

Instead, he opened his arms and invited her against his chest. Snuggling her against him, Nate enjoyed the warmth of her nearness and wrapped her tighter to himself. He buried his face in her hair and enjoyed the fragrance of plum blossoms and honey and, for that moment, nothing else mattered.

"Amber," he whispered into her hair. Capturing her face between his hands, he tilted her chin upward and lowered his mouth to cover hers. When their lips touched, Nate caught his breath, and he felt her relax into his arms.

With an explosion of sensation that ran the length of his body, Nate forced himself to step away from the kiss. He was pleased to see the deep crimson flush creeping into Amber's face and to know he was not the only one so savagely affected by the kiss.

"You have no idea how long I've wanted to do that."

"I know how long I've wanted to," she said and smiled.

Locking his fingers with hers, he began to walk again. "We'd better walk. Standing still with you for too long could be dangerous."

She wrapped her arm around his again and snuggled in close to him. For a few moments, they walked in silence, just enjoying being together and each remembering the kiss.

Startled, they looked up when they heard a man's voice calling Nate's name from across the street. "Nate! Detective

Richards! Hey, wait up." It was Eric Brodson, Butch Jensen's field man.

Nate sighed and turned to face the short red headed man. "What do you want, Eric? I've already told your boss that I had nothing to say to him. What's the phrase you guys like so much?" He looked at Amber as if he were trying to remember.

Then turning back to Eric, he slapped his forehead with the palm of his hand. "Oh yeah…no comment!"

Slipping his arm around Amber's waist, Nate turned back the direction they had come. Looking up, he saw that they had come several blocks from where they'd parked.

Eric fell instep alongside them.

Nate stopped. "Go away, Eric."

"Just one question."

Nate froze mid-stride. In a slow deliberate movement, he released his hold of Amber and then turned to face the shorter man chest to face. "What!?"

Eric stepped back, but then recovered. "So, what are you going to do now that the case has been forwarded for criminal charges?"

Nate took a step toward the man, halted, and then with curved shoulders, turned back to Amber, grabbed her hand and stalked away.

Now with distance between them, Eric called out, "What, no comment on that? Do you mind if I quote you?"

Nate stopped.

CHAPTER TWENTY- NINE

(The Present)

As NATE SPUN AND HEADED BACK toward the assistant reporter, Amber stepped in front of him, pressing her body against his. She could feel the strain of his chest muscles flexing and relaxing against her hands trapped between her chest and his. She looked into his eyes. "Let it go, Nate. Let it go."

Behind her, she could hear the sound of retreating steps as Eric fled back the way he had come. She held Nate, trembling with anger, as he stared over her shoulder.

He breathed a deep cleansing sigh and then relaxed, sinking somewhat against her. Amber looked into his eyes again. *Oh Lord, help him. Jesus, please help us.* Then out loud, "You all right?" Her voice was soft, airy, as if the words had been hollow and without substance.

She looked at her hands pressed against Nate's chest and saw that they trembled. Amber closed her eyes and waited for the tension to pass, waited for Nate to let go of the anger that held him.

After a moment that seemed like forever, Nate finally nodded but did not speak. Instead, he stood firm and erect, statuesque, then he seemed to deflate just a little. His muscles softening as the pressure drained.

Nate released a clenched hand then reached up to rub the back of his neck. He looked tired.

"Let me do that." Amber reached up and pulled Nate's forehead forward until it rested against hers. With nimble fingers, she plied the knotted coils, running lithe digits up and down the span of his neck, squeezing and releasing his trapezius. Closing her own eyes, she continued to pray while she worked.

Nate looked over Amber's shoulder one last time, his eyes boring into the back of the retreating Eric. He sighed, relaxed, and pulled Amber closer against himself, his arms folding around her and bringing him comfort in her nearness. "I—," he began, stood up straight and then continued. "I don't know...." He left the sentence hanging, dangling unfinished.

Amber stepped back, allowing her hands to slip from around his neck and tracing his arms until she clasped both his hands in hers. "Well, I do. Nate, we need to pray. We've been doing a lot of plotting and planning, a lot of running around, but not a lot of listening. Nate, we can't beat them if we play their game. We have to play our own."

Nate looked into her eyes just briefly before looking away again. "And what if God doesn't want to play at all?"

Amber inhaled, opened her mouth, and then closed it without speaking. Then inhaled again, and spoke, "Nate—"

He placed a finger across her lips. "No, don't...it'll be okay. I'm just talking out the top of my head. He pulled her into his embrace again. "Yeah, it'll be all right." He buried his face in her hair and enjoyed the fragrance of its cleanness.

Closing his eyes, Nate prayed. With silent cries, he poured out his heart to his God. Having just gotten back together with Amber, how could he tell her how afraid he was? How could he tell her how he laid awake in bed, too tense to sleep, but too exhausted to function? Wasn't he was supposed to be in control; supposed to be the man?

He smiled at her, touching her cheek with his knuckle and hoped she could not see the dread he was trying so desperately to hide.

"Come on, let's get out of here," Amber said with her face buried against his chest.

A sudden gust of wind swept across them and Nate allowed himself to drift along with the sweet fragrance wafting from her perfume. "Yeah, let's."

Taking her hand, Nate led Amber back toward his car parked along the curb in front of the lawyer's office. As he was passing the walkway that connected to the deep-set porch, Ms. Walker stepped through the lead glass front door. Raising a manicured hand, she called to them. "Detective Richards, Mr. Meir has asked that you stop by before you leave. Please."

She stepped to the side and held the door open as if the matter had been decided. Nate exchanged a glance with Amber and then pulled her along behind him back up the stone steps and onto the ancient wooden porch.

Walking through the door, Nate fully expected Ms. Walker to offer him another cup of coffee. Instead, she went directly to her desk and began working, taking further notice of neither him nor Amber.

From inside the conference room came the sonorous voice of Thomas Meir. He was talking on the phone to someone. "No, no, Lieutenant Brown that won't be a problem at all. We will be at Dr. Norman's office at 9:30 and you are most welcome to join us. As a matter of fact, I would be disappointed if you did not." He nodded as if Brown could see him.

Seeing Nate and Amber, Thomas waved them in and pointed toward the same seats they had recently vacated. "Yes I know, I've read over the first poly and I have to tell you, I have more than a few problems with it."

Nate could hear the sound of the lieutenant's voice, but could not understand the words. Across the stone table from him, Thomas smiled.

"Look, sir, we have no problem with you and one other representative being present, but just understand that we are doing this in the best interest of everyone. We wouldn't want you going forward with bad information." He laughed and swung around in his chair, much like a child at play.

Nate arched a brow and mouthed, "What's going on?"

Thomas raised a finger, halting Nate's next question and his next. Frustrated, Nate stood and paced back to the same window he had stood at before, staring at the parking lot of the hospital across the busy thoroughfare. Joining him, Amber slipped her hand into his.

"Very good, very good," Thomas said and chuckled again. "Good.... We will see you on Tuesday morning." He looked up at Nate, all traces of laughter gone. "I take it you've heard by now that the department has asked for a review of your case by the district attorney?"

Nate looked down at Amber and then back at Thomas. "How did you know-"

Thomas waved him off. "You don't survive in this business as long as I have and not develop a few friends in key places. Anyway, I expected as much."

Nate dropped into the chair beside Amber. "You expected them to charge me criminally?"

Thomas opened the file that lay before him on the table. "I see you didn't do too well on the last polygraph. You failed."

Nate started to stand.

"Sit down, Nate," Thomas said, still reading the file. "Let's see who did your test for you." He lifted and turned several pages, carefully dragging his finger down the length of each page, mumbling in soft tones as moved.

"Yes!"

Both Amber and Nate jumped at the lawyer's sudden ejaculation. "What?" Nate managed in a startled response.

"Dustin de Bon did your test."

"Yes," Nate nodded as he settled back into his chair, "some guy out of Washington, up near Seattle."

"What's so special about him?" Amber asked.

"Oh just that he's had some problems in the past. The state licensing board has had several inquiries into his practice over the past three to four years."

Ms. Walker came into the door. "Excuse me, sir, but you said you wanted this as soon as it came in." She handed the stack of papers to Thomas and then turned and walked out of the conference room, pulling the doors closed behind her as she had before.

As Ms. Walker left the room, Nate had a sense of déjà vu wash over him. Amber looked at him and smiled. "Yeah, weird, huh? It's like we've been here before," she said.

Thomas ignored them while he leafed through the new set of pages. Sobering, he looked up at Nate. "Nate, I'm going to ask you a question and I don't care how bad it sounds. I want you to tell me the absolute truth."

Nate sat up.

"If you would rather Ms. Coles wait outside—"

This time Nate interrupted him. "No, she stays. Besides, I have nothing to hide. I didn't do anything."

Thomas stacked the papers in a pile on the table in front of him, careful to make sure the edges were all aligned and neat. Sobering, he removed his glasses and rubbed the bridge of his nose. "Okay, here we go then—Kathy Kellerston."

Nate winced despite himself.

Amber looked at Nate. "Who is Kathy Kellerston? I thought this was about that woman on the rape case. What was her name?" she asked and then answered her own question. "Wanda Fuller."

Nate turned fully to face Amber. "I thought you knew. You said Haynes had told you what happened. Kellerston is the informant that provided me and Durgins the Intel on the suspect that didn't pan out. We wound up taking the guy to jail, but he wasn't our rapist.

"During the interview, she made it very obvious that she wanted to get to know me better. I explained to her that it was not going to happen, but as she was leaving, she stuck a note in my hand that I took to be more information on the case. But—"

"Let me guess," Amber interrupted, "her phone number."

"If only," Nate said. "It was a lot more than that and in very explicit terms."

"So where's the note?"

Nate cleared his throat and settled back in his chair. "Therein lies the problem, neither Durgins nor I can account for the blasted note and now Kellerston is saying she never wrote the note and I was the one that had come on to her."

Amber made the little "o" with her lips again. "It's a he said, she said, and the department is believing the she."

Thomas cleared his throat, drawing their attention back to him. He picked up his glasses, perching them on the edge of his nose. "Okay. Nate, did you ever have a sexual relationship with Ms. Kellerston while on duty or in a work capacity?"

Nate looked first at Amber then back at Thomas. "No, I did not."

"Have you had sex while on duty? Ever?"

Nate faltered, looked at his hands and then back up at Thomas. "Yes, there was once, but that was several years ago. I was engaged and I...well I did some things that I should not have." He bristled with shame at the memory. Although he had told Amber about his moment of weakness with his former fiancé, shortly after it happened, the memory embarrassed him. Even though he and Amber had been only friends—best friends then, Nate kept his eyes forward, not wanting to see any trace of disappointment in her eyes so soon after their finally deciding to come together.

Thomas cleared his throat again.

Amber squeezed Nate's hand, but she too kept her face forward.

Thomas studied Nate's face before asking the next question. "Did you make any promises to Kathy Kellerston that you would help her or assist her if she would perform for you in a sexual manner?"

This time Nate did not hesitate. "No!"

Thomas interlocked his fingers and dropped them onto the stack of papers on the table. "Good."

"Good? Is that it? I mean, what's next?" Nate asked all in a rush.

"Yeah, what are those papers all about?" Amber leaned forward and touched the corner of the stack of papers.

Thomas smiled in a patriarchal fashion and rocked back in the rich leathered upholstered chair. "What is this stack of papers," he said tapping the stack with the tip of his index finger.

Amber smiled at Thomas' playful tone. "Yes, those papers."

"This, my child, is Dr. Norman's report on Nate's initial polygraph. And I suppose you want to know why I'm smiling even though the report says Nate failed?"

Nate sat forward. "I don't know about her, but I sure do. Come on, Thomas, tell me something." Nate had managed to stretch the word out, making it sound like a plea rather than a demand.

"Well," Thomas said as he picked up the sheaf of papers. "According to Dr. Norman's review, the first poly was poorly conducted and the findings skewed."

Nate felt the faintest glimmer of hope since before the ordeal began. "Really? What does that mean in plain English?"

Thomas picked up the papers again and began laying down sheets while first reading over and selecting others. "Well, first, the blood pressure rating was not set correctly. It appears that during your test the blood pressure indicator registered a continual drop in pressure by almost a 39 percent decrease over the course of the test."

"Is that bad?"

"Well, not if you're passing out, asleep, or an eighty-year- old woman, but if you're taking a polygraph examination, that usually means bad equipment."

Nate nodded and could not stop the smile that tugged at the corner of his lips.

Thomas continued. "Also, the thoracic respiration recording was placed too high on the charts and critical data was lost as a result. In addition, the electro dermal channel was set too high as well causing an overlapping of channels."

Nate grabbed and squeezed Amber's hand. "That all sounds good, but what does it mean?"

"Oh, that's not all." Thomas smiled. "According to Dr. Norman, the score should have been a positive two at best and a zero at worst."

"Positive two, zero…what does that mean?" Amber asked.

Thomas stacked the papers back into a neat pile. "You see, the way a polygraph is scored is on a range from negative 30 on the left to a positive 30 on the right. If a person scores anywhere from positive five to negative five, the score is considered inconclusive and cannot be used to determine deceitfulness or not." He shifted his attention to Nate. "So, Nate, with a score of positive two, the best de Bon could have said was that you were inconclusive instead of reporting that you had failed."

"But—," Nate began.

"He peppered you with PLC's, probable lie comparisons. It put you in a defensive mindset, which drove your score lower. Simply, he set you up to fail."

"So not only will we be able to throw out de Bon's findings, hopefully we can finally get rid of him as well. He's been a problem in this valley for way too long. This *test* he put you through was screwed up from the beginning to the end and bespeaks of a certain lack of integrity, or competence on the part of the examiner," Thomas finished.

"But—" Nate tried again. "But that doesn't prove my innocence. That only says he couldn't prove I was lying. That's not the same thing as proving that I was telling the truth."

"No, it isn't," Amber agreed, wrapping her hands around Nate's bicep and leaning her face against his shoulder in unconscious ease.

Thomas stood and stretched his back. "These old bones get stiff after sitting for too long." Pulling a small piece of cloth from his pocket, he began to clean the lenses of his glasses. "That's where Tuesday morning at Dr. Norman's office comes into play."

Again, Nate and Amber exchanged glances. "Okay, we don't get it," Nate said for the both of them.

Thomas turned and focused his gaze on Nate and then on Amber. He smiled again and put his glasses back on his face. "Oh, Nate my boy, Sabrina did say you could be slow at times. You're gonna take another polygraph test and this time, I have no doubt you will pass."

CHAPTER THIRTY

(Tuesday Morning)

THE ALARM SOUNDED in the translucent darkness and Nate rolled over and dropped his hand on the clock, silencing it. He rubbed tired eyes and lowered his legs over the edge of the bed.

Rubbing tired eyes, Nate groaned. When he set the alarm for 6:30 a.m., he had hoped he would sleep through the night. He had not. Thoughts of dinner at his parents warmed him, and he took comfort as he remembered his father laying hands on him and praying for him before he had left to return to his apartment.

Despite himself, he smiled at the obvious pleasure his mother had taken when she saw him holding Amber's hand. "At least something's going right," he said into the air.

Nate stood and pulled on his compression shorts and grabbed his sweats and sneakers; he would follow through on his plans for a morning run. Thumbing the lamp on, he settled again on the passage of scripture he had been reading before bed the night before. It was one of his favorites; he knew it by heart and recited it to himself as he dressed.

Slipping the sweatshirt over his head, he said, "The Lord is my Shepherd."

He pulled the sweatpants on and tied them at the waist. "I shall not want." He dropped back on the edge of the bed, grabbed one of his shoes, and began tying the laces, careful not to make them too tight. "He causes me to lie down in green pastures."

Finished with dressing, Nate went into the living room and began his pre-run warm up. "You, Lord, promised to lead me beside still waters." Nate sat on the floor and spread his feet apart. Reaching for his right foot, he exhaled as his stomach compressed and whispered, "Lord, if I ever needed restoring it's now." He rested his forehead on his knee.

"Father, You know this polygraph scares me. I don't trust it…at all." Nate straightened up and then reached for his left foot. "I know I don't deserve this Lord, but I need You now more than I ever have. Thank You for being faithful and standing by me for the sake of the covenant."

This time, Nate sat up and lowered his chest while grabbing his ankles and pulling forward. Resting in that position, Nate continued to pray. "I'm in a valley and it's dark all around me, Father. Lead me through this and even in front of those who want to see me fall, Lord help me stand. Don't let them have the victory in my life."

Nate stood up, tucked the light chain with his apartment key inside his shirt, and headed for the hall. Pulling the door closed behind him, he began jogging toward the stairs. "Anoint me with your presence, Lord," then he chuckled, "especially on this run."

***

Fluorescent light gave the room a gaunt yellow haze, making the men's skin to appear slightly jaundiced. Lieutenant Donald Haynes poured himself a cup of coffee and then lifted an empty cup up to Lieutenant Brown. "Want a cup?"

Brown nodded and sat behind the metal desk he and Haynes shared in the small CID lieutenant's office. "Look, Don, I know you like the kid, but if he did this, then he's a bad seed."

Haynes didn't answer, but continued to pour coffee into the cup.

"I admit I've had my problems with Richards, but I'm not going out of my way to get him or anything."

Haynes set one cup on the desk in front of Brown and lifted the second in acknowledgment before taking a drink from his own. "Look, Larry, all I'm saying is that this job is hard enough as it is; we don't need to be taking shots at each other too. Think about it. I mean, have you ever gone through an I.A.?"

Brown took a sip of coffee and shook his head indicating that he had not.

"Well, I have and it sucks." Haynes cursed and sat his own cup down beside Brown's. "There is nothing," he cursed several more times, "nothing like it. It's like having your gut ripped out. The very people who are supposed to be on your side are the ones lining up the red dot on your forehead."

Haynes picked up his mug and took a slow drink. "All I'm saying is that the whole process is a bad deal—nothing good about it."

"I know."

The two friends sat in silence for long moments.

Brown looked at his wristwatch and then at the wall mounted clock, comparing the time. "We don't have to be over there until nine; you wanna go get a bite of breakfast en route?"

Haynes looked at his watch and stood, draining his cup in one long draft. He cursed again. "That was hot."

Brown chuckled and sipped at his own cup. "Yeah, think you'd know that since you're the one who poured it. What'd'ya think, breakfast?"

Haynes sighed and started toward the door. "Sure why not? I couldn't eat earlier; maybe now I will have an appetite."

"Express Café?"

"Works for me. I'll drive."

***

Amber parked in the driveway of the Victorian styled home of the Richards. She could see Sherri waving at her from just inside the front door. She smiled knowing how important this morning was and how hard it would be for Nate.

Against her will, Amber had agreed not to see Nate until after the test was done. She looked at the dashboard clock and saw that it was almost eight. Sighing, she opened the door, figuring the earliest she would see him wouldn't be until after one that afternoon.

As Amber made her way up the serpentine walkway, Gracie bounded through the front door embracing her. The women stood in pregnant silence for a moment before either spoke. Then Gracie, taking Amber's arm in the crook of her own, turned them both toward the front door.

"What, no quote of the day for me this morning," Amber chided good-natured, trying to ease the anxious tension. As she entered the house, she hugged and kissed Sherri who stood waiting for them both.

"Well, actually," Gracie smiled impishly. "I do have one that fits this morning's occasion perfectly."

"Are you gonna share with us or do we have to wait," Sherri asked, joining in the fun.

Gracie cleared her throat, thought for a moment, and then began to recite in clear diction, "Who, doomed to go in company with pain and fear and bloodshed, miserable train! Turns his necessity to glorious gain."

Amber looked at Sherri, "I don't get it; never heard it before."

Sherri smiled and finished closing the door, making her way into the living room behind the two younger ladies. "William

Wordsworth, the Character of the Happy Warrior. The year…1806."

Gracie squealed. "How do you do that? I thought I had you on that one. But I think you're wrong on the date though."

Amber just laughed and watched the playful banter. "I don't know Gracie, but I'm willing to bet on Mom on this one."

"You'd be wise," Sherri said.

"I-don't-know," Gracie strung the words together.

The women all sat around the dining table and Sherri poured three cups of coffee, placing one in front of each of them.

"Where's Reverend Richards?" Amber asked. "Won't he be joining us?"

"No, he got a call about an hour ago. It's Mother-Lisa. The family doesn't think she'll last the morning." Sherri set the carafe back on the table and lifted a plate of plain scones, offering it to Amber first then to Gracie.

"And Gracie," Sherri smiled, "Wordsworth wrote, Character of the Happy Warrior in 1806 in honor of Lord Nelson, the hero of the Napoleonic Wars, but it wasn't published until a year later."

Gracie snapped her fingers. "Touché, I would have missed that on my history test today, thanks."

Amber pulled her cup to her, cupping its warmth in her hands, and for a moment, her mind drifted back to Nate and how he might be doing. When she noticed that Gracie and Sherri were staring at her, she smiled. "Maybe we can pray for Mother-Lisa while we are praying for Nate," she suggested in a soft voice.

Deciphering the tone in her words, Sherri reached out and took Amber's hand. "He'll be just fine, Sweetheart. We know he didn't do this thing he's been accused of and what is better, God knows."

"But what if—"

Gracie interrupted her. "Aut-aut-aut, there are no if's in God."

"Betsy Ten Boom, I know this one," Amber said, and they all three laughed. After a brief moment, the laughter died down, and the ladies sipped their coffee in a comfortable silence.

"It's almost nine," Sherri stated in flat tones.

Gracie sat forward. "Hey, ladies, I know you know this, but in the few short years I've been a part of this crazy family, I've seen God do some pretty fantastic things. Now I'm not sure how all this I.A. thing is going to work out with Nate, but I know God is still in charge, so let's just pray about it."

"Well said."

"Okay, let's."

The three women grabbed a hold of each other's hands, closing the circle around the table and bowed their heads. What began as quiet whispers soon escalated into fervent and intense moments of groaning before the Lord. Minutes passed and soon the hour had come and gone without notice and still they prayed.

CHAPTER THIRTY- ONE

NATE RUBBED SWEATY PALMS TOGETHER and turned the ignition off, sitting for a moment longer as the car clicked and popped while the engine began to cool. Taking one moment longer to whisper a silent prayer, he opened the door and began the walk toward the one story building that housed the office of Dr. J. Norman.

Nate walked into the foyer and was greeted by the sound of a ticking clock. Exposed red brick walls were decorated sparingly with cheap prints on cardboard matted in dark wood frames. Fake plants that looked as if they had not been dusted or changed in years sat mournfully on corner tables.

The smell of coffee wafted to him from somewhere out of sight and he began to hear the sound of murmured voices.

Just ahead of him, a single door led away from the desolate waiting room. Nate walked toward the doorway and pushing it open, called through, "Thomas?"

Instead, the rosacea streaked face of Larry Brown greeted him. "Come on in Richards, we'll be done here in a minute."

Nate swallowed and looked past Lieutenant Brown and caught sight of both Thomas and Lieutenant Haynes speaking with an older and rather large white man. Nate assumed this was Dr. Norman.

The man's almost completely white hair hung on flat bangs across his forehead and was tied in the back with a single leather cord. He wore jeans and a plain white shirt that did nothing to boast of his three doctorates and numerous accomplishments in the field of polygraph science. If Thomas had not told him, Nate would not have believed that Dr. Norman had testified before the U.S. Congress on two separate occasions and provided expert testimony in almost every federal district in America.

Looking up and seeing Nate, Dr. Norman smiled and walked away from Thomas and Lieutenant Haynes to greet him. "You must be Nate. Good morning. I am glad to meet you."

Nate smiled at the warmth of the greeting and returned the handshake with vigor. Dr. Norman smiled as he rose to his full height of six feet six inches. "There's coffee and some donuts in the back. Go ahead and make yourself at home. I just have to finish getting the details from the two sides of what they expect, and then you and I can sit down and talk. You okay with that?"

Nate nodded. He hadn't been sure of what to expect, but so far this was about one-hundred and eighty degrees difference from his first experience where he felt attacked and put upon from the moment he walked through the door of Mr. de Bon's office.

Nate made his way to the small area near the back where a single coffee pot sat next to a half empty box of Crispy Crème Donuts. He selected an old fashion donut and poured himself a cup of coffee. He turned and found Brown staring at him.

He raised the paper cup. "Morning, sir."

Brown walked toward him without speaking. When he was standing beside him at the coffee pot, he asked, "How you holding up?" He did not make eye contact.

Nate drank from his cup before answering. "I guess okay."

Brown turned to look at him. "Nate, you and I have had our problems in the past, but that's been about the way you do police work." He hesitated as if he wasn't sure of what he wanted to say next, then drank from his own cup and looked up at Nate. "I'm just saying, Nate, this is not personal."

"Yes, sir."

Brown stood to his full height. "Don't get me wrong, if you did this then I don't want you wearing this uniform, but if you didn't, then I just want this over. You understand?"

"Trust me, sir," Nate said softer than he intended, "no one wants this over as much as I do. It wears on a fella."

Brown took another drink of his coffee and poured the rest down the sink. "I drink too much of this stuff. It's gonna rot my gut out one of these days." He extended a hand to Nate, and after shaking, he turned and walked away.

Nate watched him walk away, unsure of what to do with himself. So he looked around the small office kitchen, taking note of the dated pattern of the plates and cracked tiles. Finishing his donut, he rinsed his hands in the sink and began looking for something new with which to occupy himself.

Just then Dr. Norman opened the door. "Nate, come walk with me." He stepped back from the door, clearly indicating that Nate should follow him.

Once outside, the two men walked along the greenbelt enjoying the warmth and the sound of the Boise River as it splashed, hidden behind the trees. In the near distance, Nate could hear the sound of children laughing and reasoned it must be coming from the zoo.

"You know," Dr. Norman began, "you think I'd get out here more often just to do this." He raised a beefy arm and swung it in a shallow arc taking in the whole of Julia Davis Park. "I spend all that extra money to have offices near the greenbelt and don't even take the time to enjoy it."

Dr. Norman chuckled at his own joke, and Nate smiled up at him. But the lightness Nate portended did not reach his eyes, and the familiar darkness clung heavy to him.

"If you don't mind my saying so, Nate, you look a little tense," Dr. Norman said. The two men continued walking along the asphalt path occasionally moving to one side or the other to allow cyclists and joggers to pass.

Nate harrumphed. "Polygraphs. Let's just say I haven't had much luck with them, and I don't even believe in luck."

"Really? So I take it you don't believe in the polygraph process."

Stopping and forcing Dr. Norman to stop as well, Nate said, "Look, I don't mean you any disrespect, but I know I didn't lie and that machine pegged me as deceitful."

He started walking again. "By the end of today, I will have had my second polygraph test and my first experience was all bad. So you can understand if I'm not all excited about taking this test?"

Dr. Norman laughed. "Oh sure, that's an easy call." The ringing of a bell alerted them that a rider was approaching from the rear and the two men stepped aside once again allowing the bike to pass between them.

"Thomas assures me that you're an honest man and when the test is administered correctly, honest men do not fail. In that light, I am completely confident that you will do just fine."

Nate began to relax just a bit. "So was this the purpose of this walk, for you to get me to relax?"

"That's part of it. In a minute I'm going to take you into the back office and strap you in pretty much in the same way de Bon did, but we'll do it right this time." He laughed at himself again.

Nate tried, but did not feel the complete sense of ease Dr. Norman seemed to experience. He reasoned within himself that nothing would change for Dr. Norman either way. The good doctor would still be paid whether Nate passed or failed.

"Ah, we're back."

Nate looked up at the announcement, realized that they had indeed come full circle, and stood at the rear door of the small office building. He took a breath and stepped into the shadowed coolness. "Where is everyone?"

Dr. Norman came in behind him and pulled the door closed. "What? Oh, I told them to go get lunch. We can eat once we're done here."

He looked at his watch. "It's almost 10:30 now and the test will take the better part of two to two and a half hours for me to score it and all. That will put us right at one, just in time for a late lunch."

Nate looked around the office, noticing for the first time, the chair. The chair was intimidating. On first inspection, it reminded Nate of an electric chair used in the execution of convicted felons.

The high backed chair had a pressure-pad covering the seat, and cords strapped on at about chest level. Various cords draped across the chair and a blood pressure cuff hung innocently across the top. With various computer screens and printers attached, Nate knew all his vital information would be recorded during the test. What he wasn't sure of was how he would perform.

With a not so silent prayer and a cleansing breath, Nate settled himself into the indicated seat. He felt himself beginning to sweat, his breaths becoming shallow and quick.

Standing across the room Dr. Norman chuckled and crossed his arms over his chest. "You know, it's typical to wait until I start grilling you on the test before you hyperventilate."

The doctor smiled and Nate felt himself relax—just a bit.

"Okay."

"Okay," Nate repeated. He lifted his right hand while Dr. Norman clipped the skin sensor onto the tip of his index finger. He sighed and concentrated while the doctor continued to strap him into the chair and adjust various sensors.

"All right, the pad you're sitting on will simply rate the amount of unconscious movement you make during the control question, and then compare that to the contact questions. The difference between the two is where we draw our score."

Nate nodded.

Dr. Norman reached up and pulled two separate sets of straps around Nate's upper and lower chest. Nate's hands were situated on the armrest, elevated to just about shoulder level, elbows extended out to the sides and bent with the forearms forward and the hands palms down on the flat surface directly in front of him.

With the various tubes situated and the straps adjusted, Dr. Norman sat off to one side, just out of Nate's direct line of view. He cleared his throat. "You ready, Nate?"

Nate swallowed. "I guess so Doc…I'm as ready as I'm gonna get. Let's do this."

"Let's."

The questioning began just as Dr. Norman had told him it would. The control questions first: Name? City? Are you an astronaut? Have you ever stolen anything in your entire life? Once those questions had been asked and the answers agreed upon, the key questions were put forth.

"Did you attempt to have sex with Miss Kellerston while on duty?"

"No."

"Did you use your position as a detective to solicit sexual favors from Miss Kellerston?"

"No."

"Did you receive an unsolicited written message from Miss Kellerston asking you to have sex with her?"

"Yes."

"Did you purposely destroy the note given to you by Miss Kellerston?"

"No."

The same series of questions were asked and answered three more times in a different order each time. Finally, Dr. Norman stood, stretched his back and then walked over to where Nate still sat strapped in the chair. "Okay, Nate, we're done."

Nate looked up and swallowed again.

Dr. Norman began releasing the various straps and belts from Nate, allowing him to stand. "If you'll go out to the waiting room, I'll be with you as soon as I finish my initial scoring."

Nate didn't bother to wait for a second invitation to leave; neither did he look up in an attempt to read Dr. Norman's facial expression or body language. Instead, with his head down, he made his way to the waiting room.

"Pull the door closed behind you, please," Dr. Norman called as Nate made his way out the door.

Once in the waiting room, Nate checked his cell phone for the time. He couldn't believe only 90 minutes had passed. It had felt like an eternity while he sat in the chair.

In the cavernous silence, the ticking of the faded wall clock sounded large. The click, click, click of heating vents sounded from overhead as the heat alternated between its on/off positions. Nate checked his cell phone again and compared its time to that on the wall clock. The wall clock was off by several minutes and at least two hours.

Twenty minutes later, Dr. Norman came into the waiting room. Nate looked up and met his gaze. He could not get a read on the doctor's thoughts. Nate sat up, pressing his back against the vinyl chair where he sat waiting.

The heating unit kicked on again, and Nate noticed small particles of dust as they floated past a shaft of broken sunlight streaming through the window.

Dr. Norman sat on the arm of the 1970's era sofa and opened the manila folder he carried with him. "So, Nate, how do you think you did?"

CHAPTER THIRTY- TWO

NATE LOOKED FROM THE FOLDER in the doctor's hands back to his face. He sobered. "Well, I don't know what your machine said, but I know I didn't lie." He stood and paced away from the doctor. "Come on Doc, don't keep me waiting; tell me what you got." It had come out softer than he had intended and he cleared his throat and tried again. "Give it to me, Doc."

Dr. Norman chuckled. "Relax, Nate, you passed."

"I did?" The question exploded from Nate. He pumped his fist and fought to keep from dancing around the small office and hugging the doctor. "Thank You, Lord," Nate said raising both his hands and his face upward.

Still sitting on the arm of the sofa, Dr. Norman closed his folder and joined Nate in a brief celebration of laughter. "Are you really surprised?"

"Yeah, I mean no, but I told you I didn't trust that machine." Nate walked over and extended a hand to Dr. Norman. "Thanks," he said, shaking the doctor's hand.

Dr. Norman continued to laugh. "I told you innocent men don't fail. Your problem was not the machine as you refer to it, but with your previous tester."

Upon remembering de Bon, Nate soured. "But how did Kellerston pass her poly? You said the machine was not the problem and she had a different tester."

"That's what I wanted go over with you now that your test in completed. You won't see it so much in the written form of the questions the polygraph examiner asked Kellerston, but when you watch the video, you can hear the intonations of the question that allowed her to answer the questions and get the non-deception indicated response."

Nate nodded and furrowed his brows. "So, it's the way the questions were asked that helped her." It had not been a question.

Dr. Norman nodded. "You have to admit, Miss Kellerston can be charming when she wants and if you are not careful, you find yourself wanting to be nice to her, to help her out."

Nate stood again. "Wow, thank God that's over. I passed."

Dr. Norman stood. "I say you did. 28 out of 30, that is what we call statistically beyond deception. There can't be any doubt in anyone's mind, based on the polygraph test, that you are anything other than truthful."

"What now?" Nate asked as he turned and looked out at the early afternoon sun warming the grass and families taking advantage of it after the bleakness of winter.

"Well for me, I'm going to finish typing up my report, but I thought you might want to hear the result before I spent the next few hours compiling everything." He turned back toward his office door. Placing his hand on the doorknob, he stopped. "I'll call Thomas and give him the results; I suggest you go get some lunch before your blood sugar bottoms out." Without hesitating, he walked through the door and pulled it closed behind him leaving Nate alone in the waiting room.

Nate dropped back into the seat of the cracked vinyl chair and took a moment to gather his thoughts. Covering his face with his hands, he sagged. "Thank you, Lord," he prayed softly. "This can finally be over."

He rested his elbows on his knees and lowered his face into his opened hands. He sat that way for a while, not moving, not controlling his thoughts, but just following the current of his emotions.

After some time had passed, Nate grunted and stood. He looked toward the closed door that led to the back office and examination room, smiled, sighed, and turned to leave. He opened the glass door that led from the office to the outside world and was greeted by a blast of cold air. The day had grown dull, the sun having retreated behind gray clouds and the sky threatening rain if not snow.

Nate pumped his fist, too happy for his mood to be doused by the weather. He decided to skip the promised phone call and drive directly to his parents' home. Settling into the driver's seat and looking at his reflection in the car's review mirror, Nate smiled. He knew Amber would be waiting and he wanted to see her face when he shared the news in person.

***

Nate sat across the small kitchen table from his mother; Amber sat to his right, their hands entwined beneath the table. He couldn't help the smile pulling at the corners of his mouth. He sighed and turned to look at Amber, and for moment, he allowed himself to get lost in the depth of the chocolate pools of her eyes. She was smiling at something Gracie had said and the deep dimples settled into her cheeks as her face began to glow while the smile grew.

He squeezed her hand and she looked at him. He traced the curve of her lips with his eyes and studied the long smooth lines of her neck. *She's so beautiful.*

Amber watched the circuit of Nate's eyes and blushed.

"Is it getting hot in her or is Amber just blushing," Gracie asked in a teasing tone.

With a quick, but seemingly unconscious movement, Amber rubbed her cheeks, and then rested her hand on her neck. "I see your point," Sherri said joining in on the tease.

Amber stood, lifting the coffee carafe as she did. "The pot is empty. I'll refill it."

They all giggled at her apparent discomfort. "Hey, give her a break. This has been a really big day," Nate said catching a hold of Amber's hand.

"A really good day!" Sherri corrected, and then folded her hands on the table as she leaned back in her seat. "I can't wait to tell your father the good news." She looked at the digital clock on the face of the microwave. "He should be home any minute now."

As if on cue, the garage door opener began to moan, sending a slight vibration through the house. A few minutes later, Reverend Richards walked through the door from the garage. Sherri rose to meet him.

Instead of being alone, Reverend Richards was in conversation as he came through the door. "Look what I found sitting out by the curb," he said in resonant voice.

Sherri stepped around her husband to see who was following him in. Her smile grew as she caught sight of Durgins and pulled him into a hug.

Durgins freed himself from the embrace and made his way toward the kitchen. Nate stood to greet him. "Did you hear? Of course you did...that's why you're here. I passed the poly!"

The laughter and celebration began again in earnest as the girls shared and retold the story of the day to Reverend Richards. Several more minutes passed and Nate noticed that Durgins was not joining in on the fun; his smile had not reached his eyes.

Nate locked eyes with Durgins and, for that moment in time, everything else faded. He could see the smiles and could even feel the pressure of his father patting him on the back, but he could not hear the sounds. The maddening rush of blood coursing through his veins drowned out all other sounds until the only thing he could hear was his own heartbeat.

"What?"

Durgins walked toward him. "Can we go for a walk?"

Amber was at Nate's side, her fingers encircling his arm again. "What's going on Durgins?" Fear colored her voice.

Durgins looked around the small room. He swallowed. "Come on, Nate; let's go for a short walk. I promise we won't be long." He had made the final promise to those looking on.

Amber re-secured her hold on Nate's arm. "You can say whatever you have to right here. We're all family here." She looked around the circle of faces looking for reassurance. The smiles were all gone, but she could see their agreement to her sentiments.

With a slow and purposed movement, Nate removed Amber's hands and placed them into his father's. The elder Richards' had seen what his son was doing and reached out to receive the precious cargo.

Nate tilted his head toward the same door Durgins had recently entered. He turned to look at his family, allowing his eyes to linger on Amber. He nodded at her, indicating he understood her offering with the slightest dipping of his chin.

Durgins turned also and faced the small group. "I'll be saying my good-byes; I don't think I'll be coming back in when Nate and I are through talking. Evening, Ma'am," he said directing his final words to Sherri.

CHAPTER THIRTY- THREE

ONCE OUTSIDE, NATE CONTINUED WALKING until he reached the curb, then he turned and found Durgins. Soft fat flakes of snow began falling, melting on contact. Shaking his shoulders to generate some warmth, Nate flung water droplets like miniature missiles from his arms. The sun had begun setting and darkness was closing quickly.

Durgins zipped the collar closed on his corduroy jacket and paced up until he stood face to face with Nate. Nate watched as his partner's nose and ears reddened with the cold. He stilled himself.

Durgins looked back over his shoulder once before he broke the silence. "Look, man, I don't know what to say. You'd think this would be over now that you've passed the poly and all."

"Come on, Durgins, don't keep me waiting," Nate broke in impatience making him anxious. "What are you-what's going on? What's happening?" Nate's teeth began to chatter. He rubbed his arms trying to generate heat against the biting chill.

"Guess you should'a brought a coat out with you, huh, cowboy." Durgins attempted to lighten the heaviness that had settled between them. When Nate didn't respond, he continued.

Durgins cleared his throat. "I was back in the A.C.'s office this afternoon to do what I thought was going to be a final debriefing on this whole mess. I was excited because word had filtered out that you'd passed your poly and that the de Bon interview had been trashed. I thought this was all about you coming back to CID."

"But...."

"The A.C. had those folders on his desk. You know the ones."

Nate nodded.

"He started asking me questions about working with you—if I liked it, and if you had been a good partner. He even asked me how you performed in that fight we had over in Nampa a several weeks or so ago."

Nate searched his partners face trying to detect any hint of what it was the man was not saying.

"Now, I don't know this for sure, but later I was in Brown's office, and he had a copy of the upcoming duty roster. I checked for your name to see when you'd be coming back. It had been dropped. You've been marked for termination."

"Termination? Still? Why? For what?" Nate thrust his hands into his pockets and began pacing back and forth, his angry steps making soft splashing noises in the accumulated moisture on the sidewalk.

"I don't know...."

Nate spun toward his partner. "Durgins, I—" He interrupted himself. The years he'd spent living by a worldly standard came flooding back to him in a rush. Thoughts of anger and revenge washed up like a rising tide, and Nate could feel an unused portion of his vocabulary pressing against his will for expression. "I passed the stupid test, what else do they want from me?" Nate yelled at the sky.

"Hey, man," Durgins began, "you've come too far now. Don't let the system beat you. The only way they can win is if you give up." He dropped a hand on Nate's shoulder and squeezed it. "You know what they say about us."

Nate settled. "Yea, we eat our own." Running a hand roughly over his face, he turned and looked back toward his parents' home. The cold momentarily forgotten.

Nate could see silhouettes of his family posted about the window. Although he could not distinguish which face belonged to whom in the low light, he knew Amber's would be the foremost. He knew she believed in him, that she loved him for some strange reason. And even more, he knew that he loved her, deeply. A sardonic smile crept across his face.

Durgins exhaled. "I just wanted to be the one to tell you. I didn't want you finding out...you know, getting blindsided by the whole thing."

Nate shook his shoulders again. "Look, thanks for coming over to tell me." He looked back toward the house. "I'd better get in there and tell them something before they burst a vein straining at that window.

The two men laughed briefly, but it was genuine. It spoke of the bond between partners that went beyond sitting beside each other in a row of cubicles. Each knew the other would have been standing there with him if the table had been turned. "You sure you won't come back in?"

Durgins shook his head, even as he extended his hand to shake Nate's. "Naaa, I'd better be heading back to the office. I left a mess on my desk and just can't be going into that in the morning. You know me."

They laughed again, then Durgins turned toward his truck leaving Nate looking after him as the gloaming deepened. Nate looked back toward the house, stuffed his hands deeper into his pockets, smiled, but then turned and walked away from his parents' home taking slow sure steps into the darkness.

About thirty minutes later, Nate made his way back into his parent's home. Stomping slush from his shoes, he pushed open the door leading into the living room and stopped. Three sets of angry eyes and one set of very angry eyes met him, staring at—if not through him. "Nathanial Richards, where have you been?!" Sherri stormed toward him, coming within inches of her son before stopping.

"What?" Nate asked, momentarily puzzled.

"You have the nerve to ask me 'what'?" She turned to her husband. "He asked me 'what.' Did you hear that?"

Nate came fully into the room and closed the door behind him. "Ahhh, yes, sorry about that." He met everyone's eyes then focused on Amber, "I'm sorry. I just got so bottled up I needed to pray. I needed to talk to the Lord about all the junk in my head." He pulled Amber's fingers to his lips and kissed the back of her knuckles.

She smiled.

Gracie smacked him on the shoulder. "Oh no you don't get off that easy, Romeo. Just 'cause you can give her a kiss or two and her stomach goes all soft, doesn't mean the rest of us will let you off that easy."

Nate turned and grabbed his adopted sister, trapping her upper arms, and lifted her from the floor swinging her around. "Oh, you stop your barking. I said I was sorry." He set her back on her feet and kissed her forehead.

He sobered before offering an explanation of his absence as well as the conversation he'd had with Durgins. He cleared his throat. "You mind if I get something warm to drink first? I'm freezing."

"Yes, I mind," Gracie said, a hint of laughter overlapping to intended bravado.

"I bet you do," Nate mock chided.

"Oh, I'll get you a cup of coffee, but don't start until I get back," Sherri said.

The group moved en masse toward the dining table, and Nate couldn't help but think back to the night he received the call that began this latest adventure. His face darkened as he remembered Jackie had been his date that night and how he had been pretending not to notice Amber. Now it was all he could do to keep from staring at her.

"What," Amber asked seeing the change come across his face.

He squeezed her hand. "Oh, it's nothing, just thinking how much life has changed in the last few months." She smiled again and her cheeks flushed. Nate touched the corner of her smile with his thumb. He leaned close to her ear. "You're beautiful, you know."

Just then, Sherri came back into the room carrying a small tray with a coffee service along with several stacks of crackers and wedges of cheese. "I figured we might as well all enjoy ourselves," she said.

Nate poured himself and then Amber a cup of coffee before selecting crackers and cheese, placing the small sandwiches on the napkin in front of him.

"'Nuff stalling already," Gracie demanded.

Nate turned toward her and with deliberate slowness placed the cracker and cheese sandwich into his mouth. This time, Amber hit him. "Come on, Nate, we're tired of waiting."

Reverend Richards who had not spoken up until now accepted the cup of coffee from his wife and urged his son. "All right, Son, the prayer walk was a good idea, I'll give you that, but you need to tell us what brought it on. We were just celebrating your victory in the polygraph and then your partner shows up out of nowhere, and you cloud over like a storm in the Owyhee's. Then you disappear. Explain." Although his tone was soft, his had been a statement demanding satisfaction and not a question.

Nate set his cup down. "Durgins came out to tell me that I was set to be terminated, but before you ask, he didn't know why...or what the official reason was said to be. Just that it was supposed to happen."

"Can they do that?" Sherri asked.

"Right to work state, Mom," Gracie said absently as she placed a slice of pepper Jack cheese into her mouth.

"Well, it's more than that, Sweetheart," Reverend Richards said.

Everyone turned to look at the reverend, but it was Nate that answered. "Simple, I didn't violate the law, so it's harder to punish me for that, but still the situation caused a lot of trouble for the department. Somebody's gotta take the hit for that."

"Why does it have to be you? Can't they—" Amber began.

"Because I'm the one involved," Nate said, cutting off whatever question she had intended to ask. He pulled her close to him and kissed the corner of her forehead. They shared a brief moment before turning back to the circle of family at the table.

A comfortable silence settled.

Nate jumped, startled by his cell phone's buzzing in his pocket. Looking sheepishly, he smiled a wry smile and then pulled it from his breast pocket. He checked the caller I.D. "It's Thomas," Nate mouthed, barely above a whisper, then answered the phone.

"Thomas Meir, the attorney," Amber said as if she had been asked.

Nate frowned. "Tomorrow morning? Isn't that kind of quick?"

"Well," Thomas said, "after they got the results of the poly they called for a meeting with me; that was two hours ago."

Nate paced toward the living room, grabbing a Ritz cracker as he left the table and rolling it back and forth between his fingers. "I'm not sure if I'm supposed to know this yet, but Durgins told me that command was looking at terminating me. Any idea what this is all about or why?"

Thomas sighed and then laughed bitterly. Nate guessed the lawyer was driving and talking into a Bluetooth device. "Yeah,"

Thomas said, "that was part of the discussion, but I don't know how your partner found out so fast."

Nate listened as Thomas spoke to a parking attendant and then accelerated into the traffic. "So, just leaving your office?" Nate guessed aloud.

"Yeah, how did you-oh never mind," Thomas said. For a few moments neither man spoke. Nate deciding to wait until the older man chose to finish his thought. "Despite the test results, Nate, there are those within your command structure that think you're a bad element. But we will continue to fight for at least the middle ground between the positions we were presented with, termination or full reinstatement."

Nate leaned his back against the wall, not surprised when he turned and saw that Amber had wondered into the living room to stand beside him. "So what if I decide to fight their decision," Nate said.

Amber reached and took hold of his hand and Nate smiled at her none verbal motion of support. He looked at her and saw the confirmation in her eyes, as if to say: *no matter what happens, I'll be right here with you.*

Nate caressed her fingers, drawing strength from her nearness. "Okay," he finally answered, "I'll be there. What time?"

Nate could hear the sound of the vehicle's engine revving as it responded to the transmission's automatic shifting. "I told them we'd be there at 9 a.m. Oh yeah," he added as if an afterthought, "the meeting is set at the Idaho State Police CID conference room near their headquarters."

"I.S.P., why can't we meet at the Meridian office? That's where I'm assigned out of."

"The truth, I don't know. Is this going to be a problem for you?"

"No, no problem, I'll be there." Nate sighed. "See you in the morning."

***

Assistant Chief Lawrence looked at the stack of papers on his desk, comparing the information with the file he still held in his hand. "All right Durgins, even you should have made contact with Richards by now. I just hope it's enough," he said into the air. He turned to stare up at the large photograph of Gen. G.S. Patton hanging on the wall behind his desk and lifted the small glass of amber liquid. "You always made this look easy. Here's to you, sir." He drained the glass and placed both folders securely in the center desk drawer, locking it.

Returning the Podova flat glass flask and tumbler back to the side drawer, A.C. Lawrence turned off his office lights and left the building. "Sometimes, I hate my job," he muttered as he made his way toward the parking lot.

CHAPTER THIRTY- FOUR

THE MORNING BROKE IN A BRILLIANT SUNRISE, yet Nate found himself looking over his apartment complex lawn, trying to identify the heavy darkness growing in his gut. Still hidden in their roost overhead, morning birds cooed and sang a greeting to the new day as brilliant pinks infused the cobalt blue of the vanquished night sky. The valley came awake.

Nate exhaled and began his morning warm-up, anticipating a brisk run before the meeting with command.

The heaviness persisted.

Nate leaned forward from the waist, standing with his feet spread apart and began stretching his lower back and hamstrings. Almost like a mantra, he began muttering to himself, "The Lord is my Shepherd, I shall not want. The Lord is my Shepherd; I shall not lack."

After several minutes passed, Nate became aware of his mutterings and laughed out loud, standing up to look around to see if anyone had been near enough to hear him. He laughed again. "Seems like I've been coming back to this passage a lot lately, Lord," he said in a breathy voice.

Extending his right leg in front of the left, Nate bent forward, extending the stretch of his hamstring. "Lord," he said in a conversational tone, "I can't shake this feeling. Is there something I need to know…need to be aware of?" He looked at the brightening sky as if he expected to hear an audible voice.

When nothing happened, he continued his exercises and his conversation, switching the leg positions. "I guess it's just you and me against them, huh? Oh yeah, and Thomas." He tucked the cord into his shirt, securing his door key before the run.

He moved to stand against the wall, pressing both palms flat against the wall while extending one leg back, creating tension on the Achilles tendon. He switched. "You will lead me and guide me," he exhaled at a sudden twinge of pain, and lessened the stretch, "for Your namesake," he continued.

The sun rose above the mountains bathing the valley floor in a soft luminescence. Dewdrops sparkled in the new sun as light danced across their prism domes creating miniature rainbows that vanished almost as soon as they appeared.

***

"Has he left yet?" The voice sounded through the phone's speaker.

"Yes, sir. Looks like he's going on a run," the middle-aged man answered.

"Don't lose him, and let me know before he starts back toward the apartment."

The man shifted his late model nondescript car into gear and rolled silently out of the parking lot in the general direction Nate had gone. "We're clear, and I'm tailing Richards," he said into the phone then ended the call.

A few minutes later a lone figure, an older man, wearing a pair of ratty pajama pants and plaid housecoat shuffled down the hall that passed Nate's apartment door. After making it to the far end of the hall, he stopped and scratching his forehead, turned and shambled back the way he'd come.

Slipping a set of dangling metal from his pocket, the intruder quite youthful with dexterous fingers, sorted through the series of blanks and long-hook lock-pick keys. In the next moment, the hooded figure stepped into the relative darkness of Nate's apartment.

Slipping a sheath of papers from inside the housecoat, he placed the papers inside the cover of Nate's Bible. Soon the figure had gone, the only trace of his having been there tucked quietly out of sight in the binder of the black leather book on the nightstand beside Nate's bed.

At the end of the hall, crumpled in a pile in the corner of the stairwell, lay a discarded robe and a pair of worn-out pajama pants in a pile.

CHAPTER THIRTY- FIVE

AFTER A BRISK THREE MILE RUN, Nate made the final turn toward his apartment. Looking over his shoulder again, he saw the gray sedan slowly pull over to the curb. This time it stopped, apparently tired of following him. He watched as a lithe figure, a female he guessed, darted from the sidewalk, jog around to the passenger side door, and got in. The vehicle then performed a U-turn and disappeared back the direction it had come.

Nate shrugged his shoulders, but was unwilling to dismiss the incident as unimportant. It had just the opposite effect. The mystery of the situation piqued his senses, putting him on alert.

Entering the stairwell, Nate noticed the pile of clothing that had not been there when he left. He slowed his pace and scanned the area. Pulling out the cord that hung from his neck and hidden against his chest, Nate removed the three quarter-inch knife from the molded plastic sheath. While the Beretta Tomey Tactical was not his favorite knife, its sturdy blade and compact size made it useful for close quarter fighting. The flat black steel contrasted cold against the heat of Nate's hand.

He made his way to his apartment door, placing each foot carefully before advancing next. He paused and listened. Looking around before bending to study the doorknob, he steadied his breaths.

He straightened and looked around again, listening carefully for the sound of retreating footsteps. Several new scratches surrounded the keyhole.

The scarring had left bright marks in the otherwise dull bronze colored metal of the doorknob. Someone had at least attempted to enter his apartment. Nate rubbed his finger across the scratches collecting metal filings on his fingertip. *Sloppy. Must have been in a hurry.*

He slipped his key into the door and released the lock.

Nate palmed the blade, hiding it from obvious view and opened the door. Standing off to one side, away from the fatal funnel created by the doorframe and the backlighting of the hallway, he hesitated for just a breath.

After a quick scan, Nate ducked inside curling around to his right, his shoulder hugging the solid security of the wall at his back. His nerves on full alert, he waited for his eyes to adjust to the lower level of light.

After a careful survey of the living room/kitchen area, Nate knew the obvious location an intruder would hide would be the bedroom or possibly setting up for an ambush attack from the bathroom as he passed the open doorway.

A few minutes later, Nate stood back out in the living room confident that no one was still in the apartment. But he was more certain than ever that someone had been in the apartment while he'd been on his run. That also meant they had been watching him, knew his routine. The gray sedan and the male driver came back to his mind: the figure darting from the shrubs near the curb.

He studied the carpet in front of the door and saw slight impression left in the floor covering; dust, dirt, and wet grass, left in the intruder's wake. Judging from the relative shape and size of the print, Nate figure the intruder had been female or at the least a very small man.

He studied the apartment again, looking for the smallest trace of disturbance and found none. Turning, he looked at the clock on the Blu-ray player, 0810 hours. Nate ran a hand across the stubble on his chin and felt the fine film of sweat that had dried on his face. He looked back at the clock again, "Fifty minutes, shower, shave...I can make it."

He looked longingly at his Bible before heading to the shower. "I'd hope to have some time to read, Lord, but hadn't counted on a burglar this morning." Grabbing his towel, he slipped into the shower, running the water to a steam and allowing the heat and pulsating spray to massage tired sore muscles.

Twenty minutes later Nate headed for the front door, stopped and went back inside to grab his phone from the bedside table. "I should have time," Nate said aloud and grabbed his Bible as well. *I should have a few minutes while waiting at the station.*

Nate arrived seven minutes early and parked out in front of the ISP detective's office. In his rearview mirror, he could see the Meridian Station of the Treasure City Metro Police and to his surprise, a feeling of loneliness pulled at his gut. He missed being with his team. He missed being one of the guys.

It was at moments like these, the ones that snuck up on him, that made him aware of just how much being an officer meant to him. And how much it scared him to have that part of himself taken away, simply snatched out of his hands as it were.

He sighed and pulled his attention back to the building in front of him and the series of events that awaited him inside. He looked at the Bible on the seat next to him and reached for it, hoping to find some comfort from its well-used pages.

He dropped the book into his lap and began to thumb it open when someone tapped on his window. Looking up, he saw Thomas looking down at him. He closed the book and motioned for Thomas to come around and join him in the car.

"You look worn out," Thomas said as he lowered himself into the seat beside Nate.

Nate laughed. "Good morning to you too." The men shook hands and Thomas adjusted his position in the seat, turning to face Nate slightly.

"So," Nate prompted.

Thomas looked back toward the glass doors and a small sigh escaped his lips. Pushing his glasses back up the bridge of his prominent nose, he sighed again. "Nate, it's not what we wanted, but at least I think we can save your job."

"So, what...you met already? What did they have to say? Why even have me come out if the meeting is already over?" Nate slammed both hands on the steering wheel.

Thomas did not speak, but allowed Nate to vent. After a while, Nate sagged in his seat and looked over at his new friend. "I'm sorry, Thomas. I know it's not your fault. But...but I am just so tired of this. The stress of not knowing...of not understanding is taking more out of me than I knew, I guess."

Dropping a hand on Nate's forearm, Thomas squeezed it. "Trust me, son, that part I do understand. The part that confuses me is why this has gone so far."

Nate looked at Thomas, a question etched in his features.

Thomas turned back to face forward, resting his back squarely on the leather seat. "From the very beginning all they had was hearsay. The testimony of Miss Kellerston was sketchy at best." He paused and looked at Nate. "Nate, before all this your record was clean."

Nate raised a brow.

"Well, no worse than average, and you had quite a few high points. Your first homicide investigation was lead on the Abyss case, then the serial killer a few months back. You have done well."

Nate harrumphed, embarrassed at hearing the slight praise. "Apparently not well enough."

Thomas continued as if he hadn't heard him. "It's almost as if they had an alternative reason for pushing this."

"It's not like I haven't made enemies." Nate picked up the Bible again, running his finger over the embossed printing on its cover. The folded pages, secreted inside the leather cover, slipped out, falling on the center console.

Thomas reached down in an absentminded motion and picked up the folded papers. Slapping them against his leg, he continued, "That's what I thought, but in talking to Lawrence—"

Nate sat up. "The A.C.? Lawrence hates my guts. If it were up to Zachary Lawrence I would have been out a long time ago."

Thomas raised his hand, waving Nate to a halt. "That's what I thought too, but Lawrence has, in his own way, been my...been your greatest advocate."

Nate shook his head in unbelief, remembering the assistant chief's visit to his apartment and the demand for his resignation. "That doesn't make sense. The man was at my apartment not even two weeks ago demanding that I resign to save face for the department. Now you're saying he's fighting for me."

"Be that as it may...", Thomas said continuing drumming the folded papers on his knee.

The front door opened and Lieutenant Haynes stepped out into the morning sunshine. He was in uniform. Nate exchanged a look with Thomas. "I guess it's starting."

Thomas nodded, dropped the papers into his folder, and reached for the door handle. "Looks that way. I hope you've been praying." He smiled.

"Haven't stopped," Nate said, got out and walked around to greet the lieutenant. "Morning, sir."

"Morning, Nate. Thomas," he said in a clipped professional tone. Haynes looked from Thomas and back to Nate, a neutral expression on his dark-skinned face. "The chief and assistant chief are inside. They are ready when you and your client are," he said to Thomas.

"His client," Nate said under his breath, "I'm standing right here, Don."

Thomas stepped close to Nate and wrapped a restraining hand around his wrist. "Thank you, lieutenant. We'll follow you in."

"Oh, I won't be joining you. I have business at City Hall, but they are in the central meeting room."

"The one we met in earlier?"

"The same. Good day to you gentlemen." Donald Haynes turned on his heels and walked away without a look back or a word spoken directly to Nate.

"Ready?" Thomas asked.

"Yeah, ready." Nate looked back at Haynes' retreating form and began to pray. *Father, You said when I walked through the valley of the shadow of death You would be with me. Jesus, I need you now. Fight for me, Lord.*

The double glass doors swung shut behind them and it felt like a lid closing tight on a cave as a soft fluorescent glow replaced the natural light.

Nate swallowed and looked to the quasi-familiar faces of the receptionist behind the glass of the main counter. "Detective Richards, how have you been? Haven't seen you around here in a while," a middle-aged woman with glasses said, rising and coming toward the counter.

Nate fought, trying to remember the woman's name. It came to him in a sudden flash. Carol. Carol Hemmings. "Carol, it has been a while," he said and smiled.

She laughed, flattered that he actually remembered her name. "I'm surprised you actually remembered my name. Most officers just know me as the lady behind the counter." She giggled.

Nate stopped and spoke briefly with the woman, talking mostly about nothing, but giving her his undivided attention. As a slight flush began to creep up the woman's neck, Nate turned to continue his trek down the brightly lit, but somehow oppressive hallway.

Carol, unaware of why Nate was meeting, called behind him. "Well if those guys at Metro don't treat you right, you just come on over here to the State and we'll set you right up." She waved at him before turning back to her desk.

"If only she knew," Nate said under his breath to Thomas.

Thomas chuckled. "I'll grab her card on the way out just in case we need her as a reference."

When they arrived at the door of the conference room, they stopped. "Let me do the talking," Thomas said.

"Why…don't trust me?" Nate attempted at teasing, but it came out flat.

"Yeah, I trust you to be a cop, and this is not one of those times when you need to clear leather and come out shooting."

Thomas knocked on the door, two sound raps of the knuckles. "Come in." A voice called from beyond the door.

Thomas turned the knob and then stepped back allowing Nate to go in first.

Nate surveyed the room: the chief, the assistant chief, city attorney, and a H.R. representative. *Everybody but the media*, Nate thought to himself. "Morning, sir," he said to the room and then acknowledged everyone individually before taking his seat.

The chief, an older Hispanic man in his early sixties, and like the assistant chief, was in impeccable physical condition. An Ironman, Nate knew he idolized Lew Hollander, who at fifty-five years of age had run his first Ironman competition in Hawaii and most recently finished his twentieth at the age of 79. Chief J.J. Villareal did not accept weakness in himself nor tolerate it in others. Nate had not spoken to the man more than a half dozen times in his whole career.

An astute businessman, the department had seen rapid growth under Villareal's leadership. A patrol lieutenant at the time, he had been the driving force behind combining the valleys individual agencies and transforming the law enforcement community into the metro unit it had become.

"Have a seat Mr. Meir, Richards," Chief Villareal said, taking control of the meeting. He sat, back straight and his hands on the table with his fingers interlaced.

In contrast, sitting across from him, Thomas, while not slouching in his chair, sat in a decidedly relaxed posture. Nate found himself somewhere in between.

"Well, Chief," Thomas said, surprising the chief who was not used to being usurped, "you will agree, sir, that this is not in any remote fashion a Brady discussion."

Villareal swallowed and stared at Thomas, but then opened the leather binder on the table in front of him. He looked at the city attorney and nodded.

The lawyer opened his own folder and began removing papers. He passed a copy to each person at the table. "Gentlemen, you will see here a copy of the original investigation's findings. If you look at page eighteen you will see the investigators' recommendation."

Nate turned quickly to page eighteen, looked at the bold statement, and read along as the city attorney read the report out loud.

"'I recommend based on department policy section 22, subsection A, that the said officer, Nathaniel Richards be terminated for behavior unbecoming an officer. I have found that Officer Richards did pursue by using his position as a law enforcement officer and the color of authority to persuade a female citizen of this community, a Miss Katherine Kellerston, and force her into a sexual relationship.' "

Nate swallowed and sat back in his seat. He clinched and unclenched his fist. His breaths came in quick and shallow bursts.

Thomas nudged him in his side.

The attorney continued reading. "'I have not found that any force was used to obtain sex from Miss Kellerston and therefore I have no recommendation of criminal charges being filed. Also based on a violation of department policy section 7, subsection

1-A(2), which states that 'All officers shall provide truthful and no misleading answers to any department appointed investigator as part of any internal investigation. Failure to do so shall result in the immediate termination of any officer found in violation of this section. And due to Detective Richards having lied to investigators and having failed the subsequent polygraph examination, it is also the recommendation of this I.A. that Detective Richards be terminated and that all rights and privileges associated with this position be withdrawn. It is also the recommendation of this I.A. that a Brady ruling be sought against Detective Richards that will prohibit his being able to cover this behavior through lies or oversight to any future agency with which he might seek employment. Dated this 27th day of May, 2012.' " He closed the folder and sat back.

Assistant Chief Lawrence flipped open a separate folder and cleared his throat. "For the record, it should also be noted that Miss Kellerston was also given a polygraph examination which she passed and was found truthful by the examiner Mr. Dustin de Bon." He closed the folder and placed his hands on top of it.

"Yes, Assistant Chief Lawrence, but that examination was found to be flawed and the examiner, Mr. de Bon is presently under investigation by the state licensing board for a number of irregularities in his examinations," Thomas interjected.

Lawrence looked at Thomas. "Noted."

"Also," Thomas continued, "Detective Richards was later retested by Dr. Norman who had testified before the U.S. Congress on the topic of polygraph examination and the science behind it. I'd like to add, for the record, that Detective Richards was found to be overwhelmingly truthful to the point of…" he paused, opened his own folder, and looked through his papers, "positive 28 out of a possible 30." While still talking, Thomas pulled out an unfamiliar fold of paper and looked at it. Wrinkling his brow, he remembered that it had fallen out of Nate's Bible while they had spoken in the car.

Chief Villareal closed his folder with a little extra force. "Noted."

Thomas sat back and folded his hands in his lap before reaching over and tapping Nate's knee. Nate looked at the older man and saw the slightest curl at the corner of his mouth. A smile?

Looking around the table, Nate saw the assistant chief look at Thomas and tilt his head with a slight rise of the chin. He blinked, unsure if he had seen what he thought he had.

"That's all fine and good," Chief Villareal said, "but the problem we have here is that we have had a breach of trust between this department and Detective Richards and that must be dealt with."

Thomas cleared his throat again and in a manner much softer than Nate thought the situation demanded, said, "Yes, but this breach was not something created by my client. Rather this was done by a person who we know to be of questionable character and a fouled report by Mr. de Bon."

The chief leaned back in his chair. "But this brings me to the question at hand. Can this department continue to trust Mr. Richards in a position of such responsibility; can I?"

Silence claimed the room.

Nate dared not trust himself to speak. Instead, he prayed.

After several moments of silence, Assistant Chief Lawrence spoke up. "I think the six plus years that Detective Richards has put into this department must be considered in any decision this board makes."

Thomas unfolded the paper he held in his hand and began to read it. He caught his breath.

Nate turned and looked at him.

Chief Villareal looked up. "You object to the A.C.'s recommendation, Mr. Meir?"

"No, sir. It's just that I was hoping we could have a break before you inform us of your decision."

Villareal cut a quick glance at Lawrence who held a blank expression on his face. "What makes you think we have already reached a decision, Mr. Meir?"

"Your reputation, sir. You did not get to where you are by coming in to a given situation unprepared, with several viable options. Why should this be any different?

The answer seemed to pacify the Chief and he relaxed back into his seat. He looked at his watch and then at the clock on the wall as if for confirmation. It is 1015 hours now. We will be back in this room at 1100 hours." He stood, gathered his binder and left the room.

Soon only Nate and Thomas sat alone around the table. "What?" Nate demanded in a forced whisper.

"Not here. Come with me; let's get a cup of coffee."

Nate rose and followed Thomas from the building. Thomas didn't speak until they were secured in Nate's car and driving away from the I.S.P. building. "Where did you get this and why didn't you tell me you had it before now?"

Nate shook his head, while trying to focus on the sheet of paper Thomas was waving in front of his face. "What are you talking about?"

Thomas huffed. "This report," he said and shook the paper again. "Where did you get it? Why didn't you tell me you had it? This could have changed everything."

"I have no idea what you're talking about," Nate said and pulled the car into the Zamzows' parking lot, in the shadow of the yellow Meridian water tower.

Thomas turned until he was facing Nate in the front seat. "Nate, this paper fell out of your Bible this morning while we were talking in the car. I picked it up and stuck it in my folder by mistake. It wasn't until I pulled it out by accident while talking to the A.C. in the meeting that I saw what it was."

"What is it?"

"It's an employee liability list."

Nate shifted the car into park and turned the engine off. "I still have no idea what you're talking about. What is an employee liability list and what does it have to do with me?"

Thomas laughed. "Nate I'm beginning to believe that all your praying has made a difference. This was in your Bible. I watched it fall out."

Nate took the paper and began to look at it. "I've never seen this before—" Nate stopped leaving the sentence unfinished.

"What?" Thomas asked.

"This morning someone broke into my apartment…at least I thought they had, but I couldn't see where anything had been disturbed. So I dismissed it."

"You're suggesting that someone broke into your apartment to hide this in your Bible?"

Nate shook his head. "I'm not suggesting anything. You said that fell out of my Bible and I've never seen it before. When I got back to the apartment from my run, I thought I saw filings on my doorknob, as if someone had tried to pick it. Then earlier on my run, I would have sworn that some guy in a gray sedan was following me."

Thomas chuckled again, leaned back and clapped his meaty hands. "God is good."

Nate looked at the paper again. "There are," he counted, "Thirteen names on this list. My name's on here."

"I know. Keep reading"

"Hey, this has my salary listed and the amount the city pays for my benefits packet including workman's compensation insurance."

Thomas nodded. Look at the last column. That's the future liability column."

Nate looked back to the sheet of paper and began reading softly, his lips barely moving. "My accrued sick leave…my vacation time, all reduced to a dollar figure."

Thomas nodded his head. "And that dollar figure represents your liability to the city. If they cut your liability to the city, they can, in effect, save the city that amount of money."

"Wow." Nate leaned back in his seat and allowed himself to relax while trying to digest the information.

"The worse part," Thomas continued, "are the names with the X in the right margin."

Nate rolled his head to the side and looked at Thomas. He lifted the paper again and began to read the names, noting the departments within the city where the selected individuals worked: Parks and Recreation, Water Waste, Finance, Fire and the Police Department. "Hey," Nate said and sat up. "Every one of the names with an X has been terminated recently. Mine is the only one without an X."

"Yes, and every one of them represented a particularly large liability to the city. A heck of a way to make budget, huh?"

Neither man spoke for a while.

Nate drew in his breath, opened his mouth, but then closed it again without speaking.

"And you have no idea where this came from?" Thomas asked.

"None," Nate said, then raised and dropped his shoulders. "Do you think the chief had anything to do with creating this list?"

"No. No—well, not directly."

Nate raised a brow.

"I mean, part of his responsibility is to conduct the business of the police department. He has over 1700 uniformed personnel to account for and that does not even bring into consideration the number of non-sworn and civilian personnel attached to the police department—plus, equipment, building and operations. It's quite an undertaking and Chief Villareal has done a great job for the most part."

Nate was shaking his head again. "Yeah, pretty good unless your name suddenly shows up on one of these lists."

"We don't know that the list had anything to do with the I.A., Nate."

"Really? Look at the date of the list. It's dated six months before my I.A. even began. Explain how my name shows up on a termination list, and then all of a sudden I find myself in the middle of a questionable I.A. with a recommendation for termination. I don't get it."

Thomas turned back to face forward. He pointed toward an orange vested store employee making his way toward the car.

Nate turned on the electrical power and lowered the driver's side window. "Can I help you with anything?" The young man asked. Nate shook his head and showed him his I.D., just going over some paperwork. We'll be done in a minute."

The young man raised his hand and smiled. "No problem, I just didn't want to leave you hanging out here if you were waiting on propane or something. Don't want the boss thinking I'm slothful at my job." He turned and walked away.

Nate smiled and waved as the youth retreated. "I still don't see how Villareal gets a free pass on this," he said turning back to Thomas.

"What would you have me do? Charge him with what? This is still a right to work state, Nate."

"Oh, I don't know. It just feels wrong."

Thomas sighed and squeezed Nate's shoulder. Look, we have to believe that God brought us this information at a time that He saw fit. So, we will just trust that He knows what He's doing and follow His lead. We'll leave the judgment of the city and the chief in His hands, what do you say?"

Nate couldn't help but laugh. "Well, I did pray that God would lead and provide for me. I guess this is just His way of doing it."

"Looks like."

Nate checked the time. "You still want that cup of coffee?"

"No, not much of a coffee drinker, but I'd love a good cup of tea."

"Starbucks okay?"

"You buying?"

"You're the big fancy lawyer and you want the lowly street cop to buy the drinks. Let's go, it's on me." Nate laughed again and started the car. Pausing before pulling out onto Water Tower Street, he looked over at Thomas, a sly smile pulling at the corners of his mouth. "Unless you'd rather have Dairy Queen."

A few minutes later, both men sat eating a large vanilla ice cream cone; Nate's topped with chocolate. "This was such a better choice," Thomas said, around a mouthful of dessert. "It's almost 11:00, ready to head in?"

Nate nodded and opened the door to the Chrysler, took a breath, and then swallowed his last bite of cone. "Let's do this."

CHAPTER THIRTY-SIX

NATE STEPPED TO THE SIDE and then followed Thomas back into the conference room, everyone else already in their seats. The clock on the wall showed 1100 hours precisely.

"Have a seat, Mr. Richards," Chief Villareal stated matter fact.

Nate sat, reminding himself of Thomas' admonishment to allow him to speak for Nate. "Thank you, sir."

"Well, I trust you finished whatever business you had with Mr. Meir."

"Yes, Chief. I just had to go over a few details with my client, to review his options so he could better answer you when presented with your decision."

The chief looked around the room and then cleared his throat. "Very well then, if there are no further delays, A.C. Lawrence will you please read the board's ruling," the Chief announced flatly.

Lawrence opened his folder and inhaled, prepared to speak. "Excuse me, Chief," Thomas interrupted.

"What is it, Mr. Meir?" he said, irritated.

"Oh, just this, sir." He held up the liability report passing it across the table, making sure that everyone could at least see the title on the page. "I found this—someone must have dropped it, and I figured I'd better get this to you. I knew you would know what to do with it."

The chief grabbed the paper and looked at it. His dark eyes bore into the page. He looked up, first to Thomas who sat innocently across from him, and then to the A.C and finally to the city attorney. Nate didn't so much as breathe.

The chief cleared his throat. "Thank you, Mr. Meir. Where did you find this?"

"Like I said, someone dropped it, and I just happen to pick it up." Thomas said, without answering the chief's question.

Moments passed.

Assistant Chief Lawrence began to read again.

"Mr. Richards," the chief said interrupting the A.C. for the second time. "Mr. Richards, it is the decision of this board that you be reassigned to patrol. You will be stripped of the rank of detective, but your seniority will be retained." He looked around, locking eyes with Lawrence.

"Ah yes," the chief continued, "You will be eligible for reassignment in one year's time if you keep your nose clean. Any questions?"

Nate shook his head. It had all happened so fast he didn't know what to think, let alone to ask.

The chief stood. The meeting was over. The chief left the room followed by the city attorney and then the H.R. representative.

Assistant Chief Lawrence stopped in the doorway, his hand grasping the edge of the door. His broad shoulders square beneath the tailored charcoal gray suit almost filled the doorway. "Take the rest of the week to get yourself together, Nate," he said over his shoulder.

Nate nodded. "Yes, sir."

"I'll expect you back in uniform Monday morning at 0700 hours. Your assignment will be waiting for you." He walked out of the room, the door swinging shut behind him.

Chapter Thirty-Seven

Nate walked with slow measured steps as he approached his apartment door, his head down and lost in the swirl of his thoughts....

"*Head down, man down.* I thought I taught you better than that."

Nate jumped, startled by the woman's voice. He reached for his waist, seeking the Glock model 26 secured in the holster at his belt.

"Leave that Baby Glock right where it is," Sabrina Jackson said, stepping into the light from the corner. "Besides if I wanted to shoot you, you'd be shot by now."

Nate relaxed.

Sabrina closed the short distance that separated them and without hesitation took Nate into her embrace. "Good to see ya, Boy."

Nate returned the hug, pulling his mentor tighter. "It's good to be seen."

"Hey—breakable...ease up on the bear hug, Samson. Invite me in?" Sabrina said slipping from the hug and running her arm through Nate's at the elbow.

Nate turned them back toward his forgotten apartment door. Sabrina stooped and looked at the doorknob. She ran a single coffee colored finger across the brass surface. "Sloppy work."

Nate tilted away from her. "How did you know about the break-in?"

She waved away his question as if it had been unimportant. "Any idea who might have wanted to help you out?"

Nate shook his head and smiled. "Still keeping your secrets, huh?" She smiled up at him, but didn't answer.

Nate shook his head again and smiled. She hadn't changed. "Or who had it out for the chief, or the city. If old Butchy Boy had gotten his grubby hands on it, that information could have made the city look really bad."

He opened the door and they walked in together. Nate dropped his keys on the counter and went directly into the kitchen. "Coffee?"

"Do you really need to ask?"

He began filling the coffee pot with water as he gathered the coffee and filters from the cupboard. "I'm just glad this is over."

"Is it?" Sabrina had sat in the living room, placing both feet, crossed at the ankles on the low table in front of the sofa.

Nate frowned and looked up at her. "What do you mean? I lost my rank. I'm back on the streets. I mean, what else is there." It had not really been a question.

The soft gurgle of the coffee pot rose in the background as the hot liquid began to fill the pot. Nate pulled out two mugs and set the creamer and sweetener on a small tray. "Hungry?"

Sabrina just looked at him with that, *are you really asking me look.* "So you..." She left the sentence unasked.

"I don't know," Nate said as he made sandwiches for the both of them. "It's not anywhere on the plans I'd made for myself, but I have been asking God to lead me; maybe I should begin following."

The doorbell rang.

Nate looked up at Sabrina. "Don't look at me," she said, "it's your house."

Setting the tray back on the counter, Nate made his way to the door. His mother, father and Gracie made their way in as soon as the door opened. "Are we late?" Sherri asked, kissing her son's cheek as she entered.

Again, Nate turned and looked at Sabrina. She raised her shoulders. Nate looked past his mother, hoping to see Amber. When she did not follow the crowd in, he closed the door.

"Late?" Nate asked of the group.

"Congratulations, Son," Reverend Richards said, clasping his son by the shoulders. "Thomas said to meet you here at one and so we all came right over."

"This better be good, I'm missing my logic class," Gracie added. Then she saw Sabrina and ran to the older woman. "Sabrina, it's been so long."

The doorbell rang again. This time it was Don Haynes. "Don," Nate exclaimed. "Come on in." He pulled him in by his shoulders.

Don looked a little surprised by everyone else being at the apartment. Taking in his surprised expression, Nate asked, "Thomas?"

Don nodded and made his way into the apartment. Sherri was already in the kitchen making more sandwiches and putting on a second pot of coffee. Don greeted everyone. "Yeah, Thomas' secretary called and said he needed me here at your apartment today at 1:15, but he didn't say anything about it being a party."

"So tell us what happened in the meeting," Gracie said.

"Well," Nate began, but the doorbell rang again. He put up a hand indicating that they should wait. He opened the door and Durgins and Mac walked in together.

"All I know," Mac said, "is somebody better have some food on because it's my lunch time." He went directly to Sherri and grabbed her around the waist picking her up and swinging her around. "How are you Mama Richards? I know you got something for me to eat."

"Mac," Gracie screamed. "When did you get back? It's like a reunion in here."

Durgins followed in the wake of energy created by Mac. "Yeah, I'm here too," he announced to the room in general.

"Come on in, son," Reverend Richards said, extending a hand in greeting.

"Well, as far as I can see everybody is here except for Thomas," Sabrina said from her perch on the sofa.

"And Amber," Gracie added from under Mac's arm where he held her in a mock headlock.

As if on cue, a knock sounded at the door. Nate walked with a quickened pace, anticipating that Amber would be waiting at the door. Instead, Thomas stood beside Ms. Walker, his office manager. The dark-haired young lady smiled politely and then walked past Nate, the fabric of her blazer and matching skirt making a soft swishing sound as she moved.

In contrast, Thomas entered the room in as large a fashion as had Mac. "Shalom!" He almost shouted with his arms spread as if to take in everyone in a single embrace. "Labriut, BeKarov etzlecha. Bezezrat HaShem."

"Which means what?" Mac asked.

Thomas laughed, obviously pleased with himself. "Loosely translated it means, 'Good health, may it be so soon, by the grace of God.' Loosely translated."

"Yeah, very loosely, I bet," Nate added. "So what is this all about, Thomas? You've created quite the mystery here."

Thomas signaled for everyone to gather around, assuming control of the small gathering. "If I remember correctly this all began at a party, no?"

Murmurs of agreement made its way around the table. Nate remembered distinctly the night of his father's birthday party and the phone call from Sergeant Clemens that set the course of actions into play. He also remembered that he and Amber were not together at the time. He looked at his cell phone, hoping to have at least missed a call from her.

"So," Thomas continued, "not wanting to give the devil a victory where there isn't one, I thought we should pick up where the interruption came in."

He was greeted with a round of applause. Sabrina stood, lifting her cup. "I propose a toast. To Nate and his victory in the battle."

Nate stood and waved off the cheerful response. "No," he said stalling the offered blessing, "but rather to the Good Shepherd who led me even when I couldn't see the path and to all of you who stood by me during my test." He raised his cup and they all followed his lead.

The doorbell rang again and this time Gracie made her way to answer it. She pulled the door open with a flourish. "It's about time you made it here, girl. The party started without you..."

The next moment the entire room fell silent. Assistant Chief Zachary Lawrence stood in the doorway, a folder grasped in his large hand, which hung relaxed at his waist.

CHAPTER THIRTY- EIGHT

"MAY I COME IN?" the A.C. asked.

Gracie stepped back from the door as Nate made his way forward. "A.C.—Zack, come in," Nate said and extended a hand to the A.C.

"Sorry, I didn't realize you were having a party, although I can't say I'm surprised. I actually just dropped by because I wanted to give you something." He handed Nate a folder.

Nate looked at the folder and then back up at the A.C. "What is this?"

Lawrence looked at Thomas, chuckled, and then back at Nate before speaking. "It's just something someone found lying around and picked up. They brought it to me thinking I'd know what to do with it. I put a copy in your file…just in case," Lawrence finished.

The three men exchanged a knowing glance. Nate opened the folder. Everyone stepped closer and Sherri pushed a cup of coffee into A.C. Lawrence's hands. He nodded thanks and lifted the cup to his lips.

"It's the note!" Nate said to no one.

Lawrence stepped back from the small crowd and leaned a broad shoulder against the wall. "The one that Kellerston said she never wrote," Sherri asked.

"The same one," Durgins yelled. "Oh yeah!"

"But where did it come from?"

"Who had it?"

"How long have they had it?"

They all seemed to be asking questions at once. Thomas' voice rose above the din. "It's like the A.C. said…" and the shallow roar quieted, "somebody found it and gave it to him. Let's just let that be enough." Several sets of eyes met the lawyer's and the room continued into silence.

Nate looked over the heads of his friends and family and locked eyes with Lawrence. The A.C. raised his cup and smiled, Nate returned the gesture.

Durgins pulled the once crumpled sheet of paper from the folder and began passing it around; everyone wanting to touch it and see the inflammatory words that had begun this mess.

Another knock sounded at the door, but this one was soft and muffled. When no one seemed to notice, Lawrence took it upon himself to open the door. As he did, Amber walked in with an 11x16 Costco cake box in her arms. "Surprise!" She called out and everyone turned, noticing her for the first time.

Nate hurried to her, kissed her cheek, and took the box from her passing it back to Mac who had followed him over. He pulled Amber into his arms and held her for what felt like not nearly long enough. "I was beginning to worry," he whispered into her ear.

"Well," Amber began shrugging off her light jacket, "when Ms. Walker called and told me about the meeting, I figured we needed to have a cake, so…"

"So you went and got one. That's so Amber," Gracie said rolling her eyes in exaggerated motion.

Nate looked up to ask the A.C. if he would join them for cake just in time to see Lawrence's trailing shoulder slipping past the threshold and the door closing quietly behind him.

"Excuse me," Nate said and pressed another kiss on Amber's lips, "I'll be right back."

Rushing out into the hall, Nate called out, "A.C....Zack, wait up."

Lawrence stopped and turned back to face Nate.

Nate came up to where Lawrence waited. "I just wanted to say thank you and to ask you why?"

Lawrence smiled. "You're a good man, Nate. I know you, and I like what you stand for; sometimes that's all the reason a person needs. You've got a good name, Richards.

"I'm just glad Haynes and his daughter managed to get that file into your apartment in time."

Nate nodded, smiled and shook Lawrence's hand. Although his mind was flooded with a thousand questions, he knew they were perhaps better left unasked. All he said was, "Thank you, sir."

Lawrence started to turn away, but stopped. "You know things will change for you after this, Richards."

"I know, I'm just not sure how or what that'll look like."

Lawrence chuckled, a dry rumbling laugh. "Neither do I...neither do I. Keep your nose clean, Richards." And this time he did turn and walk away.

A few minutes later, Nate made his way back into his apartment to find Thomas and Durgins explaining to everyone how the I.A. had been broken. He met Haynes' gaze, and with a tilt of his head, Nate acknowledged his mentor's service.

"It all began when that little heifer lied about Nate trying to seduce her," Durgins said around a bite of cake. "When my boy turned her down, I guess it hurt her feelings." He smiled at Amber.

"But can't you charge her with filing a false police report or something?" Sherri asked.

Mac shook his head. "No charge was filed. It was simply a citizen complaint. She knew the game well enough to stay just this side of illegal."

"But the thing that made the difference was the list," Thomas added. The complaint just happened to come at the right—or the wrong time, depending on your perspective.

Everyone sobered.

Nate made his way over to Amber and slipped an arm around her waist. She looked up at him and smiled, and instantly warmth spread throughout him. He hoped those feelings would never stop. He had always seen how his parents seemed to light up with each other and hoped that he would share that kind of relationship with someone one day.

"Whatever happened with that Edna Mae woman?" Reverend Richards asked.

"Oh, don't even go there," Durgins said, exaggerating irritation. "That woman darn near drove me nuts looking for you, Nate. I think she was in love with you or something."

"Too bad, he's already taken," Amber said, leaning into Nate.

"Oh, stop it you two," Gracie said.

Nate smiled at his adopted sister and then leaned over and kissed Amber's hair.

"Is that the woman from the original rape case?" Mac asked, refilling his coffee cup. "That's the one the A.C. had me meet with. She was nuts."

"Mac," Nate chided.

Mac laughed. "Okay, she was emotionally challenged. I mean, she was schizophrenic or something. She had stopped taking her meds and got fixated on you." He drank from his cup.

"If it wasn't for the pastor guy contacting the station, you would have had a second I.A. to deal with," Durgins stated flatly.

"So that's why Pastor Luck told me that he would take care of everything," Reverend Richards said, thoughtfully.

"Pastor Luck?" Sherri asked.

"Remember at the pastors' weekly prayer meeting a few weeks back, the tall white haired fellow. The one you said looked like a stereotypical Nazarene pastor."

Sherri hushed her husband, embarrassed by having her comment voiced out loud. "Yes, yes, I remember now, but what about him?"

Reverend Richards giggled, well aware why his wife was rushing him. "Well, remember, I said how weird it was that he said he would 'take care of everything,' but neither of us knew what he was talking about? He told me later that Edna Mae goes to his church. He's known her since she was a little girl."

"Wow," Nate said.

"What?" Amber asked from beside him.

Nate sat up and looked around the room. "Think about it…all the names and faces that have had a part in this." He began naming them starting with the call from Sergeant Clemens and working forward, ending with Pastor Luck. "It's just so weird that all of these lives intersected with mine. Crazy."

"Not really," Gracie said. "It's like Corrie Ten Boom said, 'This is what the past is for! Every experience God gives us, every person He puts in our lives, is the perfect preparation for the future that only He can see.'"

"Well said," Reverend Richards agreed.

Gracie smiled at his praise and went to stand next to him, leaning against the elder Richards.

"Well," Nate said and stood, "if all of the stuff, the good and the bad was all part of God's plan to bring me to this place in my life, then I'd better not waste it. Excuse me." He walked with hurried, excited steps to his bedroom.

Laughter rose in his wake, salted with playful, but snide comments fired by Durgins and Mac.

"I guess when you gotta go, you gotta go."

"Be sure to lift the seat."

"If you sprinkle…"

A few minutes later Nate returned carrying a small box in his hand. He stopped in front of Amber and then slowly dropped to one knee.

"Oh my God!" Sabrina said, and meant it as a prayer.

"It's about time," Gracie added.

Nate took Amber's left hand in his and looked up at her. "I have loved you since we were kids. For the longest time, I was just too stupid to know it. I almost lost you once and now that God has brought you back into my life and I have this chance again.... Amber Coles, will you do me the extreme honor of marrying me?"

With a shocked, happy expression, Amber stood and looked briefly around the room. Her hands trembled. Her vision blurred. She had wanted this, had waited for it...dreamt about it. Hadn't she?

She caught her breath and looked into Nate's eyes. Tears streaked her cheeks as she fought for the control that was quickly slipping from her. For a moment she found herself standing in the third floor lobby of St. Luke's Hospital, Nate standing between her and the slowly opening elevator door. And the same fear that had controlled her heart then sprang back to life, gripping her bosom. Her breath froze in her throat and her heart seemed to skip a beat. Her mouth hung open, forming a silent O.

With a sudden intake of air, Amber moved a half step forward and looked full into Nate's face, but before she could speak, Nate's phone rang in his pocket.

Silence claimed the room.

Nate held up a finger stilling everyone. He answered the phone. "Richards."

Amber looked down at her hand and then at Sherri and smiled warily.

Nate grabbed Amber's hand and pulled her toward him. He draped an arm around her waist and kissed her cheek while still talking into the phone. "Yes, Mrs. Coles, she's here with me now."

Amber leaned away from Nate and strained to hear the voice, but it was only a muffled hum.

Nate smiled at the look of confusion on Amber's face. He spoke back into the phone. "Yes ma'am, I just asked her but...you know how stubborn she can be. She still hasn't answered yet." He smiled.

Amber stepped away from Nate and turned to look back at him. "Nate Richards, who are you talking to?" She demanded playfully.

Nate didn't answer, but instead passed her the phone. Amber stared at the phone before accepting it and placed it to her ear. "Hello."

Nate smiled and reached up to touch Amber's cheek. She looked at him with a single tear brimming in her eye. "Mom?"

EPILOGUE

TWO DAYS LATER the sun finally broke free after a night and a day of alternating rain and sleet. Nate relaxed on the sofa in Amber's small living room and watched her as she made her way toward him from the kitchen. She held in her hands two cups of coffee, steam floating upwards in lazy serpentine arcs. She stretched her left hand forward, offering him one of the cups, the half carat diamond reflecting brilliantly in the soft afternoon light.

She sat next to him, curling her left leg beneath her and tossed a loose curl of hair absent-mindedly. "Nate," she began tentatively.

He smiled and brushed her lips with a soft stroke of his thumb. "Yes?" He smiled as the dimple in her cheek deepened.

Adjusting herself on the sofa, she slipped her leg from beneath her and turned to face Nate. "What ever happened with the whole Wanda...Edna Mae thing? Did that case ever get resolved? It just weirds me out to think there's still a rapist running free here in the valley."

Seeing the worry creasing her face, Nate first sat his cup down, and then taking hers, set it beside his own. He took both her hands into his own. "I'm sorry; I should have told you all. The rapist got picked up out in Parma. He was hiding out in an old biker camp out there." He smiled again when he saw her relax.

Pulling her next to him, he held her close against his chest. She rested her face against him. Nate kissed the top of her head and played with the back of her knuckle, admiring the ring—his ring on her finger. "Yes, DNA doesn't lie." He chuckled.

"What?" Amber said, looking up so she could look in his face.

Nate kissed her upturned face. "Well he left a sample at the scene." He didn't bother to explain. "Besides, it's not so easy to hide when you're a 6'5" biker with one blue and one green eye. Especially in Parma."

She giggled along with him. "Parma." She exhaled and snuggled down against his chest. "I bet Edna Mae feels better, even if she didn't get the tall, dark and handsome detective."

Nate sighed, remembering how close it had come to having a second sexually allegation leveled against him. "Oh well, at least I have my name, huh?"

"And it's a good name," she answered from against his chest. Amber sat up, took Nate's face between her hands and kissed him, covering his mouth with her own. "And soon, it will be my name too."

THE END... BOOK THREE

ACKNOWLEDGMENT

I would like to acknowledge all the current and former police officers I interviewed to build the substance of this story. No matter whom I interviewed, male or female, officers from California to New York, all seemed to share a series of common feelings and experiences. I tried my best to capture to essence of their stories and experiences, as well as some of the resonances of my own 23 plus years in this noble profession.

A NOTE FROM THE AUTHOR

Thank you for reading *Insidious*, the third installment of the Nate Richards Mystery series. Now that you've finished this book, I would love to hear from you. You can email me with your thoughts on the book or become my friend on Facebook. You can even sign up for my newsletter, which will give you updates on upcoming releases and all the other craziness going on in my corner of the world.

If you would like to help this story succeed, please tell others about it. You can loan your copy to a friend, and ask your local libraries and bookstores to order it.

In addition, if you could please post a review on amazon.com, or goodreads.com, it would be very helpful.

My email address is:
  rayellisauthor@gmail.com
You can download discussion questions or follow my blog entries at:
  http://authorray.blogspot.com
Please visit my web site at:
  http://www.nccpublishing.com/rayellis.html
Follow me on Twitter at:
  Twitter@RayEllisWriter

MORE BY RAY ELLIS

Notorious (A Nate Richards Mystery - Book One)
Previously released as N.H.I. (No Humans Involved)

Dead List (A Nate Richards Mystery - Book Two)
Previously released as D.R.T. (Dead Right There)

"I" – A Short Story

ABOUT THE AUTHOR

A veteran law enforcement officer, former United States Marine, and ordained Christian pastor, Ray's first novel, NOTORIOUS, previously released as *N.H.I. - No Humans Involved*, was published in 2011. Since then, Ray has been selected as one of Idaho's Top 50 Authors for the year of 2011, and then as a Top 10 Idaho Author in 2012.

When not writing, Ray can be found still working as an active duty officer, speaking to student groups or teaching Bible studies in his local community.

www.ingramcontent.com/pod-product-compliance
Lightning Source LLC
Chambersburg PA
CBHW052027240626
47153CB00006B/1989

* 9 781938 596100 *